He smiled.

The night was humid and dark and he knew he was in the woods. He was in no hurry. He could kill them all, he thought. He could walk into their private lives, kill them whenever he wished. Pull out their limbs, one by one, cut their pale throats, poke out their blue eyes, jerk out their pink tongues.

He kept grinning.

Summer in the Catskills.

THE HUNTING SEASON

"Preys upon the paranoia and xenophobia all we summer people feel in our summer communities. . . . Builds a suffocating sense of dread that erupts into a terrifying, violent, and very satisfying conclusion."

—Dan Greenburg

THE HUNTING SEASON

BY JOHN COYNE

WARNER BOOKS

A Warner Communications Company

This novel is a work of fiction. Names, characters, places, and incidents are either the product of the author's imagination or are used fictitiously. Any resemblance to actual persons, living or dead, events, or locales is entirely coincidental.

This Warner Books Edition is published in association with Macmillan Publishing Company, 866 Third Avenue, New York, N.Y. 10022

Cover illustration by Mark and Stefanie Gerber

Warner Books, Inc.
666 Fifth Avenue
New York, N.Y. 10103

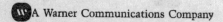A Warner Communications Company

Printed in the United States of America

First Warner Books Printing: August, 1988

10 9 8 7 6 5 4 3 2 1

For John Silbersack

Fall

It was raining, had been raining all morning, all the night before, and now there were rivers of water on the road, and thick fog blocking the valley passes, shrouding the double-lane expressway.

Whenever the car plunged into fog or hit a patch of water, April closed her eyes, thankful that Tom was driving. He was a much better driver, especially in bad weather. She tightened her embrace around Timmy, pulled the sleeping infant closer and bent to kiss the softness of his face.

When she glanced up, she saw a tollway exit for the Catskill Mountains, and then another sign: New York 125 Miles. Thank God, she thought, sighing; they'd be home soon. The baby stirred and began to cry. April unbuttoned her blouse and gave him her breast. As he sucked hungrily, her eyes filled with tears. She was thrilled that he was in her arms, thrilled she had given birth to such a lovely little boy. It was all she wanted out of life, all she had ever wanted.

She glanced up again, and through the mist, noticed a cluster of men standing at the edge of the woods. What were they doing, she thought at once, and then she spotted a deer, saw it come crashing out of the trees and charge into the heavy traffic.

April felt the heavy car begin to slide as Tom saw the deer and tried to brake.

"Darling," she said calmly, controlling herself because of Timmy, but realizing also that she was going to scream.

The car caught a puddle and the sleek tires planed across the patch of cold water. She could feel her husband fighting the wheel, but her eyes were fixed on the deer. The car spun sideways, and the huge buck leapt, as if on purpose, into the center lane, smashing into the driver's side. His spindle-legs hit the window, breaking the glass. One horny hoof clipped her husband's face and broke his jaw, another cut open his neck and popped out his Adam's apple. April and the baby were showered with the warm blood of Tom's jugular.

April was screaming into the mountain fog. Around her, brakes screeched on the shrouded highway and metal crashed. She saw bright headlights and the front grillwork of a Plymouth Fury. The old car plowed into them, skimmed the buck from the door, then flipped over and burst into flames.

April felt the heat, but she couldn't move. She was trapped, pinned down by the wreckage and her own seat belt.

In the stillness that followed the accident, she heard nothing but the wild flapping of the windshield wipers. Then her baby's screams made her realize she was alive. Her child was alive. And though she couldn't move, she managed to expose her blood-smeared breast to her hungry boy.

BOOK
ONE

...summer in the Catskills, four years later...

PEACEFUL RETREAT

Country hideaway overlooking idyllic pond. Absolute privacy for serene wknds, or year round retreat. 2 hrs from Manhattan. Circa 1820. 12 rm. rambling renovated 2 story Colonial residence. Country kit, 2 baths, 3 frplacs, 1 in master bdrm. Extraordinary views of Mad River Mountain from large, sunny deck. On secluded back road deep in the heart of the Catskills. 200 acs of woods and cross country skiing fields. Caretaker on premises.

Your wife and kids will love this peaceful spot in the Catskills. Great Buy!

Helen Smythe Ely
Specializing in Fine Homes & Estates

One

April Benard turned from the family tree she had diagrammed on the blackboard and faced the students around the seminar table.

"As this family tree shows," she went on, "a group can be isolated by any of a number of factors, including religion, politics, culture or geography. Group members mate only with each other, thus limiting the gene pool, and, therefore, causing a greater number of stillbirths, congenital malformations and higher sterility rates." She paused a moment to see if the ten seniors in her advanced anthropology class were following her, and then summed up her lecture.

"Okay, we've made several points today. First, that most societies have prohibited the mating of parents and offspring, or brothers and sisters. Two exceptions are the Egyptian pharaohs and the rulers of the Incas of Peru. And most societies avoid first-cousin marriages. As I mentioned, the incidence of first-cousin marriages in the U.S. population is less than one in one-thousand.

"Nevertheless, even today, we have societies in the United States where inbreeding still occurs. There are three well-known communities. The Amish, a religious group, in Pennsylvania, Indiana and Ohio. The Hutterites, another religious group, in South Dakota and Canada. The third major group, dating from the late 1700s, are part American Indian, part

Caucasian and part Negro. They live in small clusters of families stretching from New Jersey south to Mississippi."

She paused a moment and then saw James Galvin timidly raise his hand.

"Yes, James?" she asked, encouraging him. Most of the undergraduates she encountered at Columbia University were aggressive and intense. James was not. He was one of the sweetest and shyest young men she had ever taught.

"What about Mad River Mountain in the Catskills?"

April smiled. "Yes, James, thank you for my cue." April paused a moment and scanned the students, seizing their full attention. "I should explain that this semester Mr. Galvin worked with me in developing a computer program on a cluster of consanguineous relationships located in an isolated area in the Catskill Mountains. And this summer, I plan on conducting some research there."

"The Borscht Belt!" someone called out.

April raised both her hands, signaled the class to stop laughing.

"All right! All right!" She glanced at the wall clock, saw she had five minutes left, then nodded to another student.

"Yes, Alan?"

"I went to camp as a kid in the Catskills. Where was the inbreeding?"

"Not in your tent, Schwartz," a student called down the table.

"Enough!" April banged a piece of chalk on the seminar table. She stood perfectly still and stared at the class, waited for them to settle down. It was late on a Friday and she knew they were tired of being in classrooms all week, but she also knew that, as a woman teacher, she had to be fierce with her discipline. Otherwise, the kids would take the class away from her.

"You're too beautiful," her husband had told her when they first started seeing each other. "If I'd had teachers like you when I was at Columbia I would never have graduated."

When the room was perfectly still she turned back to the blackboard and pulled down a New York State map.

"Here, at this corner of Ulster County, there is a mountain called Mad River. A community has existed there since the early 1770s, before the Revolutionary War." She pinpointed the spot and glanced back at the seminar table. "We don't know much about the community. Dutch immigrants settled in the valley after the Revolutionary War, and by the early 1850s two neighboring families, the Tassels and the Holts, began to intermarry. By the 1890s, according to a few county records I've been able to find, first cousins were marrying. Some members, of course, moved out of the region and married outsiders, but there is a core population of perhaps one hundred people still on that mountain."

"What kind of research are you going to do?" Alan asked.

"What any anthropologist would do. I'll go up there and try to meet some of the family members, begin to get to know them, hoping that they'll trust me enough to talk about their lives and relationships. Also, I want to see what kind of statistical data I can begin to gather about the number of consanguineous marriages taking place today."

"But will they talk to you?" another student asked.

"I hope so, but I'm not sure." She nodded again at James. "This winter James could find only a handful of references to the Mad River people in the journals. Somehow they have successfully kept themselves away from researchers, and are really unknown to the outside world. There's a local Catskill warning that you don't go alone into Mad River Mountain."

"Why?" several students asked in unison.

"Because they shoot you," April said, smiling; then added, "No, they are peaceful people, like all isolated societies that have been left alone, they have no reason to fear outsiders." Then, as if on cue, the bell sounded. Class was over.

"All right, listen, please!" she said quickly, speaking over the noise of moving chairs, the shuffling of books and bookbags. "Next Friday is the final examination. Remember, it will be four essay questions focusing on material in chapters fifteen through twenty. Come prepared to think, and write, and then write some more."

She stepped to the seminar table, scooped up her papers, textbook and purse, and without breaking stride headed for the door. It was 4:45, she saw, and she began to calculate how long it would take her to get back downtown to SoHo, bathe and dress, then meet Marshall to go back uptown. They were due at the Morrisons by 7:30.

She was on the steps of Low Library before James Galvin caught up.

"Dr. Benard? Do you have a moment?"

"No, Jim, I'm sorry." She smiled, tried to seem as if she wasn't trying to get rid of him, and explained, "I'm running late. Can it wait till my office hours?"

"Oh, sure, I was just wondering." He had fallen into step with her, his long legs easily matching her hurried stride. "If, you know, you needed someone to help you up in those hills. I mean, I've got the summer off. And it would look good on my résumé, doing research like that. If you don't have room at your place, I could camp out. I've got a tent and everything." He spoke to her in quick bursts of sentences.

April suppressed her smile. She was used to undergraduates becoming infatuated with her, and she did not want to hurt his feelings as she turned him down.

"Thank you, James, but my husband and I don't know yet how much time we'll be spending upstate. His daughter will be visiting us from California, and I'll have my little boy with me. We don't know how they'll adapt to country living; it will be quite a culture shock. Also, I want to go slowly; give these people a chance to get to know me gradually. Perhaps next summer they'll be ready to meet someone else." They reached the campus gate and she stopped walking, out of breath from her hurried pace.

"Next summer I'll be gone. I'm a senior, Dr. Benard." He sounded depressed.

April resisted an urge to reach out and touch his arm.

"I'm sorry, Jim. I forgot you'll be graduating. I do appreciate your offer. You were a big help this winter, collecting all the documentation, and it would be wonderful having you this summer." She kept smiling, trying to ease his disappointment with the warmth of her voice. She could hear the downtown subway rumbling into the station under her feet, but she couldn't just brush him off. Students should come first, she believed, before any research or university committee assignments. "Look, I'm planning on taking the fall term off to continue work on this. Maybe you can come upstate then, on weekends.''

He nodded reluctantly, shy, then said without looking at her, ''You won't do anything stupid?''

''Stupid?''

''I mean, dangerous. You know.'' He was embarrassed now and shifted his bookbag from one shoulder to the other.

''I'll be careful,'' April said softly. Then she gently patted his arm as she stepped around him and moved toward the subway station. ''I'll keep you posted on my research. Now go over to Butler and start studying for that final. I want to be able to give you an A.''

James Galvin stood at the gate of Columbia and watched Dr. Benard rush to the subway entrance. He should follow, he thought; it was dangerous on the subway, especially for a beautiful woman. But that would have been pushing his luck. She might not like it, his bird-dogging.

Still he couldn't take his eyes off her slight body, the slimness of her legs, the smooth roll of her rear as she strode off. He swallowed hard. She looked more like a model than an associate professor.

He was being an ass, he knew. He had seen her driver's license: November 21, 1957. She was too old for him. Ten years too old.

Besides, she had just married a hotshot lawyer. He had read about Marshall Benard in the *New York Times*. There had been a picture of him with his ''anthropologist wife'' in snowy Central Park. They were pulling her four-year-old son on a sled. The article mentioned how they had met, how she had been married before and lost her husband in an automobile accident.

When her blond hair disappeared at the bottom of the subway stairs, he reluctantly turned and walked back onto campus. It wasn't fair, he told himself. He should have majored in prelaw, not anthropology. He should never have taken her class in the first place and then he wouldn't be in this fix.

And then he realized he didn't have to work for April Benard that summer. He didn't have to camp out on her front lawn. He could just borrow his mother's car and drive up to the Catskills, cruise through the hills, find Mad River Mountain himself, stop by and say he just happened to be in the neighborhood. She'd like that, he thought, grinning now. After all, he wouldn't be just another one of her students this summer. He'd be a graduate of Columbia.

And besides, he reminded himself for the thousandth time, she liked him. She really did! He could tell by the way she smiled at him. He picked up his pace and broke into a trot, ran toward the library to study for the final. He was going to ace that exam. He was going to make April Benard proud of him, dazzled by his knowledge. And then he was going to go upstate and visit her when her husband wasn't around, when she'd be glad to see him on some warm night when she was bored and lonely and wanting company. His company! Yeah, he thought, getting excited with anticipation. This summer he was going to make April Benard forget she was even married.

Two

"You're late," Marshall said to April as he slipped into the backseat of the yellow cab.

"But I'm beautiful," April retorted, smiling, and leaned over to let her husband kiss her cheek.

"And you smell beautiful, too."

"Thank you, darling. I miss you." She always said she missed him in the present tense. And it was true. When she was with Marshall, she seemed to miss him most of all, as if she were secretly afraid that someday he might not be there by her side.

"Frantic day?" he asked, settling down into the seat as the taxi pulled away from the Athletic Club and started for the Upper West Side.

"Yes, the usual." She sat back to take in her husband, to enjoy the brief moment alone with him in the taxi, without ringing telephones and demands on his attention. "You look beautiful, too," she told him.

He was wearing the new Armani suit she had picked out for him at Barneys. In the ten months that they had been married she had worked on his wardrobe, getting him away from his drab navy suits, buying him shirts with stripes and colors, and picking out Italian silk jacquard ties so that when he went off to work in the morning, he didn't look like every other Wall Street lawyer.

"How was the game? Did you clean Oliver's clock?" she asked, mimicking his jock talk.

"Of course!" He stretched out his legs, sat sideways and rested his head on the back of the seat.

"Exhausted?"

"Exhausted," he whispered, closing his eyes.

"Maybe we shouldn't drive up to the Catskills tomorrow," she suggested, snugging down close to him. She loved the way he smelled, clean and damp from his shower, and she was aroused just being alone with him.

"No, the kids want to go see the place. And I think you should get moved in, set up your computer, get ready to work. Did you tell the driver where to go?" he asked abruptly, as the cab turned onto West Street.

"The Dakota, right?"

Marshall nodded, settled down again, and said reluctantly, "Oh, I've got to go into the office tomorrow. . . ."

"Marshall!" She looked hurt.

"It's okay. Just for a couple of hours. I've got an emergency meeting with attorneys from California. They want me to look at their draft of the brief on the RamDisk appeal case. They're scheduled for the second circuit on Monday morning. But I'll be out of the office by noon. I promise."

April looked out the taxi window, towards New Jersey, as the car went up onto the West Side Highway. She knew they wouldn't be driving upstate by noon. He was going to avoid the trip as long as he could.

"Are you sorry I forced you to buy the place?" she asked next.

"You didn't force me, April!"

"You make me feel as if I did."

"Oh, for Chrissake." He pulled himself up in the backseat of the taxi and looked away from her.

"You said it made you uneasy, being up in those mountains."

"That was because of the weather. I was afraid we might be snowed in on top of Mad River Mountain."

April didn't press. Marshall had wanted to buy a summer place across the Hudson River in Columbia County, but she had insisted on the Mad River Mountain farmhouse. It was located in the center of her research area. He had gone ahead and bought the property to please her, April knew. She also knew there was something about that remote end of the mountain that troubled him. She didn't know what it was that bothered him. And she was sure Marshall didn't know either. And that had struck her as odd, because his family, his great-great-grandmother Boyd, had come from Mad River Mountain.

"How were the kids when you left them?" Marshall asked next, shifting the conversation.

"Greta was playing a computer game with Timmy. And I told Sara that Timmy could stay up until ten o'clock. They're going to order pizza."

"Sounds great to me. I'd love a pizza right now." Marshall smiled, thinking of the children at home.

"They're getting on great, don't you think?"

April nodded. "Yes, they are. I'm sure they'll be at each other's throats at times over the summer, but Greta, I think, likes the idea of having a little brother to boss around, and Timmy, naturally, idolizes her."

"She's really a California kid, isn't she?"

"It's mostly her clothes and hair," April answered, and thinking of how Greta looked reminded her to check her makeup. She was always apprehensive when she went to a dinner party at one of Marshall's partners' homes. The other wives lived such different lives, spent most of their time on clothes. She was just getting used to having money for expensive things, and once again she made a silent prayer, thanking God for sending her Marshall. She would have had a lifetime of loneliness, April knew, if Marshall hadn't asked her to marry him.

"What possessed her to cut her hair like that?" Marshall asked next.

"It's a phase, honey. By the time she goes back to L.A. she'll be trying something else."

"Green dye, probably," he sighed.

"Probably." April glanced at her husband, smiling at his discontent. "There's not much you can do about it. Besides, she'll grow out of it, and so will her hair. She loves you, that's what's important."

"She does, doesn't she?" Marshall said, grinning.

"And who wouldn't?" This time April leaned over and kissed him, nuzzling his ear. "You're a wonderful man. A wonderful husband. And a wonderful father. How's that? Enough praise?"

"More. More."

"Well, it's true."

"Then why do I feel guilty that I'm not spending more time with the three of you?"

"Once this appeals case is done, you'll have time."

"There's always something else, another important case." Now he sounded depressed.

"Honey, it's your work and I'm proud of you. Not everyone is married to the litigator," April said, teasing him with a quote from the *New York Times* article.

"You're my life. You and Timmy and Greta," Marshall said.

April placed her head lightly on his shoulder, whispering, "We understand, darling."

"Does Greta?"

"I think so. She wants to see more of you, of course, that's only natural. We all want that. But she's proud of her Daddy."

The taxi had turned onto Seventy-second Street and was slowing as it approached the massive, turreted apartment building that was the Dakota.

April sat up and caught a glimpse of herself in the driver's rearview mirror. She did look beautiful, she thought, permitting herself a moment of vanity. She was wearing a linen jacket and cropped linen trousers that she had bought the week before at Bergdorf's. And she had pulled her blond hair off her neck, and clipped it together with the silver clasp from Neiman-Marcus that Marshall had given her at Christmas. She had worn no other jewelry. All the firm wives were at least ten years older than she, and, April thought, they wore too much jewelry, too much make-up. She was just thankful that she could rely on her youth, her clear skin, and God's gift of clear blue eyes, the warm shade of soldier blue.

"You look like Cybill Shepherd tonight," Marshall said as the taxi stopped.

"Thank you. You mean, a younger Cybill Shepherd," April answered back, smiling.

"Yes! Yes!" Marshall said quickly, stepping from the taxi and offering his wife a hand.

"What do you really think?" April whispered, letting an edge of her insecurity show as they walked with the doorman to the entrance of the Central Park West co-op.

"I think you're more beautiful than Cybill Shepherd."

"Liar! I've noticed how you're always home on Tuesday night to catch *Moonlighting*."

"I'm in love with Bruce Willis."

"Oh, great. Well, I've got a twenty-year-old boy who wants to spend the summer with me up on Mad River Mountain."

"Over my dead body!"

"That could be arranged," April smiled back as they stepped into the waiting elevator, and the doors slid closed behind them. "That could be arranged."

Three

The buck was pinned by the high-beam headlights, his eyes wide open and unfocused in the glare. Marshall stopped the car and whispered to the children, "Look! Timmy . . . Greta. A deer!"

"Please, darling, the bright lights." April touched her husband's arm, and immediately began to feel herself tense up.

"Where, Daddy?" Greta asked. She had pulled herself up from the backseat and was leaning forward, pushing her head between April and her father.

"Ahead! See? Where the road bends."

"Timmy?" April glanced around and saw that her little boy was asleep, curled up in the wide, soft backseat of the Volvo. She resisted the urge to wake him.

"He's beautiful, Daddy!" Greta whispered.

April said nothing. She hated deer since the accident, but she knew it was irrational, and she did not want the children to develop her fear.

The deer moved then, slowly turned and jumped into the thick trees that edged the dark country road.

"Are we there?" Timmy asked, waking and scrambling up beside Greta.

Marshall took his foot off the brake and the car moved slowly forward.

"Almost, honey," April said.

Marshall had been reluctant to buy the property. It was too isolated, he said. But April wanted it. She loved the old farmhouse, and she wanted to be in Mad River Valley, close to her research.

"It's a lovely house," she said next, turning to Greta. "I hope you like your room."

"There aren't any streetlights," Greta said, looking out at the dark night.

"No, Greta!" Marshall laughed, "I'm afraid not. You're a long way from L.A., sweetheart."

The teenager fell silent and April stared ahead as the headlights sliced the darkness. She found herself listening to the wheels crush the gravel as they went slowly along the mountain road. It wasn't going to be easy, she thought again, for Greta to adjust. They were asking a lot of this little girl, having her leave California and her friends to spend the summer with them in the wilds of New York State. Well, April would do her best. Marshall had promised that this summer belonged to his family, not his law practice, and she had promised to help him make sure Greta had a good time.

"There it is," Marshall announced.

"Where?" Both children climbed forward.

Marshall flipped on the high beams and stopped the Volvo. They were on a slight rise in the mountain road, and the car's headlights spotlighted the old wooden farmhouse.

April had only seen the house twice during the winter, when there was heavy snow on the ground. She had loved the place because it had seemed safe and secure, there at the edge of the mountain road: a warm haven in the winter weather.

Now in the gloomy glow of the bright lights, the house did not seem as inviting. It was much bigger than she had remembered, and more ramshackle. The front porch sagged, there were shutters loose, and a broken pane of glass.

"The repairs are cosmetic," she said, anticipating Marshall's reaction. "Remember, the place hasn't been lived in for over a year."

"And it looks like Luke Grange, this tenant/caretaker of ours, hasn't been doing his job."

"It's old," Greta said, sounding disappointed.

"Yes, it is. Part of the house was built before 1820, when there were Indians living in these hills," Marshall explained, trying to make it sound exciting.

"Indians!" Timmy shouted.

April bit her lip and smiled to herself. She had known Timmy would love the house. It was so much better for him than being in the city, having to be taken by subway to Central Park. Here in the Catskills he could play outside all summer long without fear.

"Well, there aren't Indians anymore, Timmy, I'm afraid. But we own all these woods, and across the valley. Tomorrow we'll go look and see if we can find some old Indian arrowheads." Marshall reached back and ruffled Timmy's blond hair. "How'd you like that?"

Everything would be all right, April told herself. Marshall loved her son, and Timmy was thrilled to have a father. It was up to her to make Greta love her. Still she was worried. It was what her friend Susan had said after Greta's short and tense Christmas visit: Greta's relationship with her father was Oedipal. "You're the evil stepmother, April, that's all," Susan had summed up.

Well, that situation wouldn't last long, April promised

herself. She would win this child's love before the end of summer if it killed her.

Four

"Okay, gang!" Marshall announced. "Let's park and get unpacked. Is anyone hungry?"

"What's that?" Greta asked, looking away from the house. "There's a light in the trees."

"That's Luke's house," Marshall explained, rolling the Volvo down the hill and parking in front of the house. "He has a log cabin down there beyond the pond."

April looked out the window at their new house. It was above her, a dark form at the end of a flagstone walk.

"Mommy," Timmy whispered, "do I have a room to myself?"

"Yes, darling, of course you do!" April turned to her son. "You both have lovely rooms and you can fix them up any way you like. Now what do you think of that!" She leaned over and kissed her son's warm nose.

"Wait here," Marshall instructed. "I'll go up and unlock the front door and turn on some lights."

"Can I come?" Timmy asked, climbing over Greta's long legs and reaching for the door.

"Timmy!" Greta shouted. "Oh, God, you're messing up my clothes! Daddy! I'm coming too!"

As they walked up to the house, squabbling, the children's high voices carried clear through the cold night air.

On the porch Marshall's footsteps sounded heavy and alarming. April could see him struggling to unlock the door in the darkness.

"Marshall?" Her voice lost all its authority against the sharp wind. He didn't hear her. "Marshall, do you need a flashlight?'' she asked again, then opened the glove compartment and dug through the road maps looking for it. When she looked up again, Marshall and the children were gone.

''Oh, dear,'' she whispered, feeling abandoned. She went behind the car and opened the hatch of the station wagon and began to unpack, keeping busy and trying to warm herself. She had forgotten how cold a May night could be in the mountains.

They had jam-packed the rear of the Volvo, filling the car with everything the children might need for the summer, and what April knew the house required just to make it livable.

She pulled the kids' sleeping bags off the top of Greta's three pieces of Gucci luggage and set them down on the lawn. Then, with room to maneuver in the wide hatch, she quickly unpacked the car. The backpack that had once been Tom's which she had kept as the one tangible reminder of her dead husband. Marshall's two pieces of soft luggage and his garment bag full of summer shirts. Timmy's things, stuffed into Marshall's old air force duffel bag. She set it all out on the lawn, then pulled out a box containing Greta's Walkman, her tapes, and her small Sony TV, all of which she had brought with her from California. Wedged between the luggage and April's boxes of linens were Timmy's toys, his new bike. She had made a special trip up to the East Side with Timmy to make sure he got just the one he wanted.

When the toys and luggage were unpacked, April paused to catch her breath. Up at the house lights were being flipped on, first one, then another. Seeing them made April feel better.

''Hello.''

The man's voice was gentle and close. April jumped away, terrified, and stumbled against the car, losing her balance.

''I'm sorry.'' The man reached for her.

April felt his strong hand on her arm. In the moonlight, all that was visible was the shape of his head, his long hair, his broad shoulders.

''Let go!'' she demanded. She had been mugged once near Columbia and had scared the attacker away with her shouting. ''Who are you?'' she asked illogically, as if the question might stop him.

"Mrs. Benard? It's me. Luke. Luke Grange." He let go of her. "The caretaker." He stepped away, as if to give her room and seem less threatening.

"Damn it! You frightened me to death. . . ."

"I'm sorry, Mrs. Benard. I heard the car."

". . . Sneaking up behind me in the dark." April kept talking, gaining confidence from the sound of her voice. Her whole body was trembling. She stepped away from the caretaker, went back to unloading the Volvo, pulled another small trunk to the open hatch.

"Let me," Luke offered, reaching for the heavy box.

"I can handle it!" April insisted. She was embarrassed that she had been so frightened, that she had shouted at the hired hand.

"It's my job, Mrs. Benard." Smiling, the caretaker took the liquor box from her grasp.

The porch light flipped on and the front door opened. Marshall stepped into the bright light, followed by the children.

"Mommy! Mommy!" Timmy shouted from the porch, "It's a big house. Mommy! A big house."

"Luke?" Marshall called, "is that you?"

"Yes, Mr. Benard." The slim young man carried the box up the flagstone, explaining as he approached the house, "I heard the car and thought you might need help."

"The house is freezing, Luke. Can you start a fire in the front room?" Marshall asked.

"I wasn't sure if you were planning on arriving tonight," Luke kept explaining, "I'd have put down a fire."

"Make sure the flue is open," April instructed, feeling a need to establish herself with the caretaker.

"I'm cold!" Greta complained.

"Yes, Greta, we all are," April said, following after Luke, "but we're going to build a nice warm fire. Now you and Timmy come help carry some of your things to your rooms." Shivering herself, she stepped past the young caretaker, looking up at him as she did. April had not met the man before and was surprised by his looks. With his finely shaped face and strong, angular body, he looked more like a male model than a mountain type. "While Luke makes the fire, Marshall, would you bring the luggage up from the car?'' she said quickly, making an effort not to stare openly at Luke Grange. ''I'll start getting Timmy and Greta something to eat.''

The kitchen was at the rear of the house, through the pantry. April guessed that it had been a summer kitchen, only later connected to the main building. Once they were settled she would remodel, making the kitchen bigger and not so separate. For the next few months, though, it would have to stay the way it was, tucked away and out of sight at the back of the big house.

''Well, Greta, what do you think?'' April said as the teenager followed her and Timmy into the kitchen.

''I'm still cold.''

''Not for long,'' April said as cheerfully as she could. ''I'm going to give you both hot soup to eat. Meantime, Greta, would you see if you can find the dishes? The realtor said we had a complete set in one of the cabinets.''

''What are we having, Mommy?'' Timmy said.

''Here, I'll show you!'' April bent over and, picking up her four-year-old son, set him on the butcher-block counter. She began unpacking groceries as Greta checked the cupboards.

''They must be in here,'' Greta announced, reaching the pine cabinet door.

As she pulled it open rats came screeching out, two large, gray rodents tumbling down onto the wood floor. In the shocked stillness of the moment, April could hear their tiny nails scratching frantically on the wide barnwood floor as they ran for dark corners.

Greta was screaming. One heavy rat clung to the sleeve of her blouse, its tiny feet tangled in the fine weave. The girl swung her arm and banged the rat against the refrigerator. It thumped against the metal, and dropped to the kitchen floor.

''Christ! What's going on?'' Marshall ran into the kitchen and swung his screaming daughter up into his arms.

''Rats!'' April said calmly. ''We have rats in our cabinets, that's all.'' She went to Timmy, still perched on the counter, his legs tucked under him. He was laughing.

''Mom! Open another door!'' Timmy shouted.

''They left food in these goddamn cabinets all year,'' Marshall said, glancing inside.

"They're just rodents, Marshall," April said. "This is what happens over the winter. All sorts of animals get into an empty house."

"Rats, Daddy! Rats!" Greta shouted, trying to regain her father's full attention.

"It's okay, sweetie. Everything is okay," Marshall whispered, calming himself as well as his daughter with his voice.

"Marshall, go upstairs with the children and help them unpack," April asked. "I'll get dinner on the table. Everyone will feel better once we eat. Okay?" Then, as if to prove to everyone that everything was under control, she turned and pulled open the top drawer of the pine hutch. There were no rats, no squeals.

Behind her, she heard her husband organizing things in his best attorney's tone. "Okay, gang, let's go see your bedrooms and then, guess what? ... I brought marshmallows. We can roast them in the fireplace, once Luke has it going. How does that sound?"

The two children cheered loudly and April turned to see the happy smile on Timmy's face. He was looking up lovingly at his stepfather, reaching out for him, waiting to be lifted off the butcher-block counter and carried upstairs.

Marshall glanced over at April and winked. He had a wonderful wide smile that made him look like a kid himself, full of deviltry. His blitheness was what had drawn her to him. He wasn't like the other men she met in the months after Tom's death, men obsessed with getting ahead in their careers. Marshall had had all the time in the world for her. At least he had had time when they were first married, she thought again, and quickly reminded herself how Marshall had promised to spend more time with them, with his new family.

"Okay, darling?" Marshall asked, watching her, responding to the curious expression on her face.

April nodded and smiled back. She looked at her family, all standing together, as if in a family portrait. Her dark handsome husband and his lithe blond daughter; her little Timmy, all freckles and golden brown cheeks, with his father's almond-shaped chocolate eyes, and she thought: This is my life now.

And everything would be okay here in the country, she told

herself. Her son was happy and safe. She was out of the hot, humid city, and she had the whole summer ahead to get to know Greta, to do her research, to spend time with the man who had saved her life, who had found her when she thought she'd never again find peace, happiness and love.

Yes, she told herself, she had nothing to worry about at all.

Five

Marshall picked up the bottle and divided the last of the Bordeaux between them.

"No, darling, I've had enough," April said. Turning, she stretched out in front of the fire, felt the heat burn her face. She was drunk, she knew.

"This is great, isn't it?" Marshall asked. "I'm glad you talked me into buying this place." He shifted around on the floor and slid down beside her. "Happy?"

April nodded, but did not open her eyes. She would fall asleep there in the warmth of the blaze. It was a lovely thought.

Marshall kissed her eyelids, her cheek. She smiled but did not stir. He touched her breast and she shivered. His fingers were cold from the wine bottle.

"Sweetheart," she said sleepily. "Not tonight, okay?" she asked, not opening her eyes, not moving. She wished she wouldn't have to move for the rest of her life.

Marshall did not stop. Abruptly and roughly, he ran his fingers down the slope of her stomach and drove his hand beneath the tight waist of her jeans and grabbed her crotch.

In the firelight, his face looked cold and sullen, and April was immediately angered by his actions. At home, he was always slow and gentle in his lovemaking, and his sudden crude behavior upset her. He had had too much wine, April rationalized.

She turned away and faced the flame. The heat of the fire flushed her face. Marshall kept unbuttoning her white blouse. She closed her eyes. He liked her to be passive when they made love. It was something he had not told her in words, yet she knew. He made love much differently than Tom, and it surprised her that two men could find pleasure in such different ways. Tom had liked her to be aggressive and demanding, to seek her own satisfaction. Marshall was put off by her sexual hunger, and after their first time together, she had learned how to respond to his desires, to be shy and pliant when he took her.

"We should go into the bedroom. The kids." And without waiting, she scooped up her clothes and, picking up her glass, finished off the last of the wine, then walked across the front room to their bedroom. There were no curtains on the windows, and she finished undressing while watching the dark woods. She could hear Marshall walking through the house, checking the doors. He was truly a city person, she thought, slipping into bed. The sheets were cold and she shivered, wishing Marshall would hurry.

He came back into the bedroom and stood at the front windows, looking out. The full moon filled the bedroom with its glow. "Darling?" she asked, keeping her voice low. "What is it?" she asked, when he didn't respond.

"I thought I saw something."

"Maybe it was a neighbor," April said, snuggling down into the pillows and blankets.

"It wasn't a neighbor. There aren't any houses on this road," he answered, sitting down on the edge of the bed.

April poked her head out of the blankets.

"Was it the caretaker?"

In the dark room he shook his head. "I guess it wasn't anything—just the shape of the trees."

"Where?"

"Across the road, by the barns."

She was out of bed at once.

"April, it's not anyone! I mean, we're the only house up at this end of the valley." He turned around to watch his wife. "Stay away from the window! You can be seen if someone is out there." He climbed into bed and shuddered. "The bed is freezing! Hurry up!"

"Once," April whispered, coming back to bed and hugging Marshall, "when I was at summer camp, I thought there was someone in the cabin. The noise kept getting louder and louder, and I was driving myself crazy, imagining who it might be. I was sure it was some mad mountain killer, or something. And . . ."

"And it wasn't?"

"Of course not. It was a brown squirrel that had gotten caught in the wall. We just have to learn to live with the peace and quiet of country life."

"And the animals."

"Animals are better than muggers," she said, and thought at once of Tom, of how he had been killed, and as always, deep in a secret corner of her heart, she felt the pain of her loss.

Marshall grabbed her breast then, alarming her, and she started to protest, but thought no, tonight she'd let him have his way, even if he did bruise her. If nothing else, it would take her mind off Tom.

Timmy woke, was fully awake, but did not open his eyes. He never opened his eyes until he was sure he was safe. For a moment, he wasn't sure where he was and it scared him. He began to breathe quickly and almost called out for his mother, then he remembered: the long car ride, the house in the woods, Greta, rats. He grinned in the dark, thinking of the rats scurrying across the kitchen floor. He opened his eyes and looked for Sam. The teddy bear had slipped off the bed. He reached down, picked it up, tucked it into his embrace, and looked around.

His mother had left on the hall light, and his bedroom door was open. He sat on the edge of the bed, letting his bare feet dangle, and tried to think what he should do. His feet were cold, and he pulled his legs up under him, staring across the new bedroom. He was crying, he realized, but he did not know why. He often cried and it always made him feel better when he did. He wiped away the tears, then blew his nose on the sleeve of his wool pajamas.

Smokey moonlight filled the room, spread over the furniture like white sheets. He listened for his mother, for Greta, sleeping down the hall. He couldn't hear them, there were no muffled voices from down the hallway, no one spoke, but there were noises. The house was squeaking, pulling, tugging at itself. And there was wind. It blew against the walls and howled. Then, in the window, a huge bird flew down to perch on the sill. It looked like one of those creatures from his *Wild Things* book, with the body of a owl, and a hog's face. It kept watching him through the glass, yet when he waved, the bird flapped its wide wings and sailed off.

Timmy jumped off the bed and ran to the window. The bird hovered over the pond, then soared over the trees that framed the side lawn. Timmy laughed, thrilled by the way the bird sailed on its wide webbed wings. He wondered what the bird was, and thought again of running downstairs to ask his mother.

Then he saw more creatures on the lawn. They had come crawling from the woods, as if called by the bird. Timmy pressed his face against the cold pane of glass as the animals raced across the lawn. They were all the size of dogs, but with odd shaped bodies. Some trotted on four feet, while others, waddling on their hind legs, ran in quick bursts of speed. They all had furry bear bodies, short turkey legs, and the round yellow faces of jack-o'-lanterns.

Timmy slipped down from the window and ran back to his bed, crawled quickly under the quilts and buried his head. He was asleep, he knew, having a "bad dream" as his mommy said when he woke up crying in the dark. There were no funny animals on the lawn. It was only a dream, and, sighing, he fell swiftly back to sleep.

Six

ZZZZZZZZZZZRRRRRRRRRRR

"God! What was that?" Marshall bolted up in bed.

"A chain saw," April muttered. She rolled over, but did not open her eyes. "Your caretaker must be cutting down a tree."

"The hell he is!" Marshall swung his legs out of bed. He reached into his open suitcase to pull out fresh underwear. "It's the middle of the goddamn night," he swore, standing and pulling on his shorts.

"It's seven, honey." April raised her head to read her watch on the night table. "And I'm sure Luke has been up for hours. This is the country, darling. Everyone has a day's work done by dawn." She lay back and closed her eyes. Her body hurt, as it always did after she had made love with Marshall.

"Not on my land, he doesn't!" He reached for his jeans and pulled them on.

From across the backyard and pond came another long roar as the chain saw cut into wood.

April watched Marshall pull on his shoes and lace them up. The shoes were new, thick hiking boots that he had bought from a mail order catalogue. Since closing on the farm, he had been buying a lot of things like that—new equipment and outfits for the country. The shoes were better for the Rockies than the Catskills, but men, like boys, she had learned, needed their new toys. She smiled. She found it endearing.

"I'll be right back." He slipped on his tan hat and bush jacket.

"Honey, wait!" April couldn't stop herself from smiling. "Look at yourself, please." She bit her lip, trying not to laugh. "You look as if you're going on a safari. All the way

28

to the other side of the pond! Take off the bush jacket, sweetheart. This is the Catskills, not Kenya."

Marshall paused, frowning into the small mirror over the dresser. Then he threw off the bush jacket and stormed out of the bedroom, his boots thumping across the wide barnboard floors.

If the chain saw didn't wake the children, his boots would, April thought, and as if on cue she heard Timmy calling to her from upstairs.

"Yes, darling, I'm coming," she answered. On the second floor landing she paused and looked out the window.

Marshall was below her on the back lawn, circling the pond, heading for the caretaker's cabin. His footsteps cut a ragged edge through the lawn's deep frost. Then April lost sight of him in the mist as he went down the path into the woods.

"Mommy!" Timmy shouted from the back bedroom.

"Coming," April answered, and then to include her stepdaughter, she said quickly, "Greta, are you awake?" The teenager did not respond.

All right for you, April thought, annoyed. She went by Greta's door without a word and walked into Timmy's room.

"Well, good morning, darling! Did you have a nice sleep?"

Her son was curled up into the corner of the bed with the blankets pulled around him. He was rubbing the sleep from his brown almond eyes.

"Are they gone?" he asked.

"Gone? Who?" It was the rats, she thought. He had been frightened after all. "Yes, darling, the rats are gone. You don't have to worry about them." She slipped her hand under the covers and touched him. His small feet were warm. "Timmy, do you feel okay?" At once, she felt his forehead and cheek with the back of her hand. "I think you're running a fever, honey," she said softly. That was all she needed: Timmy sick on their first day in the country.

"Are they gone?" he asked again, looking up.

"Who, darling?" She slid her hand beneath his pajama top to feel his body.

"The wild things."

April studied her son.

"There aren't any wild things, darling, in the trees. Wild

things and little people and fairies are just in your books.''

''But I want to play with them,'' he said, flopping down in bed again, yawning.

''Who, darling? What?''

''Those wild things. They were cute.'' He rolled over, grinning.

April shook her head. At times she had no idea what he was talking about. He would wake in the morning chatting away about some bit of an event that had happened the day before at nursery school, or in the park. She simply nodded, smiled, tried to keep him cheery.

''Let's get up, honey, and we'll go downstairs and have French toast. How would you like that?'' She nuzzled her son and kissed his cheek, hugged him tightly.

From behind her, Greta announced, ''I saw them too. . . .''

April glanced at Greta, frowning.

''Well, I did!'' The teenager came into the room, circling around to the side windows, but keeping her distance from her stepmother. ''Last night I saw these weird things running across the lawn. You were already in bed and they came up to your windows and peeped inside. They were watching you.''

April glanced at Timmy, then at Greta. The thin tall girl was wearing a Miami Vice T-shirt, panties, and nothing else. Her legs were long and lovely. She would be a beautiful woman when she grew up, once she got rid of her punk haircut and let her blond hair grow out. April found she was slightly jealous and also annoyed at Greta for feeding Timmy's fantasies.

''Well, there's nothing on the lawn now but wood-chucks,'' she replied. Maybe, she thought, Greta just wanted to be included in the conversation, to be considered part of the family.

''Where's Daddy?'' Greta said as April helped Timmy pull on his clothes.

''He's off to see Luke, but he'll be back in a few minutes. I'm going downstairs to start the French toast.''

''Mommy always has pancakes on Saturdays,'' Greta said.

''That's nice. We're having French toast,'' April answered back. ''Your father loves it.'' April smiled down at her stepdaughter and said, "Okay you two! Breakfast is in twenty minutes. Let's get a move on."

"April?"

"Yes, Greta?" April paused at the doorway.

"I'll cook my own pancakes."

"Fine as long as you clean up your own mess." And she went on downstairs angry now at herself for letting Greta put her in a bad mood.

Seven

Down in the kitchen, April reached to open the pine hutch and stopped. Something moved inside the cupboard, toppling the canned goods. Her hand halted in mid-air.

"Oh, shit!" She knew at once what had happened. The night before Marshall had set a rat trap and now one was caught, thumping itself to death in the cupboard.

Without opening the cabinet, she spun around and went back through the house, grabbing her heavy Irish sweater as she walked, and ran out into the cold morning.

Another roar of the chain saw met her. She went down off the porch and onto the lawn, following Marshall's footsteps in the frost. Her Reeboks and wool socks were soaked before she had reached the edge of the pond. Still she kept running, following the sound of the chain saw.

She hadn't been into the woods before. When they first saw the house, the fields and woods were under two feet of snow, and she had not come back with Marshall to walk the property line before the closing. But the path into the trees was well worn, and the sound of the chain saw grew louder once she entered the woods. Then she spotted Marshall's bright red shirt, and slowing, exhausted from her running, she stepped off the path and went through the underbrush to where her husband stood with the caretaker in the middle of a birch grove.

"Listen, you fucking redneck!" April heard her husband shout at Luke Grange. "This is my property, my trees, and I'll kick your goddamn ass off this land if you don't do what I tell you, boy."

The caretaker stared back at Marshall and then without speaking, he squeezed the trigger of the chain saw, and its noise roared into Mad River Valley.

ZZZZZZZZZRRRRRRRRRR

April stood trembling at the edge of the clearing. She had never seen her husband so angry, never heard that tone in his voice, and Luke Grange had completely ignored him. The caretaker was now working his way down the length of a fallen tree, cutting fireplace lengths off the birch. Bent over, with his legs spread to handle the weight of the heavy chain saw, he moved quickly, whipping the long bar from one cut to the next. Within minutes, he had reduced the slender tree to a dozen logs.

April ran across the clearing to her husband's side and quickly slipped her arm into Marshall's as the caretaker turned off the chain saw and standing up, nodded to her.

"What's going on? Why are we cutting down birch trees?"

"We're not!" There was still an edge to Marshall's voice. He nodded toward the caretaker. "Luke says these trees are blighted. They could ruin the whole birchstand if he doesn't trim them out." Slowly he was regaining control of himself.

"That's right, Mrs. Benard," Luke added. He took off his John Deere cap as he addressed her.

Now, in the bright daylight of morning, April saw Luke clearly for the first time. He was the same size as Marshall, but not as tall as Tom, and she thought he was about twenty, younger than she by ten years. But then he brushed back his long blond hair, and she saw his eyes. Soft and brown, they nonetheless resembled Marshall's, and then she realized it was his facial expression, the way he bore down at her, seized her up, that made her think of her husband. He was standing close to her, still breathing deeply from cutting the wood. He was wearing a SUNY college sweatshirt over a heavy blue workshirt. His blond hair was shoulder length but he had swept it back and tied it with a shoelace. Her head was level with his chest.

"Are you sure you don't just need firewood for next winter?" April asked coolly. "Or are you selling off cords of wood?"

She felt, rather than saw, Marshall stiffen beside her. "Okay," he said, suddenly stern, "don't cut down trees unless you talk to me first. Understand?"

April looked away so as not to catch the caretaker's eyes. She glanced up at the tips of the tall white birch trees still caught in the fog. There were a few birds in the high branches and as she watched, a large bird dropped off its perch, sailed down into the small clearing where they stood, where her husband was telling Luke Grange what to do. It took a moment before April realized that the bird was a hawk and it was diving at them, at Marshall, and she shouted too late as it struck.

It caught Marshall's new hat. Its claws bit into the cloth and plucked the hat away, then beating hard with its wide wings, the hawk rose gracefully, sailed off into the trees and mist, brushing April's face with its feathered wing. Marshall fell back, swearing and swinging his arms to protect himself, then stumbled into the deep soft mat of fallen leaves.

"Are you okay?" April asked, kneeling to help him. She had never seen an attack like this, but she knew hawks did swoop down on farm animals.

"Jesus, yes, but just. Did you see that goddamn bird?"

"It happens sometimes," Luke said. "Hawks become confused or are attracted by a particular color. Misty weather like this fouls up their radar."

"He could've clawed out my eyes," April said, shaken. Then she remembered the rat in the cupboard. "Marshall, I need your help in the kitchen," she said vaguely, not wanting Luke Grange to know why. "Would you come up to the house?"

"What's the matter?"

"More rats," she said reluctantly. "At least, I think so."

Marshall laughed. "April, if you're going to live in the

country, then you'd better not be afraid of a few rats." He wrapped his arm tightly around her shoulders.

"Don't!" she said, wriggling free, then shot him a glance. He had let the caretaker see that he was afraid of the hawk; now he wanted to show Luke that he was the man of the family. Boys, she thought, they never stop trying to prove themselves.

"I mean, you make it sound as if you cornered a brown bear in the kitchen," Marshall went on.

"It might be a snake," Luke said quietly.

"Snake!" Marshall's casual pose shattered.

Luke nodded. "This time of year, first thing after the thaw, snakes come out of hibernation. That's an old stone foundation you've got on that house, and in the fall snakes burrow down into the crevices for the winter. I've been seeing snakes round my place this whole last week."

"What kind?" Marshall asked, the bravado gone.

"Oh, you know, milk and garter, some Queen and Copperhead. But you don't get many Copperheads up around the house." He glanced at both of them. "You want me to take a look?"

"Yes," April said quickly, before Marshall could decide not to admit they needed help. "Could you come now?" she went on quickly. "The children are awake and I don't want them frightened."

"Oh, they'll get used to snakes," the caretaker remarked, as he lifted the chain saw and the can of gasoline. "That's the great thing about kids, you know. They adapt lots better than we give them credit for."

He smiled at April, ducking his head as he did, and she was immediately taken by his gentleness. Luke would be all right, she thought. She wouldn't be afraid to have him living on the property, so close to the house.

"Do you have a family, Luke?" she asked as they walked through the woods.

Luke laughed softly and shook his head.

"Oh, no, ma'am. None of my own, just lots of relatives hereabouts."

"And why is that? My guess is that all the girls up here in

the Catskills would be calling on you," April teased, but also wanting to learn more about the young man.

"No girls up here, I'm afraid, except my kin."

"Then what about all the city people?" April pressed. "Camp counselors? Summer renters?"

"Let's concentrate on those snakes, okay?" Marshall interrupted, pushing by both of them on the narrow path. "After I get back from town, Luke, I want to go around the property with you and work up a flow chart on all the major projects for this summer. We've got a lot of cosmetic problems right off. The house is in terrible shape. It needs repairs and a fresh coat of paint. Be ready to talk first thing after lunch." He took off for the house, almost at a run.

April smiled at Luke to soften Marshall's rudeness. They had both been abrupt with the caretaker, and now she wanted to smooth over any bruised egos.

"You'll be in the country all summer then?" Luke asked, falling in step.

"Yes. With the children." April glanced up again. There was something so familiar about him. "You're from here?" she asked.

"Yes."

"You don't sound like it." She was about to say more about her research on the area, then decided it was best to keep quiet. It might make her work harder if everyone knew why she had picked that piece of property on Mad River Mountain for her country home.

"I couldn't be more local," Luke said. "I was raised in the mountains, south of the highway, in the lower valley. One of my ancestors was among the first settlers in Mad River. That's the family story anyway."

"When was that?" April asked, now very interested.

"That would have been in the late 1760s. His name was Richard Ely and he was an immigrant, an indentured servant from Scotland. The story is he jumped ship in Kingston and disappeared into these mountains, hid from whatever law there was, and settled with the local Indians. He was the first white person, they say, to build a homestead on Mad River."

"But there is no river."

"There once was, but rivers shift. There's nothing left but dry gullies deep in this valley."

"Did the Indians call it Mad River?"

"The Indians called it Muddicaia but gradually it became Mad River."

They had reached the back lawn and the pond. Marshall was already halfway across the wet grass, going toward the back deck and door. She saw the children on the deck and she waved.

"Your daughter," Luke said, "is quite a little beauty."

"Yes," April said, surprised by the comment, then added carefully, "She's actually my stepdaughter, and she's also very young."

"Oh, she's not that young," Luke commented vaguely.

They all assembled in the kitchen. Marshall stood back, content to let Luke handle the job. The caretaker opened the pine cupboard doors without apprehension, as if he knew there was nothing in the house, no rodents or vermin anywhere on the property, that could harm him.

A three-foot snake, its flat head caught in a rat trap, flung itself out and dropped noisily to the worn floor.

Greta screamed.

"Jesus!" Marshall swore, jumping back.

The snake thrashed back and forth, trying to free itself. Greta was screaming uncontrollably now, choking on her fear. Yet she didn't run or hide her eyes. She seemed hypnotized by the sight of the long, gray snake, and watched as it wrapped itself around a leg of the counter, then curled into the corner of the kitchen, trying to escape.

Luke crouched and seized the reptile behind the head to lift it up. The long, limbless animal hung loose, its dead white underbelly twisting and jerking in the air. The snake had swallowed a mouse, April saw. Beneath where Luke had pinched its scaly body, there was a fat bulge.

"Get it out of here!" Marshall demanded, going to his daughter. Turning her around, he pushed her gently toward the pantry and out of the kitchen.

April saw Timmy then. He was staring at the reptile in wide-eyed fascination.

"It's just a garter snake, Mrs. Benard," Luke said, removing the trap. "They're big, but harmless." He spoke calmly, as if a snake in the cupboard with a mouse stuck in its belly was something they could expect every day.

"Thank you," April said quickly, trying to bring order back to the kitchen. "If you could just get rid of it . . ."

She and Timmy followed Luke through the pantry and dining room and out onto the deck.

"Can I go with him, Mommy, please?" Timmy asked, hanging onto April's arm.

"Luke, do you mind?"

"No, no. Come on, Timmy. I'll show you what to do with snakes."

"Let me carry him, please!" Timmy shouted, skipping after the caretaker.

"Where are they going?" Marshall asked, appearing on the deck. Timmy, still begging for the snake, was following Luke toward the path in the woods.

"Beyond the pond," April explained, "so the snake will be too disoriented to crawl back to the house."

"Why doesn't he just kill the goddamn thing?"

"He won't," April answered. She stood with her arms crossed, watching Luke and her son. "The snake is harmless, and mountain people won't kill anything that's harmless to them."

"We'll see about that. I won't have Greta terrified again by that snake," Marshall announced, starting off the deck after them.

"Marshall, don't!" Timmy was close behind Luke, still excited at having the snake caught, at being so close to it. "It will only upset Timmy. Just let Luke turn it loose. God knows, it's not the only snake in these hills."

She turned away from Marshall and went back into the house. Something was bothering her, and for a moment she couldn't pin it down. She wasn't that afraid of the snake. Nor was it Greta's hysterical outburst.

No, it was Luke, she realized. Luke bothered her. And at first she didn't understand why. There was something about him, the way he walked, the sly, little-boy way he looked at her, the way he spoke to her, the intimacy of his tone, and then she recognized what it was.

Luke Grange reminded her of Tom.

Eight

Marshall stopped the Volvo as they came out of the trees. They had crested Mad River Mountain and the town was below them, wedged between cliffs. Built up the steep slopes were several rows of wooden frame houses, nestled between the rocks and outcroppings. There were half a dozen streets, all short and irregular, dark patches of black-top beneath the thick new green leaves of spring.

"That's the town?" April asked.

Marshall nodded. "Not much of a place. You'll need to drive down to Kingston for any real shopping. Or I can bring up what we need from the city when I come on Friday."

"If I can buy milk and the *Times*, I'll be okay," April answered, being positive.

"It's ugly," Greta stated.

"Well, it ain't Beverly Hills, honey," April laughed. "But maybe it has its own tacky charm," she added as Marshall started the car and went slowly down the steep mountain road, heading for the little town.

April eyed the road nervously as they descended. The spring rains had already washed out sections of the gravel, leaving ruts and a soft shoulder. Glancing down, April saw they were only inches from the deep gorge.

"Is this the only way?" she asked.

"No. You can go out the way we came in last night and take the highway around the valley. That road is better, but it takes twice as long. There's no easy way to get into this town.''

Just then a pickup truck came around the turn, spinning on the gravel and tearing up the road. Reacting suddenly to the sight of the truck, Marshall jerked the big station wagon out, toward the edge of the mountain road.

"Marshall!" April shouted as the heavy car slid toward the soft outer shoulder, then broke through the gravel, and tipped to one side. April screamed.

"Mommy! Mommy!" Timmy's head bounced first against the front seat, then against the back door.

"It's okay, sweetheart. It's okay.'' She said quickly to calm the child. She reached back to him, and said quietly to Marshall, "Be careful, it may give way.'' As she spoke the front of the car shifted again toward the edge. Out the side window the valley loomed up, the steep tar roofs of the houses angled sharply. It made her dizzy, as if she were falling through space. She looked away.

"Get out of the car!" Marshall ordered.

The heavy front end shifted as he spoke and the second front wheel broke through the soft edge. The car lurched.

Greta screamed.

"Easy, easy,'' April whispered, speaking softly to them all. She wondered why she didn't feel more terrified, then realized it was because of Timmy. She had to act calmly because of him. "Okay, Greta, Timmy, we're getting out of the car, but slowly, all right?'' She forced herself to smile.

"We're going to die,'' Greta whispered. Her face had paled and she kept staring into the deep gorge.

"No, we're not, Greta!" April said confidently. "Now open your door slowly and step out.''

"Daddy?" Greta asked.

"Go ahead, honey, do what April says. You'll be okay.''

"I can't open it.'' Greta pushed against the heavy door.

"That's okay,'' April said quickly. "Try Timmy's side, Greta, slowly.'' The frightened girl moved cautiously as she reached over the boy, realizing that the car might slip again if their weight shifted too suddenly. Straining, and breathing quickly, Greta pushed hard, but the door would open only a few inches. It was being blocked by a lump of grass. April looked to Marshall. "It won't open because of the angle."

"The window! They can get out that way."

April nodded and immediately rolled down the back window behind her. "You first, Timmy. I want you to climb out, then go stand on the other side of the road. Away from the car." She helped her small son over Greta's knees. He slid easily out the window.

"I can't! I'm too big!" Greta cried, panicking.

"No you're not, sweetheart."

"Yes, I am! I am!"

"Honey, honey! Now stop it!" Marshall ordered his daughter. "Do what I tell you."

He reached back carefully, to calm Greta and help her start the climb, but the terrified girl pulled away violently. In response, the car lurched again in the soft earth, tipped up and over the edge, and slid several feet farther down the embankment.

Greta screamed. April screamed. Marshall threw himself back in his seat, as if his weight could stop the car from sliding.

"Jesus," he whispered, staring at his wife and realizing how precarious the car was, how close to death they were, there on the edge of the road.

"Greta!" April said, trying to control her fear. "You have to get out on your own. Your father and I can't help you. Do you understand? Are you listening?"

Greta shook her head, too panicked to move.

"Greta," April said again, encouraging. "Move yourself closer to the door." April took her time, waited for the child to do just that. One step at a time, she kept telling herself.

Slowly, carefully, Greta slid nearer the door.

"Wonderful!" April whispered. "Wonderful. Now, Greta, I want you—we want you, your father and I—to slip out through that window."

"I can't." The terror in the young girl's eyes nearly broke April's heart, and for the first time, she felt genuine affection for Greta.

"Yes, you can. Reach out with your hands, grab hold of the roof and pull yourself up. The car will move a little.

That's okay. Don't stop. Just pull yourself up as you do on a gym bar. Understand?''

Greta nodded slowly.

"Good!" It was a risk, April realized. Greta's weight might be all that was keeping them from crashing down through the evergreens and into the valley. "Get a tight hold," April instructed. "And when you're ready, pull yourself up and out in one motion. Don't stop." She took a deep breath as the child shifted herself. "Okay, honey, go ahead."

"Daddy?"

"It's all right, darling. Do what April says. You'll be safe and sound in a second. Daddy loves you," he added, as he, too, realized what might happen to April and himself once Greta started moving.

"Mommy! Mommy!" Frightened by waiting all alone, Timmy was running back across the road to her side of the car. "Mommy, let me back in."

"Timmy! Away from the car, now!" April shouted, her control breaking at last.

Timmy stopped. He had never heard his mother speak to him in that tone before.

"Greta, go!" she said in the same voice, and this time Greta obeyed, frightened by April as well as by what she had to do next. She lifted herself up and out of the window, clearing the car in one quick motion. As she propelled herself outward, the big station wagon shifted in the mud. As she tumbled free and landed safely, it swung slowly, steadily toward the driver's side, with Marshall's heavier weight. April screamed.

The car stopped. Its rear axle was wedged against a boulder so that the front dangled over the cliff, poised in space. April couldn't look. She buried her face in her hands. She had moments more to live, she realized, becoming suddenly and strangely calm, as if her life was no longer hers to control. And she thought at that moment of the car accident years ago and the endless time it took for Tom's car to spin on the icy highway and hit the charging deer.

Then she heard the truck.

It was the heavy sound of an old V-8 laboring up the

steep mountain road. April looked up. Marshall was staring past her, his eyes wide with anticipation.

She turned her head cautiously, fixed her eyes on the corner of the empty road. An open-bed hay truck pulled into view and stopped, halted by the sight of the two children standing in the middle of the gravel road, and the station wagon, pinned against the rocks, dangling in space.

A group of men and boys jumped from the flatbed. There were more boys and girls peering at them over the wooden sides.

Inbreds, April realized at once. The clan she had been seeking were now around her. As they approached, she recognized from photos the strange deformity of their faces. They were either Tassels or Holts, and even in her fear, with her life in peril, she was thrilled by her first actual sighting of them, this lost, anthropologically precious race.

They were all small, dark and wiry, with flat, blunt noses, large watery pink eyes, and enormous, pumpkin-shaped heads. They were like creatures from another place and time, another planet. Even the photographs had not prepared her.

"Jesus! Who are they?" Marshall whispered.

"They're the people I want to research. There are two families, the Tassels and Holts. They don't look very human, do they?"

Marshall took a deep breath. "I've seen worse, I guess, but this clan could give anyone a race."

The older men and boys circled Timmy and Greta without a word and came to investigate the car. Then from the back of the truck, a few of the young men pulled out planks of wood, carrying them to the road's edge. April started to say something, to shout instructions, but Marshall said quickly, "Let them be."

They went to work immediately, without speaking, and without, it seemed to April, any fear for their own lives. Several of the young men jumped over the edge of the road and went beneath the Volvo to shore up the station wagon with the wooden planks. Then they turned around their battered old truck and backed up behind the car to hitch a heavy chain to the Volvo's rear axle.

"I hope to God they know what they're doing," April said.

"They do," Marshall answered. These strange people gave him an odd confidence. The chain could break and even now, as they were being helped, the car might tumble down the mountain. But Marshall didn't think so. He looked at Greta and Timmy, signaled that they should move away and keep clear of the men. Then he held his breath and listened to the truck's engine roar and strain as it tried to drag the heavy station wagon back to safety. "Come on, baby, let's work," he whispered.

The Volvo tipped and swayed and April grabbed Marshall, dug her nails into his arm. Then she felt the car's wheels grip the long planks, begin to roll and in one quick and sudden jerk, pulled onto solid ground.

"Thank God," April exclaimed, exhausted by her tension. She was safe, she realized, and she opened the door and swept Timmy up into her arms, hugging him tightly as she turned to the men and began to thank them.

They shied away from her, ducking their heads, hurrying to climb back onto the truckbed. They moved quickly with awkward and jerky strides. There was nothing feeble about the young men, April saw. Their limbs were short and deformed, but with the muscle development of body builders. Their strength, the deformity of their gourdlike heads, and their large pink and watery eyes were frightening at close range.

Marshall came around the car, thanking the men and talking easily to them. April was surprised, seeing the ease with which he dealt with the local people. Watching him, April saw that her husband had a natural gift with the strange mountain clan. Well, she thought, perhaps everything would be all right for him on the mountain. She wondered if it was because of his law experience, of having to deal with so many diverse types, that made him handle these people with such ease.

Two of the dwarfish men ducked beneath the station wagon and unbuckled the towing line, silently working, dragging the heavy chain back to the flatbed.

"Marshall! Perhaps we could give them some money for helping us," April suggested, stepping over to her husband.

"It doesn't work that way," he said quietly. "It's not . . . neighborly."

She smiled up at the collection of mountain people standing in the flatbed truck. They were staring silently at her and Marshall, peering at them through the slats and hanging over the wooden sides, their heavy pumpkin-heads lobbed to one side or the other, too much, it appeared, for their short necks.

"Thank you for your help." She called out and kept smiling, pleased that her family's first encounter with the inbreds had gone well. It would make it easier, she thought, to spend the summer up on the mountain.

The driver poked his head out the cab window and stared down at them. He was older than the others, April saw, grandfatherly. A leprechaun of an old man, with a Santa Claus beard and a full head of white hair. April stepped closer to hear him over the roaring truck engine.

"You people called Benard?" he asked.

"What?" April glanced at Marshall, not understanding the old man's diction.

"Yes," Marshall replied. "I'm Marshall Benard and this is my wife. Thank you for the help, for saving our lives, I guess."

He kept talking, speaking slowly, April noticed, measuring out his words, spacing them, so that the stranger would understand. But as Marshall talked, the man kept staring down at her, canvassing her body as though she were his prey. She moved back from the truck and stepped behind Marshall, as if to hide herself.

"You bought the Smythe place?" the old man asked, nodding up the hill.

"Yes, Smythe," Marshall answered, and then quickly to April. "That name is on the original deed. I saw a copy of it at the trust office. The land grant to this valley, all of Mad River, was given originally by the Dutch to a family called Van Smythe. It's in the papers at home."

"But that's from Colonial times." April looked up again at the old man and noticed for the first time that there were women as well in the crowded front seat of the truck. Two girls peered down at her through the grimy window. They were teenagers with the same distorted faces, unkempt brown hair, and pink eyes. Oh, Lord, she thought. The clan's abnormality suddenly seemed worse when reflected in the faces of young women.

"Marshall, let's go," she said. Then whispering, added, "I'm afraid Timmy and Greta are getting freaked out!"

"You know the boy? Luke?" the old man asked suddenly.

"Yes, Luke. Luke Grange," Marshall shouted back over the noisy engine. "He's our caretaker."

The old man grinned, displaying his raw gums, black from tobacco and age. Then he added, "Good boy, Luke."

"You know him?" April asked.

"Of course he knows him," Marshall said, glancing over at her. "All these people knew each other's families, have known them for generations. No one moves out of these hills." He turned back to the driver and waved good-bye, then stepped back and gave the man room to move the old truck.

Without waiting for Marshall, she walked across the road, taking the two children with her to get them off the road. The truck engine raced, then the old man shifted into first, grinding gears. April moved to the edge and pulled the children protectively into her arms. Marshall stepping to the other side and standing clear of the truck, waved good-bye to the truckload of Tassels and Holts.

April waved too as the lumbering truck churned up the gravel road, waved until she realized that the large, round, pink eyes of the young men hanging over the sides of the flatbed were not riveted on her at all. They were hungrily watching Greta Benard, standing by her side.

Nine

"Where do people like that come from?" Marshall asked once they were on the narrow tarmac road into town. "Mad River Mountain isn't that far from civilization, never has been."

"Oh, there are often many reasons for such inbreeding bottlenecks," April said, happy to talk about her research project. Marshall never seemed to have much time to discuss her work, but now that they had met the inbreds, he was curious. "Inbreeding can be caused by religion, politics, culture or geography. The Samaritans, in Israel, for example, have two small communities of no more than 500 and follow a religious tradition from prerabbinical times. They keep their identity by marrying first-cousins, usually. —And they never marry outside their extended family."

"What about deformities?" he asked. "Are the Samaritans like that crowd we just saw?"

"One study done at Tel Aviv University showed that since 1963 the rate of inbreeding has increased, and so has the incidence of genetic defects. Something like 30 percent of Samaritans are color blind."

"Color blind! What we just saw is a helluva lot worse than that. I mean, Jack Nicklaus is color blind and he just won the Masters!"

"You're right. The mutations we saw are caused by the wrong combination of genes. Sometimes the zygote, or fertilized egg, gets a double dose of an abnormal recessive gene. What we don't know is what happens when all the genes are recessive. The common belief is that this would produce a real monster."

"I'd call these people monsters," Marshall said. They

had reached the edge of the small town and he began to slow the car. "They're dangerous."

"They're incestuous, not dangerous."

"You don't know that. Enough recessive genes, I bet, and you can get some real wackos."

"Marshall, the Amish of Pennsylvania have had generations of consanguineous marriages and they're called the harmless people."

They were in town now, and April looked out the window, watched the beautiful Victorian homes set back from the street. "Why is it," she commented, "that all the charming old houses are located in places where you wouldn't want to live?"

"You said it," Marshall agreed, sliding into a parking space on Main Street. "This town looks like the Twilight Zone."

"More like the thirties."

"What?" Greta asked, leaning forward again and looking out the front window. "What are the thirties, April?"

"The Depression, honey. When people couldn't find work. Everyone was very poor and wore old clothes like those people you see on the sidewalk."

April had read in the *Times* that some upstate towns were dying, losing their local industries, losing their young people, and becoming part of the new Rust Belt of America. Here was the proof in the boarded-up Main Street stores and on the sullen, gray faces of the people. Of course, April reasoned, it had been a long winter. She knew how difficult it must be to spend half the year in the cold and snow of the Catskills.

"I think we might be a little overdressed for this crowd," Marshall commented wryly, turning off the engine.

"They're dressed like bums," Greta said. "Oh, God!"

"I'm afraid they just don't have money to buy nice clothes," April replied. It was time, she thought, that this child learned how most of the world lived.

"That's not my fault," Greta answered, and then announced, "I won't play with any of these weird kids!" She sat back and crossed her arms, making her point.

"Well, you don't have to play," April said patiently, and

then to Marshall. "Let's divide the chores and get out of here." She, too, did not like the looks of the town.

"Okay. You go buy the liquor. I'll find the hardware store."

"I want to go with you, Daddy," Greta announced.

"Fine," April replied at once. "Timmy, come with me, sweetheart." She stepped out of the car, telling Marshall. "I'll meet you two back here in twenty minutes, okay?"

April opened the door to Gordon's Liquors and guided Timmy inside.

"Hello!" Timmy said cheerily to the man behind the counter. April smiled as she entered and took in the dark room with a quick scan. There wasn't much of a selection, she saw at once, but then reminded herself that this was small town America, not New York City.

She let the door slam behind her and said hello to the storekeeper who slowly—cautiously, it appeared to April—moved from the darkness of the room into the daylight that filled the front of the store. "Hello," April said again, continuing to be friendly.

The man looked surprised, as if he were startled to have a customer. He nodded, but did not speak.

"You're open, aren't you?" April asked, glancing around. She saw then that there were dust and cobwebs on the rows of red wine. This place really is out of the Twilight Zone, she thought, and protectively placed her hands on Timmy's thin shoulders.

"Oh, we're open sure enough," he said, moving slowly, cautiously up the counter in front. April was amused, thinking: What was so unusual about a mother and child?

He was a slight man in his sixties, balding and gaunt. April saw at once that the old man was sick. His heart, she guessed, looking at his trembling hands and gray skin. His heart could not supply his body with sufficient blood. She felt immediately sorry for him, trapped in this dying Catskills town when he should be retired, living in Florida, having a final few peaceful and pleasant years in the sun.

"Sorry to bother you," April apologized.

"No problem. It's my business, but we don't often get

you people this early in the day." He managed a vague, unfocused smile as he went behind the counter and then, pulling himself together, asked, "What will it be then, ma'am?"

"Oh, well, I just want to buy some..." April stopped speaking, realizing that she had raised her voice and was shouting at the man. "... some wine."

"Where are you from?" the storekeeper asked, cocking his head.

April saw then that he was also physically deformed, that his withered right arm flopped loose by his side. He had concealed it in the sleeve of his checkered wool shirt, the useless fingers stuffed like a broken toy into the pocket of his baggy trousers. April glanced away, embarrassed. "We just bought the farmhouse up at the top of Mad River Valley."

"The Smythe place?"

"That's right!"

"You're up on the mountain then."

"That's right."

The old man shook his head and said flatly, "A mean bunch, that lot. You've seen any of those Hill People?"

"Pardon me?"

"The Hill People! The inbreds. You've seen them, or you ain't. No way to forget them, not them, if you seen one." He turned then and began to take dusty bottles of red and white wine off the shelves, talking as he set them on the counter. "If I were you, I'd keep away from them. No good, the whole damn godless lot. I bet you don't see many like them down there in New York City. You live in that SoHo place, don't you?"

"Yes!" April drew back, startled by how much he knew about her.

"It's a small town, ma'am," the storekeeper went on, registering the surprise in her voice.

He turned around and asked, "What about the Italian wines? Do you drink those Italians? I got a case of Barbera in the cellar."

"Excuse me," April said. She saw that he had set a magnum of expensive champagne on the counter. "I didn't ask for Dom Pérignon!"

"Oh, you'll want to have your friends up for a weekend.

Celebrate your new house." He was smiling for the first time, and seemed to be enjoying himself, having a customer in the dingy place.

"We don't have any plans for that!"

"You'll be meeting other city folks. These mountains are crowded with 'em in the summer. You'll stick together. Have parties."

"I won't be doing much entertaining," April insisted, and then immediately felt foolish that she was even arguing with the old man.

"You will. Ain't much to do up here but drink."

"Please!" April interrupted. "I have a few bottles of wine I'd like to buy." She glanced down at her crumpled list, upset at the man's presumption. "Do you have Spanish wines? I'd like a bottle of white Monopole."

The man pushed one of the bottles on the counter toward her and then paused, waiting for her next request. April realized he was amused by this game and was grinning at her. "And two bottles of a chardonnay."

"Mâcon-Villages, '84," he answered, pushing another bottle across the counter. "These are very good—dry and inexpensive. I have some good, but expensive, white burgundies. They're from La Guiche and Folabere, but we're talking twenty-five dollars a bottle. You plan to have a nice dinner with just your husband and yourself, you let me know."

April studied her list for a moment, taking some time to think, wondering how this storekeeper in the Catskills knew so much about wines, knew which ones she'd prefer. Then she continued slowly, saying, "My husband likes red wines, and he recently found a Bulgarian . . ."

"Trakia! A '78 cabernet sauvignon. I have it at $5.99." He pushed the last bottle on the counter closer to her, explaining, "It's from the southwestern slopes of the Sakar mountain range. They make a solid cabernet, but 1978 was a very good year. Serve it with a spaghetti. Do you have a good meat sauce?"

"Yes, I have a good meat sauce," April answered slowly, staring at the man. He had begun to carefully package her order, slipping cardboard between the bottles as he filled the plastic shopping bag. "Excuse me," she asked. "How do you know exactly what wines I want? We've never met. I've never been in your store, or in this town."

"You're city folks, ain't you?"

"Yes."

"All you city people buy the same wine, same brandy. I stock up this time of year in the fancy labels, you know, Rémy Martin. I can give you people a better cognac at half the price, but no, you all want your Rémy Martin." The man reached for April's money.

"That's two twenties and a ten," she said placing the bills in the man's thin fingers.

"Oh, you won't cheat me," he answered, smiling and moving to the cash register. "That's one thing I can say about city people. I don't know what they do to each other down there in that place, but they're honest folks up here in the mountains. We think highly of you. And your money." And then he laughed. "Your change, ma'am." He held up the few dollars for April. "How 'bout a licorice stick for the little fella?" The storekeeper lifted the metal top of the large glass jar and waited for Timmy.

"Go ahead, dear," April nodded okay to Timmy when he looked up to her.

"Thata boy, Timmy. You're a fine boy, aren't you?"

"Thank you," Timmy whispered, taking one black licorice stick and then stepping closer to his mother.

"Let's go, honey," April said, as a way of leaving the store. She backed away from the counter and toward the front door, saying, "Many thanks for all your help."

"Any time." He nodded in the direction of their voices and then added, "You have a nice time up there on Mad Mountain now. Give my best to your husband. Timmy, you stay away from those dry river beds. Catch a bunch of rattles in those hot spots, this time of year. Ma'am, you want anything special, you give me a call, and I'll order it from Albany. Have it down here within the week. No problem." He kept talking, chattering away, pleased by his morning sale.

On the sidewalk April paused, and took a deep breath to calm herself.

"Mommy? What's the matter?" Timmy asked, clutching his mother's hand.

She shook her head. "Nothing really." She smiled at her

son to reassure him and kept thinking: How did that store-keeper know Timmy's name? She had not said it when they were in the store. And why was he watching them now, standing in the grimy front window as she protectively tightened her grip on the hand of her little boy.

Ten

That afternoon, when Marshall went off for a walk and the children were playing on the back lawn, April went into her new office to power up her computer and begin work. She took out the box of files that James Galvin had developed that winter, slipped the directory diskette into the 0 drive, and loaded the program.

She entered the Search mode and typed Mad River Mountain. A half dozen references flashed on the screen. She scanned them until she spotted one that looked likely, typed in its reference number, and watched as the file appeared on the screen.

Item 23.
AUTHOR	Pettit, John
TITLE	Kaatskill: Facetiae, Folktales, Legends
PUBLICATION	Spencer, N.Y.: Spencer Press, 1836.
DESCRIPTION	xi, 404 p. illus. 24 cm.
SUBJECTS	(1) Frontier and pioneer life—New York (State)—Catskill Mountains—Anecdotes, facetiae, satire, folktales, legends, etc. (2) Catksill Mountains—History. (3) Catskill Mountains—Social life and customs. (4) Mad River Valley—Families.
CALL NUMBER	IRM (Catskill) 76-534

Using the telephone modem hookup to the Columbia library April called up the document. It was an abstract of the Pettit book. To save time, she looked at the contents page, seeking the reference to Mad River Mountain. Finding it, she typed in the page number, waited a moment for the text to appear on the screen, and began to read carefully.

"I found myself, in the fall of 1834, passing through a remote, mountainous area of the Kaatskill locally called Mad River Mountain. It was an area worthy of Mr. Irving's Rip Van Winkle, with wild mountains, ravines and hollows, small grottos, and perpendicular precipices.

"It is a land of great physical beauty. Vast lawns of green, clumps of gigantic trees, rich piles of foliage. Deer trooped by in silent herds. And hare! They bounded by in legion. There were sequestered pools with fearless trout deep in the limpid waters. I stopped at one of these rustic temples, and stood in marvel at nature's way.

"And then I met the human inhabitants, and theirs is another tale indeed.

"I came across a community of strange folk named Tasel, the tragic issue of generations of sinful inbreeding. This prodigious incest produces very many children who either die at birth, are deformed, or retarded, but the tradition of large families, numbering often in the teens, allows their population to continue to grow.

"Some of the men will occasionally leave the clan, seeking employment downriver in Kingston or north along the Erie Canal, carrying their peculiar traits outside of the immediate community. However, as no outsiders come to this secluded, savage mountain range, the inbreeding continues, and as time passes, the interweaving of the family trees grows so tangled that it is impossible to discern who is brother, who is sister, who is father and child.

"I have myself seen boys and girls who suffer from mental retardation, congenital deafness. I have seen hemophiliacs, bleeding to death in poor, dank log cabins, and six-fingered dwarfs. I have seen blind men walking the trails unassisted, never venturing beyond the few paths leading from cabin to cabin and into their small village, situated on the banks of a small lake they call Secret.

"These clannish families, having little contact with outsiders, often disappeared from the mountain path when I rode by, and it was only their pastor, a man by the name of Richard Ely, Reverend Ely, who spoke to me on the banks of what the local Indians call Mad River."

Richard Ely. April stopped reading.

Luke's relative. He had told her his ancestors had come into the area in the late 1760s, that Richard Ely was the first white person to build a homestead on Mad River.

April went back to the directory, selected the document utilities, and then searched for her demographic data file. She slipped it into the expansion drive and pulled up its directory. During the winter James Galvin had typed in all the articles that had a reference to Ulster County. Again she hit Global Search and typed in the names Ely and Grange.

Two dozen references with cross references appeared, and she scanned that list until she found the one she wanted.

The study was by James Thompson, Ph.D. It was Doctor Thompson whom April had first heard lecture about inbreeding populations when she was an undergraduate at Barnard. Thompson had shown slides of Mad River Mountain, and he had called the population, April remembered, the Hill People.

April keyed in the file and began to scan the pages of the study from the Annals of Human Biology. She moved the document further along on the screen, still searching for any reference to the names Ely or Grange, but pausing now and then to read bits of the old anthropological study.

"The only components of human movement which are genetically significant are those which lead an individual of one population to contribute his genes to another. This is commonly called 'exogamy' or may be placed under the more general heading of marital movement.

". . . Whereas children of unrelated parents have a one-in-thirty-two probability of abnormalities, an incestuous couple's child would have a one-in-four risk."

". . . From within the area, movement was found to be limited to paths over the crest of Mad River and between the towns of Secret and Elyville. This was the only direct way out of the hills, and then only in good weather. It forced people to travel either east or west, or by-pass the ridge itself, and isolated the rural community on Mad River.

"In their early study Miller and Johnson (1937) surveyed the demography, anthropometry, and genetics of a portion of Ulster County, including Mad River, whose inhabitants were referred to as the Hill People. This population sample was believed to be the remnants of a once large biracial population (Iroquois and Euro-Americans) which occupied an extensive area in and around Mad River Mountain.

"Their conclusions were that the gene frequencies noted for the Hill People population sample resulted from racial intermixture which had become established in this group over a long period of reproductive isolation. They further concluded that this isolation

may in time produce not only grotesque deformities, but descendants who are also severely psy-
chopathic, although this abnormal trait may not
turn up for generations.''

April stopped reading and searched further, locating the
tables that were attached to the scholarly article. There she
found what she was looking for, a string of family names
listing the consanguineous marriages which had produced
the Mad River inbreds. They were Tassels and Holts, but
there were two other families whose genes had mingled with
theirs over the years. There were dozens of references to
these other two families. Their names were Ely and Grange.

Luke Grange was one of them, she realized. Luke Grange
was connected by birth to the genetically defective marriages
that had produced these strange, pumpkin-headed families.

He was their kinfolk.

April turned off her computer, too excited to work longer,
and walked out onto the deck and into the bright sunlight.

Luke wasn't like his deformed relatives on the mountain,
she thought, reflecting on the information she had just read.
Among all the genetic abnormalities, this long history of
consanguineous marriages had also produced a handsome
young man. A model human being. It had produced Luke
Grange. It didn't seem possible. Given what she knew,
anthropologically, it wasn't possible. And were there others
like Luke somewhere in the mountains, she wondered next. A
moment later she realized what this meant for her, and she
smiled, staring off across Mad River Valley. Mad River wasn't
just going to give her a research study. Whoever delivered the
mystery of Luke Grange to the academic world would be the
next Margaret Mead. Mad River would make her career.

He had come up out of Mad River Valley, come up through
the dark cool trees, come up to the edge of the woods and
crouched in the underbrush, to watch her there on the deck.
She was staring off across the lawn, staring at him, but even
in the bright sunlight, she would not see him, would not
know why he was there.

What was it, he wondered, that had brought him back to

the house, that made him hide in the woods and watch the woman. It was not right, but he was thrilled at seeing her alone, seeing her helpless even, if he decided to do more, to run out of the trees, to frighten her, or something else perhaps, to rape her, or cut her up, to have fun with her flesh and make her die.

Yet he didn't move, and he knew why. He was hiding, but not from the woman. He was hiding from himself and what one day soon he would do to April Benard.

Eleven

The green expressway sign said Park And Ride. Marshall moved into the right lane, turned onto the exit ramp, and left the highway. As the Volvo slowed and curved, April spotted a dozen cars parked in the waiting lot. The city commuter bus hadn't yet arrived and its lateness upset April. She had hoped they'd miss it and Marshall would be forced to spend another night upstate. They had spent very little of the week alone, and it disappointed her.

"I'll call when I get to the apartment," Marshall said, pulling into the lot and stopping the car.

He was already in his "departure mode" as she termed his tone, and that upset her further.

To keep from shedding the tears she felt welling up, April concentrated on the other couples and families. She saw at once that it was the men who were carrying the overnight bags, heading back to the city for the week, leaving the wives and children upstate at the country homes. What she should do, she knew, was to get out of the car and begin to introduce herself, push herself forward and make some new friends.

"Is there anything you want from the city? I can do some shopping at Zabar's if you give me a list."

He was being nice and cooperative, but she saw it as manipulation. She didn't answer.

"We both agreed to this arrangement," he finally said. "You said you'd take care of Greta. You wrote to her, remember, inviting her to spend the summer in New York."

"Don't bring Greta into this! It's not Greta that's upsetting me."

"April, I have to work. I've got a job, you know."

"I know," she sighed.

"I'll try and cut down on the travel, okay? You know how my work life is. Some months are real bears."

"All of your months are bears. You haven't had any real time off since we came back from the honeymoon."

"I'm sorry." He reached across the seat, took her hand, and squeezed. "Let me wrap this case up. A week or two at the most, and then I'll be here all summer. Meanwhile, why don't you try and get a chunk of that research done?" He flashed his wide smile.

"I'm sorry. I just miss you, that's all."

"Yes, but you have that great bit of news about Luke."

April nodded. "I've just got to get him to talk to me, that's all."

"You will. Just blink those beautiful eyes of yours and all men talk." He leaned across the seat and kissed her softly.

"Thank you, sweetheart," April whispered. When she pulled back, she spotted a bus slowing on the expressway, flashing its lights as it exited the slow lane. She heard the hiss of the air brakes as the driver moved the oversize vehicle onto the steep, curving ramp.

The sun had slipped behind the distant hills, turning the late May afternoon suddenly cold. A breeze had come up with the setting sun and it whipped across the open parking lot. Other wives and children were saying quick good-byes and getting back into their cars.

"Bye, kiddo," Marshall whispered, opening the front door.

April stepped out of the car and followed her husband around to the back of the Volvo. He opened the rear hatch and took out his brown duffel bag and a gray Square Rigger bag that he used as a weekend briefcase.

"I'm going to miss you," she whispered. And then admitted, "I'm always scared when you leave me. You know that." Now she wanted to be nice to him, to have him miss her, too.

He kissed the top of her head while glancing across the parking lot to where the bus had circled to a stop. "You'll be fine. You're not alone in the house, and there's Luke right on the property."

April saw the other men walking quickly toward the big bus, picking up at once the harried gait of New Yorkers.

"I'll call as soon as I get to the City."

She buttoned her parka against the wind and walked with him toward the waiting bus. The driver had opened the luggage compartment and now stood by the door collecting fares.

"Do you have enough money for the week?" Marshall asked.

"Yes, I'm fine. There's nothing to buy up here anyway."

"I've got to go," he said, bending down and kissing her lightly on the cheek. "I love you, kiddo." He paused a moment, studying her face. "Are you going to be okay?"

April nodded, drawing herself up. She wouldn't allow herself to cry, to make a show of herself there in the public parking lot.

"Yes, I'll be fine." She was upset at herself for acting foolish. She was the one, after all, who wanted to be on Mad River Mountain. And in some ways, she knew, it would be easier without him there. "I'll be okay," she said, forcing a smile. "In a day or two, I'll have the house in order. Next weekend it will look like home."

"Have Luke help you. Remember he gets his place free for taking care of the property."

April nodded. Luke had already been nice to her, agreeing to take care of the children while she took Marshall to the bus stop.

"Don't worry, we'll all be fine." She smiled up at him. She was all right again. She kissed him and stepped back, letting her husband leave Mad River Mountain.

Twelve

April recognized the battered truck when she topped the slight rise of the country road and came to a stop in front of the farmhouse. The truck was pulled into the trees, near where the deer path went up the mountainside to the open meadowland behind the barn and apple orchard. The cabin and open bed of the old truck were empty.

She got out of the Volvo and called for Timmy and Greta as she went up the path. She had left the front door unlocked and as she stepped onto the porch, her footsteps thumped on the old boards. The house was quiet, deserted, and she stopped, suddenly afraid to go in.

"Shit," she swore.

She backed off the porch and started around to the back lawn, calling for the children. Her voice bounced off the water and echoed across the valley. It startled her, hearing her voice reverberating against the hillside, but it also made her feel better.

The children were not outside. She had half hoped they'd be down by the pond, playing innocently near the water, but the lawns were empty. She stood still for a moment, listening for voices, and the serenity of the scene, the peacefulness of the mountain spot, touched her and lessened her fear.

She looked out over the valley, beyond the pond, and saw half a dozen high-flying birds in the empty sky. They were swooping low over the trees, then soaring off, circling high several hundred yards from where she stood on the level lawn. They were hawks and vultures, and she guessed that somewhere on the valley floor near where Mad River Creek had run dry, an animal was dying in the underbrush.

It made her shiver, thinking of the birds up there waiting.

Then she remembered Timmy, and called for him and Greta as she walked along the edge of the pond.

The path she was following led to the caretaker's cabin, but it took a circuitous route, curving through the woods and bringing her into the open so that she could look back at the pond and the house. The views of the property were beautiful and she wondered if the caretaker, or perhaps a previous owner, had cut the trees and bushes so that the landscape was visible from the path. April was delighted by the picture-perfect views of the farmhouse and barns, the teardrop pond, and the acreage of smooth green lawns cut to the rough edges of the woods.

It was at the next opening, farther along the path and at the highest point, that she spotted the deer. It had stepped from the thick woods and walked the dozen yards to the water's edge. There it stopped, held its twelve-point antlers erect, and sniffed the evening breeze.

April stopped walking, afraid to move and break a twig, to do anything that might alert the deer. She was afraid the deer might see her. Afraid he might attack her.

His color surprised her. The white-tailed deer she had seen were often honey brown in the early spring, but gradually over the summer their buckskin turned dull, and easily camouflaged them in the bright foliage of fall.

This deer looked golden. She thought that perhaps it was sunlight reflecting off the pond, but there was no light on the water, no lengthy shadows across the lawn. In the gray light of evening, the huge buck was naturally gold, unlike any deer she had ever seen, and she regretted that she didn't have her camera. It would be such a breathtaking photograph: the motionless and poised deer, his golden reflection in the pond, and the white farmhouse in the background.

She inadvertently moved and his heavy antlered head went up as he sniffed the breeze. Slowly, he turned his head as if searching the lawn and then the bushes. April stood perfectly still and breathless until his eyes found her.

For a moment longer he looked across the small pond toward where she stood in the break of wood. Then, as unexpectedly as he had appeared, he bolted, spun on his spindly legs and sailed out of sight into the woods.

April calmed her racing heart. He was afraid of her, she saw, and she walked up the path, realizing for the first time since the accident that she had nothing more to fear from wild deer.

When she came out of the woods, Luke's cabin was below her in the clearing. April had only seen the cabin from a distance, and now saw that it was older than she thought. But someone had rebuilt the roof and added to the small original building, extending a deck on the back, and, on the southern side, installing skylights.

April went down the path and across the bare front yard to the porch. At the bottom of the steps, she called for Luke, and when he didn't reply, she went up to the cabin door and knocked. The unlocked door swung open.

"Luke?" she called into the silent house. She could see the length of the living room, a row of ceiling-to-floor bookshelves, bright spring flowers on a pine table, and several tall green potted trees, lit by the skylights. There was a Indian design rug on the polished barnboard floor, a leather couch facing the stone fireplace, and on the thick wooden mantel, several ceramic serving plates.

The room surprised her. April had not expected Luke to be so neat. This cabin appeared to have been decorated by a woman. Of course, she reasoned: As she'd suspected, Luke Grange had a girlfriend.

Turning back to the doorway, April let out a small shriek of alarm. Below her on the lawn were a dozen of the inbred children, the boys she had seen on the back of their father's truck.

"Hello," April said, smiling.

They were all eleven and twelve years old, small, dwarfish, undernourished and slightly built. Their limbs were rickety, their heads large and misshapen. Their features seemed to have been shaped with soft reddish putty that had melted into odd forms, leaving sunken sockets and heavy, bagged eyes, blunt stubby noses, and very small mouths. They had jack-o'-lantern faces, April noticed. But their smiles startled her most: thin, irregular lips curled into permanent sneers.

One of the boys screamed. He waved his skinny arms and

kept shouting, spitting out a string of high pitched utterances through his small mouth.

April shook her head, not understanding.

He screamed again, more slowly, but still it was an incomprehensible babble. April smiled her encouragement, straining to understand. She glanced at the other kids, looking for some sign of comprehension on their part, and then slowly, as if speaking in a foreign language, "I am sorry. I do not understand you."

They glanced at each other, as if unsure of what more to say, and then the first boy said "Luke," grunting out the caretaker's name.

"Yes. Luke," April seized on the caretaker's name.

"I am looking for Luke. Have you seen him?"

The boys shook their awkward heads.

April sighed. At least they had understood.

Another one of the boys spoke up, again too rapidly for April to understand. It sounded to her as if he were chipping words off a block of ice, showering her with syllable slivers. She wished now that she had her tape recorder. If she could record their speech and play it back, maybe she'd eventually understand them. She might even be able to do an article on their speech patterns.

"Luke. Do you know where Luke is?" she asked again.

Slowly, one at a time, they began to shake their heads, and then, as if by a secret signal, they moved forward, started to encircle her, and close in on where she stood.

Oh, dear God, she thought, backing up, trying not to show how frightened she was. One of them said something, spitting out the words, and the others laughed and slapped their thighs.

"Get away!" April demanded, but they kept coming, edging closer. Then over their heads, on the path toward the farmhouse, she spotted Luke and the children, and she shouted out the caretaker's name.

The inbreds bolted, ran for the woods, fleeing the yard and log cabin, and April reached out and grabbed the porch rail to steady herself, to stop herself from trembling.

Thirteen

Luke opened the bottle of wine and filled two glasses. He did it slowly, carefully, as if all he had to do for the rest of his life was complete this simple task, standing there on the deck of the farmhouse, with the late afternoon sunlight turning the glasses golden in his hands. He carried the drinks to where April sat. She had closed her eyes and was facing the sun, catching the little warmth that was left in the day.

"Thank you," she said, when he set her glass down on the wooden bench and stepped away to sit on the railing.

"Where's Timmy?" she asked, sitting up to drink the wine.

"He's fine, I can see him down by the pond. Greta's there, too."

Luke did not raise his voice and April was immediately comforted by his presence and assurance. It was nice, she thought, to have someone to do little household tasks, to open a bottle, to pour her a drink.

She sipped the wine, and then said casually, "Oh, I ran into some mountain children the other day. The same family that helped us with the car."

"Those were the Holt boys," Luke said, looking off across the lawn. "They're really pretty harmless."

"Their English isn't much."

She had decided not to ask him questions directly, but to try to draw him into random conversation that she hoped would lead in interesting directions. But Luke didn't respond to her opener.

"Why were the boys looking for you?" she tried again.

"Oh, the kids are always coming by; I give them candy."

April glanced at the small bouquet of mountain flowers on

the railing. Luke had brought them for her; a small present, he had said, his way of welcoming her to Mad River Mountain.

"What kind of flowers are these?" she asked, wanting him to see she appreciated his gesture.

"The purple are trillium; the white, hepatica; and the others are white shadbush. They're spring flowers that grow up in the hill. Later in the summer we'll have all kinds of flowers."

"Did you plant them?"

"Oh, no, they grow wild." He smiled and looked away, as if embarrassed by his gift.

April heard Timmy's laugh. His voice filled the valley like the song of a bird, and she thought he was never that excited in the city. Luke turned and glanced behind the house.

"I see them. They're playing by the cluster of maples. If you want, I can build a tree house for Timmy. A kid should really have a tree house when he's growing up." Luke smiled. "I remember when I was about his age. I had one down there in the valley, in a small area we call Secret Lake. Some of the old boards are still in the trees. I use them as a blind during deer season."

"That reminds me," April spoke up. "I saw this beautiful buck before, down by our pond." April sat forward in the chair to show Luke the spot. "He had a beautiful head of antlers and the slanting sunlight made him look gold."

"Don't tell anyone in town," Luke said quickly. His face had lost its softness and now there was an edge to his profile.

"I'm sorry. . ."

"He's very rare, Mrs. Benard," Luke went on. "I didn't mean to startle you, but we try to keep his existence a secret. If hunters found out about him, we'd have every jerk from New York shooting up Mad River Valley."

"I'm surprised he hasn't been killed already," April replied, standing. She was cold now, and also she needed to get dinner started. "Have you hunted him?" she asked, picking up the wild flowers.

"We'd never do that. He's protected by those of us who live on the mountain. Hunters have heard rumors about him, and sometimes during deer season they'll drive through the valley looking, but we make it hard on them."

"I'm sure my husband would agree with that. I know he'll post our land during hunting season. It's awfully dangerous, especially with children around."

"They don't like it when land is posted," Luke remarked.

April stopped and stared at the caretaker. She noticed she had been wrong about his eyes. They were not a light color, but a deep fudge brown. He was a chameleon, she thought; his looks changed with his mood.

"Who doesn't like it?"

"Town folks."

"Did Barbara Olsen let them hunt here?"

He shook his head, watching her as he did, as if he expected more questions about the previous owner. Instead, April said, "Don't worry. People from town don't intimidate us."

"Does your husband hunt?" Luke walked across the deck and handed April his empty wine glass.

"No, of course not!" She opened the door and stepped inside. When Luke followed her and closed the door behind him, her heart did a quick flip.

She entered the dining room, passing through the connecting pantry into the bright kitchen, and kept talking. She heard her own voice, yet she had no idea what she was saying. Her voice ran on like a phone message out of whack.

She set down the two glasses on the butcher-block counter. Her hands were trembling and she knew, too, that she was blushing.

"I'm going now," Luke said from the doorway. "I'll tell the kids to come inside for dinner. If you need anything, give me a call. The number at the cabin is taped on the wall next to your phone."

April forced herself to make eye contact. "I'm sorry that I seem nervous, Luke," she said, trying to make an excuse for herself. "It's just that I'm alone up here with the children for the first time, and this weekend has been trying."

"You've got nothing to worry about, ma'am."

"I know." She gestured with her hands, sighing. "I'm afraid, I guess, to be in such a big house by myself."

"I'm out back if you need help," he said again, and then paused by the door, watching her, deciding what more he might suggest. "Why don't you and the kids come to my place for dinner? It's nothing special, but you wouldn't have to bother about fixing anything." He was smiling, making his invitation as pleasant as possible, a neighborly gesture.

April shook her head. "Thank you, Luke. That's kind of you, but it's easier on Timmy if he eats at home and gets to bed." She smiled at him. "But why don't you join us instead?"

"I wouldn't want to be any bother. . . ."

"Please, you won't be. Timmy adores you, and I wouldn't be surprised if Greta did too." April laughed, teasing. "I'm just going to fry some chicken, and I still have some of the Zabar's goodies."

"Zabar's?"

"Yes. From the City." She saw his puzzlement. He had never heard of the famous gourmet food shop, and for some reason that pleased her. It was refreshing to be with a person who did not know or care about what was trendy in the city.

"Okay, I'll come if you let me bring dessert."

"Of course! That would be wonderful."

"I baked a pie this morning with the last of my canned apples."

"You bake!"

Luke nodded, and then smiled, as if embarrassed by April's look of astonishment. "A little," he admitted.

"And you can fruit in the fall?"

"Well, we have long winters up here, and the county road is the last to get plowed out. It's more of a precaution for the bad weather."

"Well, Luke Grange, you'll make some woman a good husband," April teased, glancing up at him as they walked off the deck and across the lawn. The two children were playing by the water, chasing frogs into the lily pads.

"Oh, there's no wife for me," he said, laughing.

"Now, don't tell me again that you don't have a girlfriend," she taunted. The good-naturedness of his laugh made her bolder. They had reached the children, and Timmy turned around at once to show her his find.

"Big, fat, green frogs!" he exclaimed, all excited, going back at once to comb the long grass at the edge of the pond with a stick.

"They're slimy," Greta announced with disdain, and stepped away from Timmy to stand near Luke, as if to show him that she was really too mature for such child's play.

April smiled, amused at how Greta had maneuvered herself next to Luke. Now she was telling him that in Beverly Hills the boys in her class caught frogs to race on the streets behind their school.

April stepped over to the pond's edge and knelt beside her son, "It's getting cold, darling," she said softly.

"No!" he announced, beating the thick grass. A frog leapt from the marshy bank and she jumped away, startled.

"Oh, April!" Greta cried. "Don't be such a sissy! They don't give you warts, you know."

"Yes, they do," Timmy said, keeping up his search. "John Kerwin says his father once touched a frog and now he has two warts on his hand. I've seen them!"

"Do you know how toads came to be, Timmy?" Luke asked. "And why they make their beds on lily pads?" He lowered his voice, beginning a story.

Timmy was shaking his head, and April saw how wide his eyes were as he listened. She moved next to Timmy and pulled him into her arms, smiling at Luke, but hoping it wasn't a tale that would give Timmy nightmares.

"Toads are like frogs," Greta said, edging closer.

"They are, Greta," Luke agreed, and then whispered theatrically, "and once they were the most famous creatures in the forest."

"They were not!"

"Greta, please!"

"But toads are ugly and those stories are just for kids!" Greta turned on April.

"I'm a kid!" Timmy protested.

"Tell us the story, Luke," April asked.

"Well, once in the days when kings ruled the world there was a wise king who had three sons. He wanted to give his kingdom to one of his sons, but didn't know which. So he decided to give his children a difficult task, and the son who did it best would inherit his crown.'"

In the growing darkness, April smiled. She recognized the Grimm story, and was glad she had never read it to Timmy. It would be such a pleasure for him now, hearing it for the first time.

"Two of the king's children were very bright, but the third child, a little boy, didn't say much, and his older brothers called him a dummy. His name was Timmy."

"It was not! Oh, God, I can't stand this!" Greta threw up her arms in protest, but Luke kept going.

"The wise king told his sons that whoever brought him the finest carpet in the world would be the new king after his death. And to set the children on their quest he went outside his castle and threw three feathers into the air. One feather flew east, the other west, and the last feather only went a few feet before it fell to the ground.

"Well, one brother went right, the other went left, and both of them laughed at Timmy, calling him a dummy because he stayed where the last feather had fallen.

"Timmy sat down and started to cry, not knowing what to do, but then he saw that beside the fallen feather was a trap door. When he lifted it, he discovered stairs into the ground, and he went down into the earth.

"At the bottom of the steps, Timmy came upon another door, which opened by itself, and when he entered the room, he found a big, fat toad sitting there, surrounded by other toads."

"Ugh!" Greta announced, but, April saw that she, too, was caught up in Luke's story.

"The big toad asked Timmy what he wanted," Luke went on. "And the boy said he was looking for the most beautiful carpet in the world. The toad gave the boy a carpet so beautiful and so fine, that when his father saw it, he told his young son, 'Why, none better could be woven on this earth.'

"His brothers came racing back to the castle with the rags that they had taken from shepherds' wives, and the king told them that it was Timmy who had inherited the kingdom.

"Well," exclaimed Luke, throwing himself further into the story, "the older brothers started yelling and demanding that their father give them another task, some other prize to win."

"That's not fair," Timmy shouted, suddenly teary, "the little boy won!"

April tugged him closer to her and whispered, "Listen, honey, Luke isn't finished with his story."

"Well," Luke went on, "the king told his sons to find the most beautiful woman in the land, and whoever did would be the next king.

"Timmy went at once to see his good friend, the fat toad, and told him that he was supposed to bring home the most beautiful woman in the whole wide world.

"The toad thought a moment before doing anything. He sat there on his lily pad smoking his pipe and then gave Timmy a hollowed-out yellow turnip to which six tiny mice were harnessed."

"God, that's stupid!" exclaimed Greta. "Just like all these stupid fairytales."

In the darkness, Luke raised his hand, motioned Greta to be silent. He was still kneeling and leaning forward, concentrating on Timmy as he told the end of the tale.

"Little Timmy looked at the yellow turnip and the tiny mice and then politely asked what he should do.

" 'Put one of my little toads into it,' said the fat toad.

"And when Timmy placed a little toad inside the yellow turnip, it suddenly became a beautiful woman, and the turnip turned into a carriage, and all the mice became handsome white horses.

"Happily, and in love with this beautiful woman, Timmy returned to the castle and even his brothers, who had found only fat peasant women for their wives, admitted their defeat. And their little brother was crowned heir to the castle and the kingdom."

"I know a story," Greta said at once. "It's about this beautiful princess who is given a necklace by her mother and is getting married, but she has to go to a strange land, and her mother . . ."

"I'm cold," said Timmy. "I want to go in."

"No! I want to tell my story!"

"You can tell your story," April said quickly. "Tell us all later, at dinner." She was sorry Timmy had interrupted, but he was right—it was freezing. And she had to start cooking. Maybe Greta would come quietly—but no, April could see she was going into one of her sulks.

"Yes, tell us at dinner, please," Luke asked. As he stepped by the young girl he touched the top of her head, and then gently, slowly, let his fingers caress her smooth cheek as he passed.

April was surprised. She walked up the slope of the hill with Timmy, then turned back, but the caretaker was on his way around the pond, heading back to his cabin. He paused only to tell April that he would be up at the big house within the hour.

April nodded, not sure of what to say. She glanced at Greta. The teenager was looking away, staring off across the pond and over the tips of the valley trees. She seemed frozen in the moment, stunned by Luke's touch. The evening light shone across her face, lighting her like a Botticelli Venus.

April could feel the cold rising off the water, chilling her, and she thought that she should have worn a sweater out onto the lawn. Then her mind flipped back to what she had just seen, and she didn't know whether she was jealous of Luke's attention to her stepdaughter, or enraged by his bold behavior. To keep herself from dwelling on her emotions, she turned abruptly and hurried into the house. She never noticed who was in the woods, who was watching the house, watching the children, watching her with Luke.

Fourteen

Greta woke screaming.

April jumped from her bed, stumbled into the living room and up the stairs, not fully awake, but knowing the child needed her. Something was terribly wrong.

When she rushed into Greta's room, the girl was standing, rubbing the sleep from her eyes.

"Honey. Did you have a bad dream?"

"Get away from me!"

"Greta, please. Wake up, honey, you're having a nightmare." April moved closer, but slowly, aware that the child might lash out at her.

"No!"

April stopped.

"They're after me," Greta cried.

"No one is after you."

"I heard the music."

"Honey, it was just a dream. A very bad dream," April whispered, realizing what was wrong. It was her fault. She shouldn't have let Luke tell the story.

Yet it had been so pleasant. Everyone had been sitting in front of the fireplace, while Luke told them about the Algonquin Indians who had first lived in the mountains, hunting wildlife and trading with French trappers. Then he had gotten up to clean the hearth, sweeping back the ashes, and she had said, "Oh, Luke, I'll clean it in the morning." He had casually remarked, "You never want to leave a fireplace dirty. The Sidhes don't like slovenly housekeepers."

"Sidhes?" Greta had asked. "What are Sidhes?" She

had been that way all evening, asking questions, pulling Luke's attention to her.

"They're fairies, honey," April interrupted. "You know, little people."

"There are many kinds of little people," Luke went on, "and the greatest of them all are the Sidhes. They are all beautiful young women with soft skin and long blond hair, just like you." He smiled at Greta.

"Am I a Sidhe?" she asked, giggling, pleased by his attention.

"I don't know. You might be. Sidhes are great beauties and their queen is so beautiful that it's dangerous for humans to look at her."

"Then I'm one!"

"I wouldn't be so enthusiastic if I were you," Luke shook his head and sat back again in the armchair. "They're also very dangerous and if you're touched by them, you can be driven mad with rage." He began his story then. At first, April had thought it was just a harmless folk tale, a fable like *Rip Van Winkle*. She, too, had been caught up in the telling and did not realize what the story meant.

"There was a girl once," Luke began, "who was no older than you, Greta."

"I'm almost fifteen," Greta spoke out.

Luke smiled, wiping away her defenses with the warmth of his eyes, then went on speaking softly and slowly.

"... There was once a young woman who went out every day into the woods here in Mad River to gather nuts, and one day she heard music.

"It was such beautiful music that she stopped her work and stood still to listen. The music continued all afternoon, until the valley filled with darkness, but still she could not guess where it came from.

"She told her mother about the music that night and early the next morning she rushed into the woods, stood again in the small clearing, and listened hard. All day the music filtered through the tall trees, growing softer as the sun faded over Mad River.

"But that night the music did not stop. When she went home the music followed her. It came into her farmhouse and went up the staircase and filled her room. Only then did it stop.

"Later that night, her mother asked her, 'Where's the music?' And the young girl said, 'There is no music, Mother. You don't know what you are saying.'

"But the next morning, the young girl didn't come downstairs. Her mother went up and found her dead, lying stone white on the bed.

"She ran from the house, screaming for help. But when the neighbors went into the girl's bedroom, they found not a young, beautiful woman, but an ancient hag with black, ugly skin and shriveled limbs."

"Oh, Luke," April had protested, surprised by the story's ending. She had expected something sweet and loving, like the folktale he had told Timmy.

Now she was paying for it, April realized, as she dealt with Greta.

"Do you want to sleep with me, Greta?" April offered.

Greta shook her head and crawled back under the covers. April went to the bed and rearranged the quilt.

"I did hear the music," Greta said. She was wide awake.

"Nightmares are like that, honey. They sometimes seem realer than real."

April waited a moment, watching the young girl. Now she felt terrible that she had been so hard on Greta during the day. She had to keep reminding herself that the child was still very young and having a hard time growing up.

"I heard it," Greta flatly announced and turned her face away from April.

April waited a moment, stayed kneeling beside the bed. She debated whether she should say anything more, try to get the child to talk about the nightmare. But now was not the time. In the morning it would be easier. In the light of day, April decided, Greta would be more reasonable.

"Good night, honey," April whispered, and walked to the door. Greta called to her before she stepped into the hall.

"Yes?"

"Don't call me 'honey.'"

April paused a moment, thinking how to reply, then she said quietly, "All right, Greta. Whatever you prefer," and stepped out into the hallway. Closing the teenager's door behind her, she took a deep breath.

As she walked down the hallway she heard Timmy cry out softly. She peeped into his room. The bright moonlight shone on that side of the house and spread a soft glow over him. He had turned himself around in the bed and had thrown off his covers. April softly crossed the room and carefully pulled the quilt up over her sleeping son. She leaned forward and kissed him.

His face was warm and soft to her touch. He smelled of his bed and his warm pajamas. April smiled, reminded of earlier days. Right after Tom's death, when Timmy was very small, she would go into his room late at night to nurse him, and sit in the dark silence of their apartment, holding him in her arms, knowing that whatever else happened in her life, she had to take care of him. She owed him that because he would never know the wonderful man who had been his father.

She stood and went to the window. The entire lawn was brightly lit, and the moonlight was silvery on the still water of the pond. She could see beyond the pond as well, over the tops of the trees that edged the lawn and grew thick across the narrow valley.

She started to turn away from the window when something caught her eye. Something was in the thick growth of trees beyond the lawn, less than fifty yards from the house. A deer, she guessed. She waited and watched, tried to separate the shadowy forms and pick out what it was there, half hiding, standing close to a tree, obscured and camouflaged.

Then the figure stepped away from the tree and stood out of the shadows. The sudden sight of a man startled April. A cold shiver ripped down the length of her spine. He waited a moment in the clearing, as if staring across the lawn, watching her where she stood petrified. Then she remembered that the light was on behind her in the hallway, that she was silhouetted in the upstairs window.

Still she did not move, not wanting the man to know that he had been spotted. She had made a mistake. She had left lights on in the house, and the windows were without shades and curtains. Now a man had come through the woods and seen her, watched her walk from room to room, watched her put the children to bed, then take a bath, and walk naked through the downstairs rooms and into bed.

She would telephone the police. There were highway

patrols on the interstate. They could be at the house within
ten minutes. No, she would telephone Luke. He could run
up through the woods and be there even faster.

April stepped back but did not look away from the figure.
She wanted to fade into the darkness of Timmy's room, and
run for the telephone, but the man moved then. He turned to
go back into the trees, and the moonlight caught him. The
same man who had sat at her dinner table was now spying
on her like an animal in the woods.

Fifteen

April waited until the children were eating breakfast and
then walked down to Luke's cabin. The lawn was still thick
with dew and her shoes and feet were soaked before she
reached the woods. She should have known better than to go
out so early, but she wanted to confront Luke before she lost
the edge of her anger.

She had not been able to go back to sleep after seeing him
in the trees, but lay awake listening to all the night sounds
of the old farmhouse. She had thought of getting her mind
off the incident by reading, but was afraid to turn on another
light, afraid that he might still be out there, watching her
through the curtainless windows.

April did not go to the door of the cabin when she came
out of the woods. Instead she stood below the porch and
called for him. There was smoke coming out of the wood-
stove chimney, but Luke did not come out of the house.
Instead, he appeared from below, running up the path that
led into the valley.

He was barefoot, wearing only jogging shorts and his
SUNY sweatshirt. He slowed as he approached, and smiled,
nodding hello. He was out of breath, and stood with his

hands on his hips, breathing deeply. His shirt was dark with sweat.

"Luke, I want to talk to you," April announced, and without waiting for a response, told how she had seen him watching her, watching all of them, from the dark.

He listened without protesting, but kept walking around her, stretching his body as he cooled down. April turned with him, as if she were the eye of a camera.

"It wasn't me," he replied when she finished. He climbed the steps to the front porch and sat down, finding a spot in the morning sun.

"It was!" April answered back.

The sunlight was directly on him and outlined his head, as if his face had been sketched by bold, black strokes. His blond hair, the smoothness of his cheeks and his quiet manner had persuaded April that there was a softness about him, but the morning light framed his face, and showed the hard edge of his profile, the squareness of his chin.

"I do know who it was though," he said quietly, not looking at her, but pulling on thick white socks and Nike shoes, now that he had finished running.

"Who?" April demanded. She pressed her fingernails into her soft palms, forcing herself to feel pain.

"My brother Mark."

"You have a brother living here?"

"He doesn't live here. No." Luke stood up. "Come with me please," he asked, opening the screen door of the log cabin.

April hesitated. She felt safer in the open, but there was a note of sorrow in Luke's voice, a touch of lament. And then he looked back at her with his sad eyes and she realized it would be an affront not to trust him.

Still nervous, still with her fingers clutched in her palms, April stepped up onto the wooden porch and into the log cabin.

It was much warmer inside and the rooms smelled of baking and of burning logs.

"Would you like a cup of tea?" Luke asked. "I'm afraid I only have herbal."

She noticed now that the cabin was just one large space with counters, furniture, and large plants breaking it into rooms. There was an open second-floor loft. A mattress was on the floor, and she could see the clothes he had worn the day before neatly hung on open hangers.

"Do you have coffee?" she asked.

"No, sorry. I never drink it. Coffee's bad for the body."

"You're much more virtuous than I am," she said smiling, trying to make a momentary peace. "I bet you also eat berries and nuts."

"Raspberries, chokeberries, white mushrooms, apples and pears, whatever," he grinned, pulling out two glass jars. "The woods are full of good things to eat."

It was his way of disarming people, April realized. He had a way of edging around a problem, sometimes with folk stories, sometimes with humor. He made people respond to him by a show of humility and by his simplicity. April recognized the behavior. She had students at Columbia who would press their poor, disadvantaged backgrounds just to get an extra grade.

"So where does your brother live? In town?" She wasn't going to let him get away without answering her.

"No. He doesn't even live in New York State. I didn't expect him myself."

"I didn't hear a car, or anything. And you know the house is right on the road. We hear every car or truck that passes."

"He came up from the city by bus and walked in from the expressway," Luke answered quickly, as if he had prepared himself for this cross-examination.

He went back to the stove, took off the kettle and filled two cups, using tea caddies for the loose leaves, and gave one of the cups to April, though she hadn't asked for tea. Then he sat down at the table and dug a spoon into a jar of honey.

April did not move from where she stood at the counter. The sunlight had found him again. It came from above, through the skylight, and the delicate, interlacing shadows crossing his face made it seem as though she were seeing him through the tracery of a Gothic window.

"Why did he move away?" she asked. "That's pretty unusual around here."

"He's been serving a life sentence at Joliet Federal prison for first degree murder," Luke said. "He was paroled on

Friday after fifteen years for good behavior, and because he volunteered for federal drug experiments.''

April was silenced.

"He killed a man. A man and his wife, really." Luke stirred the thick honey into his tea.

"Who? City people?"

"No, cousins of ours, actually. He was our relative. Burke Hickey was his name. His wife was Mary Sue. Mary Sue Watson Hickey. Mark fell in love with Mary Sue. He's a lot older than me. I was just a kid, not much older than Timmy, when it all happened.

"He killed Burke with an axe one Sunday afternoon, after church. And then when Mary Sue still wouldn't go off with him, Mark did her in as well."

"With the axe?"

"No, he took her out behind her place and dumped her down the spring well. And when she tried to climb out, he cut the well rope. They say he just stood there screaming down at her, asking her to marry him, but I guess she was out of her mind with fright. She drowned before anyone could help her.

"Pinky Ely, he's a few years older than me; Pinky was tied to a rope and lowered down the well to get the body. He still talks about it. Hauling Mary Sue Watson out of the Hickey well was the great achievement of Pinky's life."

"Oh, dear God," April whispered.

"Killings like this happen all the time in New York City," Luke went on calmly, sipping the hot tea. "It just sounds worse happening here. You people come to the Catskills thinking it's a quiet little world, with friendly folks." He turned toward her and added, almost a warning, "You scratch the surface of anyone's life, April, and you'll find some real raw stuff."

"Where is he?"

"My brother? I suspect he's at Mary Sue's house. He said he was going down there this morning."

"Where's the house? On this land?"

"It was once. After he killed her, Mark set the house on fire. That's how the neighbors knew something was wrong. It lit up the whole valley. There's nothing left there but the stone foundation. Even the well was pushed in. No one

liked the idea of drinking from it, not after they pulled up
Mary Sue's body.''

"You people are all crazy!'"

"Some say," he answered calmly. He had gone to the
windows of the kitchen and was looking out across the front
lawn. "There's Greta and Timmy.'"

"Damn it. I told Greta to stay up at the house." She
turned to the door.

"April?" Luke asked, stopping her. "I'm not sure if you
know it or not, and it's really, I know, none of my business,
but you seem to push Greta a little hard."

April stopped, her hand on the handmade door pull. She
looked back at Luke, studying him for a moment.

"Yes, it is none of your business," she said quietly.

Then he stepped closer, edging her back against the door.
He did not touch her, yet she could feel his presence, smell
the sweat from his jog. She wanted to say something, to
stop him before he did something, but she couldn't move.
She was holding her breath, staring into his eyes, as if she
were a deer blinded by bright lights.

But Luke didn't touch her, or speak. He reached out and
pushed open the door, letting a burst of sunlight fill the log
cabin, then he stepped past her and casually walked out onto
the front porch, calling to Timmy, telling him that his
mother was there.

"Anyway, you don't need to worry about Mark. He's
going down to the City today," Luke added quietly, as
Timmy ran toward the cabin.

April leaned back against the wall. She was trembling
again. Her legs were weak and she could feel the perspiration under her arms and at the base of her neck. She pulled
a tissue from the back pocket of her jeans and wiped her
eyes. This was stupid. What was she doing to herself? She
followed Luke onto the front porch, wanting the distraction
of her child.

Timmy came running down the path, out of the trees and
across the lawn, shouting at her, enjoying the bright warm
summer morning. It made her feel immensely better, seeing
his pleasure. She raised her arms to welcome him into her
embrace.

The moment with Luke was over. She would not think about it, April told herself. Luke's brother wasn't hanging around. And Luke had meant nothing, stepping close to her.

Sixteen

"He's not here," Greta complained as April pulled into the parking lot. "We could have stopped at that diner for ice cream, but you always have to be early."

"I don't want to have your father waiting for us, not after a long bus ride," April replied coolly. Since the night Luke had come for dinner, Greta had been increasingly testy with her. April wondered if it was because she felt abandoned by her father.

"Where's the bus?" Timmy bounced up from the backseat.

"The bus is late, Timmy," April said sweetly. "See all the boys and girls waiting for their fathers?"

There were at least fifteen cars already in the Park And Ride lot. A handful of young children were out of their cars and playing King of the Mountain on the grassy mounds behind the blacktop lot.

"Greta, why don't you take Timmy over to where the kids are? You might meet a new friend."

"I don't want to meet any of these creeps."

"You don't even know who they are. I'm sure they're all from the City."

"New York kids are creeps," she announced.

April wanted to point out that since Greta had spent most of the week before they had gone to the country in her room, listening to tapes on her Walkman, reading *Seventeen* magazine, and styling her hair, she didn't actually know any New York kids. She had appeared only for meals, and to watch cartoons with Timmy late in the afternoon.

"Well, I think I'll meet some people," April answered instead, sizing up the crowd. Several of the wives were standing together on the blacktop. April noticed that they were all wearing dresses and make-up to meet their husbands coming from the city. She regretted now that she was still in jeans and her old work shirt.

"Timmy, come with me," April said, grabbing her purse and opening the door.

Timmy scrambled out of the backseat, following her.

"Greta?" April asked, gently.

"I said I don't want to meet them!"

"Fine!" April closed the door and protectively took Timmy's hand.

She walked across to a cluster of three women, determined to introduce herself.

The women noticed her approach and broke off their conversation, glancing over and smiling.

"Excuse me," April asked, smiling back, "is the bus from the City usually late?"

"Always," a dark-haired woman said quickly and, extending her hand, added, "Hello, I'm Betty Banks. And this is Lynn Grossman; Ann O'Malley. Welcome to our club. We take as our motto Milton's line, 'they also serve who merely stand and wait.' "

"I'm April Benard. And this is my son, Timmy." She smiled warmly at the women, immediately relieved by their openness. Ruefully, she added, "I guess these buses are a lot like the IRT."

"The only difference is that no one gets mugged while waiting. At least not so far," Ann O'Malley answered, "Is this your first trip to Park And Ride?"

April nodded. They could all be friends of hers from the city.

"We were guessing who might own the Volvo," Lynn laughed. She was blond and perky, like a high school cheerleading captain. "After a season in the Catskills, you know everyone's car. You're new to the hills?"

"Yes. My husband and I bought a house on Mad River Mountain. Do you know the area?" April scanned their faces.

"You bought the Olsen's place?" Betty asked immediately, and her saucer-y brown eyes widened.

"Why, yes." April smiled nervously, glancing again at the women. "Don't tell me you know something I don't?" She forced herself to laugh.

"Oh, no, of course not," Betty Banks said at once, stepping closer to April, as if prepared to give her physical protection. "But you know how it is in the mountains. There are always stories. You're from the Upper West Side?" she asked next, shifting the conversation.

"SoHo. We have a loft on Greene Street. This is my son, Timmy. And Marshall's daughter, Greta"—April turned around and nodded toward the Volvo—"is in the car. I can't seem to separate her from her Walkman."

"Well, she just has to meet children her own age, that's all," Lynn advised. "I know my Debbie would love to have a new girlfriend. It can be lonely for city kids up here. They never seem to have anything to do once they're in the wilds."

"It would be wonderful for Greta to have a few friends. Her father, unfortunately, has to work most of the summer, and Timmy is just not in her league. And the local children . . ."

"You've met the Tassels and Holts?" Ann O'Malley asked next.

"Yes, a few . . ." April paused and waited for the woman to go on. She was curious to see how much contact the mountain people had with outsiders.

"A strange lot, aren't they?" Lynn added. "But they're good people, once you get to know them. Honest. You know, Alan, my husband, hires some of them every spring to clean out the pool. They're weird, all right, but they work cheap."

"So you've dealt with them?" April asked next.

"We all use the families one way or another. They're kind of frightening to look at, but harmless."

"That's what the caretaker says."

"Luke Grange?" Lynn asked quickly.

"Yes. Do you know him?"

Lynn laughed, "Everyone knows Luke Grange. Especially the local girls."

"He's something of a rogue?" April asked, kidding.

The women exchanged glances.

What was wrong here, April asked herself, waiting for the women to respond.

"Well, he does have a reputation, let's say that," Betty said, summing up for the others.

"There it is!" Lynn announced. The bus had appeared over the rise and was slowing, its brakes hissing as it left the expressway and curved down the exit ramp. Car doors opened and more wives appeared, and the children came running and shouting to greet their fathers.

The three women began to say good-bye, and April said quickly, "Oh, may I have your telephone numbers? I would like the children—Greta especially—to meet some other kids." April reached into her shoulder bag and searched for a pen, thinking that if she had the children meet new friends and be away from the house, she'd have more time available to work on her research.

She scribbled her farmhouse telephone number and handed it to Lynn, then April smiled at all the women and said, "I'm planning on having a party soon." She suddenly felt guilty that she was trying to palm off her children. "Perhaps you and your husbands could come . . ."

"We'd love to," they said, almost in unison, laughing at their eagerness.

"To tell you the unguarded truth, we're all dying to see the inside of that house," Lynn admitted, touching April's arm in a gesture of understanding. "It's such a lovely old-fashioned place, and such a pretty setting, with the pond and the hillside. I believe Mad River Mountain is the loveliest spot in the Catskills when the leaves turn."

The bus door hissed opened, and men in suits and ties stepped down, to be swarmed upon by their excited children. April saw Greta running for the bus. She was pleased for Marshall, but also momentarily jealous. Greta had yet to show any affection toward her.

"Maybe I should show the house and sell tickets," April joked, watching Greta as she spoke. Marshall stepped down from the bus and swept his long-legged daughter up into an embrace, as if she were his wife and he had returned from the wars. Absorbed, she missed Lynn Grossman's answer.

"Pardon me?" She forced herself to turn away from the sight of Marshall and Greta.

"I said you should sell tickets to meet your caretaker," Lynn smiled, moving off to meet her husband.

"The Catskills are famous for their long, hot summer days, April," she called back. "And their long, hot summer nights. I'll phone you tomorrow about the party. 'Bye."

And then Marshall was by her side, bending to kiss her hello and saying, "It looks like you've met some new friends. Good for you!" he said.

April let herself be swept into his hug.

"I'm not sure," she whispered against his neck, "if they're friends or not."

Seventeen

"I went for a swim," Greta announced, strolling into the farmhouse kitchen.

April glanced around at her stepdaughter and asked innocently, "In what?"

"My suit, of course!" She lifted her oversized Puma sweatshirt and showed April the bottom of her bikini. "Do you think I'd swim naked in the pond?" As she talked, she went to the cupboard and took down the peanut butter jar.

"I'll fix you breakfast," April said. "How about some hot cereal?"

"I hate cereal." Greta spooned a thick glob of peanut butter onto a slice of whole-wheat bread. "This is better for me, besides. No artificial ingredients."

"I didn't see you swimming when I woke up," April remarked, shifting the conversation.

"I went early. I couldn't sleep. I keep having this weird dream. You and Daddy weren't even awake when I went out; I could hear him snoring from the deck. How can you sleep with someone who snores like that? Do you think that's why Mom divorced him?" Greta came back to the butcher-block counter and slid up onto a stool beside Timmy.

"What's the dream, Greta?" April asked casually, not responding to her questions about Marshall. "The one about the Sidhes?"

"No. Another one. I don't know." She shrugged.

"Well, was it a nightmare?"

"Yeah, kinda. It's weird." She paused a moment, as if trying to think how to explain the dream. "I'm swimming like in a pond. This pond," she nodded toward the back lawn, "and there's this weird outer space creature swimming with me, you know. Remember in *Close Encounters*? Those guys that got off the spaceship. He was like those guys, but ugly. It was this thing, like an extraterrestrial or something, swimming next to me. Nothing happened; we just swam. But it was yicky. Then I couldn't breathe, and I started to swim like crazy for the surface." She licked the knife clean with a long swipe of her tongue.

"Greta, please, don't! You'll . . ."

"I won't cut my tongue, April. Give me a break!" She tossed back her head as she always did when she was upset, but her blond hair was damp and heavy on her shoulders.

"Did you see *E.T.*?" Timmy asked. "He was cute." He looked up at Greta, waited for her to answer, but she ignored him.

"Did you see your father outside?" April asked next.

"Nope, I was down at Luke's."

"I hope you weren't bothering Luke this early in the morning," April said casually, but glancing at Greta, surprised by her answer.

"I wasn't bothering him. He was swimming, too. He swims every morning."

"He does?"

"He asked me if I wanted to have a cup of tea. He makes this wonderful herbal tea. Apple Spice with honey. He makes honey himself." Greta bit into her slice of bread and peanut butter and with her mouth full, asked, "Why can't we ever have anything good like that to eat in this place? I mean, we're like camping out here."

"You can have anything you want, Greta," April said softly.

"Can I have chocolate fudge ice cream?" Timmy asked.

"No, sweetheart, not for breakfast."

"Ice cream is bad for you," Greta told Timmy. "It makes you fat. Didn't you ever see all those ugly women in laundromats? They got fat like that from eating chocolate fudge ice cream. You're going to be big and ugly like that when you grow up, Timmy."

"I like chocolate fudge," he protested.

It was the first time all week that Greta had been so talkative. April wondered if it was because Marshall was back, or because she had been up for hours, swimming half naked with Luke Grange.

"How did you know Luke swims every morning?" April asked.

"I see him. I can't sleep, I told you. This weird dream . . ."

"Greta, have you had nightmares all week?" April asked, concerned now.

The tall teenager thought a moment, then shook her head. "I don't think so. I mean, sometimes when I wake up I can't remember what I dreamed. There's Daddy!" she announced, pointing out the kitchen window.

Marshall came out of the woods then. He was walking quickly with his head down, rushing, as if he were back in the City and late for an appointment. One of April's greatest hopes was that Marshall would learn to relax upstate, that he'd fall into the easy routine of country living.

There was a sudden roar from the woods.

ZZZZZZZZZRRRRRRRRR

"That son-of-a-bitch," Marshall swore, banging into the house.

April glanced at the children and Greta, looking back at her, grimaced and whispered, "I guess Daddy didn't get his way again." She giggled.

"Marshall, we're all here in the kitchen," April called to her husband.

"That bastard!" Marshall came into the kitchen, peeling off his leather jacket and tossing it down on the low pine chest that filled one wall of the room.

"Now he tells me he has some rights in perpetuity that not only let him harvest wood and sell off cords, but that also allow him—or any one member of his family—to stay on the property as caretaker. He says it's in the deed, a covenant. Any coffee?"

"What does the deed say?"

"I don't know. I don't remember. I let Foster handle it in the office when we went to contract. That bastard!"

"Marshall," April nodded toward Timmy.

"When I told him I didn't appreciate being woken at the crack of dawn, he looked at me as if I were a goddam dodo bird and said he waited especially until nine o'clock. As if 9 A.M. was an hour to be awake on Saturday morning."

"I told him it was okay," Greta announced.

"You told him?" Marshall stopped pacing and stared at his daughter.

"It seems Greta went swimming with Luke this morning."

"Swimming?"

Greta nodded. "Luke swims every morning at dawn. He saw me watching him and asked if I wanted to come along. It's fun. I mean, it's something to do around this dumb place." Greta finished her peanut butter and bread and began peeling a banana.

"I don't want you hanging around that guy, Greta!"

"Why? What did I do wrong?" Greta pulled herself up on the tall stool. Sitting, she was as tall as her father.

"Nothing, yet! But I don't like him."

"He's cute," Greta answered back.

Marshall glanced at April, seeking help. There was a look of uncertainty in his eyes, as if he realized he had pushed himself into an uncharted region with his daughter. April shook her head. She wasn't going to get into the middle of this argument.

"I don't trust him," Marshall said, but his tone of outrage was weakening.

"April does," Greta remarked.

April had turned on the water to do the dishes, but she

turned it off to explain to Marshall. "We had Luke for dinner during the week."

"April is down at his cabin all the time, Daddy. I don't know why you're picking on me."

April smiled, said sweetly to her son, "Have you finished breakfast, honey?" She reached for Timmy's bowl.

"Can't I go play with Luke?" Timmy asked.

"Yes, sweetheart, but let me clean your face."

"Luke is going to show me where the Indians sleep at night."

"He is? That will be fun, won't it? But there aren't any Indians alive in these hills," April added.

"Luke says there are," Timmy answered with conviction, climbing off the tall stool.

"Timmy, they're just stories, like you see on television," April told him. "They're fun, but they're not true."

"They are!" Timmy insisted. He looked up at his mother, defying her, "There's an old Indian ghost, Luke says, who lives up in the graveyard and she comes out at night when everyone is sleeping and she has this long kitchen knife and she cuts the ears off people if they've been telling lies or hurting the wild animals, or doing bad stuff like that."

April knelt beside Timmy and took hold of the four-year-old.

"Timmy, those are just fairy stories. They are not true. There is no Indian ghost in the graveyard."

"Yes there is. Luke said so," Timmy answered back.

April stared at her son. She was furious now at the caretaker for what he had told Timmy. He had no right to tell such stories to a four-year-old.

"Let it go, April," Marshall commented. "He'll just get more confused. Let him get dressed."

"I'll take him," Greta offered, jumping off her stool. She took Timmy by the hand and pulled him after her.

"All right," April agreed. "But put a sweater on him. It's chilly this morning."

"No it isn't, April. It wasn't cold when I went swimming."

"Greta! Do what you're told."

"Marshall, please." April touched Marshall's arm, then waited until Greta was out of hearing before she added,

"You'll only make it worse if she knows she can get a reaction from you."

"She's behaving like a snotty teenager."

"And that's what she is. A teenager." She turned back to the sink and finished the dishes, not saying anything more, just waiting for Marshall to ask about Luke. She didn't have to wait long.

"Kiddo, why are you being so nice to Luke?" He asked obliquely.

"I wasn't being 'nice to Luke,' as you say. He's the only adult contact I have all week, so I had him for dinner."

"What about Greta? I was hoping you two would get a chance to know each other up here."

"Greta spent her time locked away in her room."

"How's your work going then?"

"Oh, I'm just getting started. I spent most of the week going through computer files that one of my students developed."

"Then you weren't spending all your time hanging around his cabin?" He had poured himself another cup of coffee, but did not move away from April.

"Marshall, enough! You're not amusing." April did not enjoy being questioned like a witness. "I did go down to see Luke Thursday morning. I needed to speak to him in private and away from the kids."

"How come?"

"There was a man watching the house on Wednesday night. I thought it was Luke, but it turned out to be his older brother Mark." She told him the rest of the story and enjoyed his shock—and letting him know what she had to deal with up here.

"Where's this brother now?"

"I told Luke to get him off the property. Luke said he had already passed through, was on his way to the City."

"This is getting out of hand. I've got to break that covenant," Marshall said, thinking out loud. He had stepped to the windows and was staring across the pond toward the log cabin. From that angle, only part of the slate roof and the rocky chimney were visible, and in another week, April knew—once the trees were in full bloom—they wouldn't be able to see the cabin at all from the main house.

"Do you believe him?" Marshall said, "I mean, that he even has a brother? Maybe it really was him and he made the rest up."

"I don't know." April shrugged. She, too, was staring out the window. "The story was weird enough to be true."

"Was the brother normal, or one of those pumpkin-heads?"

"I don't know—I didn't see him very clearly."

"Could Luke be normal and have a pumpkin-head brother?"

"That might happen. I'm going to find out for sure with my research. Basically, we all carry three harmful, recessive genes. For example, I might carry a gene for albinism, a gene for muscular dystrophy and a gene for congenital deafness. You might carry genes for blindness, dwarfism, and anemia.

"Our children, however, would not be affected because they must receive two of the same recessive genes for a trait to appear, and it's very rare that unrelated spouses have the same bad gene. Inbreeding, however, increases the chances that two people will carry the same recessive gene and produce an abnormal child."

"By limiting the gene pool."

April nodded.

"What kind of odds are we talking about?"

"If first cousins marry, the chance they'll have the same gene is one in eight. If a brother and sister produce a child, the odds are one in four. I'd actually love to get a better look at Mark, and find out from Luke the exact genetic makeup of his family."

"Well, you'd better ask him soon," Marshall said dryly, "because I'm going to kick his ass off this property."

"No!" she answered back. "I need him."

"Need him for what?"

"He's my contact. I can use him to reach the others."

"You don't mind him around here? Him and his killer brother?"

"Luke is harmless," she said quickly, remembering that he had said the same thing to her about the Hill children.

"I thought you were worried about Luke and the kids? The folktales, all that shit."

"I'm concerned, but I'll handle it my own way. I don't tell you how to litigate, do I?"

"Sorry." He raised his palm, backing off.

"Well, sometimes you just build up a head of steam, get onto one of your lawyerly rolls."

She was upset and overreacting, she knew, and she stopped harping. She did not like to fight with Marshall, especially when he was just up for the weekend and they had so little time together.

Marshall wanted to make peace too. He began putting away the breakfast dishes.

"What was that, by the way, about Greta's not being able to sleep, being awake at dawn? In California, her mother says, she doesn't get up till noon."

"She seems to be having a recurring dream. Something about swimming in the pond and suddenly having an extra-terrestrial swimming by her side."

Marshall shook his head, "If she didn't go in that dirty pond water, she wouldn't have nightmares."

"That's not true."

"You don't think that's the reason?"

April slowly shook her head and then said quietly, "Last night I had the same nightmare."

Eighteen

Marshall slowed the Volvo as they came out of Mad River Valley, just before reaching the interstate.

"What's that?" he asked, nodding toward the crowd of people on the lawn of an old Victorian house.

"An auction," April said, seeing the auctioneer holding

up a household lamp. "An estate sale, it seems," she added, spotting the sign on the lawn.

Marshall pulled the car to the edge of the road and parked behind a pickup truck. There were cars and trucks on both sides of the gravel road. April looked at the grand Victorian house with its wide front porch and third floor of high-peaked gables.

"Are we stopping?" April asked, surprised. "We have shopping to do."

"We've got time," he smiled. "These country auctions are fun, and sometimes you can find a good deal."

"Marshall, the children aren't up for an auction."

"I am," Greta chimed in from the backseat.

"Well, I guess that settles it." Marshall looked over at April and unbuckled his seat belt.

"All right, let's go." April stepped out of the car. She took Timmy and walked ahead, across the lawn and into the crowd of people that clustered in front of the wooden porch.

The auctioneer called out, "Okay, we've got a fine piece of furniture here, it's an 1890 breakfront. You all knew Miss Rotherham kept her china in this piece, back there in the parlor. What am I offered? Let's start the bidding at seventy-five. Do I have seventy-five? I have seventy-five. Do we have eighty dollars?" The auctioneer's high voice sang into the warm midday air as he pointed, nodded, kept scanning, smiling and chewing on tobacco as he worked the crowd.

"Aunt Anita must be turning in her grave," a young woman blurted out as April pushed into the crowd. "It makes me sick, seeing her things sold off like this."

April glanced at the thin rail of a woman. She was wearing jeans and a cotton T-shirt that advertised the Campbell Feed Depot.

"You want this junk?" the man beside her asked, pushing up a John Deere cap. "We got no goddamn room in the trailer, Cindy."

"I just don't want it sold off to these city people. And it ain't junk, Ralph! Those city people call her things antiques."

"Let 'em! I'll take their money and buy me a pickup." He was grinning, showing his bad teeth.

"Ralph, you know what? You're really an asshole!"

Cindy said without looking up at him. "Just because they got money, ain't living on welfare, they think they can come in here, buy our belongings, everything Mommy and Daddy had, what Aunt Anita kept all those years, and you don't give a good goddamn."

She saw April then, glanced at her, but kept talking, this time speaking straight at April, her gray eyes flashing in her narrow face.

"Ain't I right, lady? You city people buy our things real cheap, take them into the city, to those fancy high-price places you got, and leave us with what?"

April backed away. "I'm not buying anything."

The thin woman hooted. "You'll buy fast enough, once you see some of what we got. We got good furniture, here. It's worth good money. They don't build furniture like this, not no more."

April kept backing away, edging her way out of the thick crowd. She was perspiring and she realized how conspicuous she must look in her fresh white linen skirt, the flowered blouse. It was the wrong thing to wear, she realized, glancing around.

"Mommy!" Timmy grabbed her arm.

"Timmy, please don't pull me," she snapped. The heat was terrible, she realized. Abruptly she took Timmy's hand and pulled him toward a cluster of trees.

Stepping into the shade felt like entering an air-conditioned room, and April breathed deeply.

"April! It is you!" Ann O'Malley ducked her head, peering at April. "Are you hiding from the great unwashed?" she whispered.

"Actually, I was just looking for a cool spot," April smiled, matching Ann's tone as she examined her clothes. Ann was wearing tight jeans, heelless sandals, and a thin white oversized T-shirt. The outfit was too young for her; April thought the older woman looked like she was wearing a costume.

"Is your cute husband with you? Or are you soloing?"

"He's parking the car."

"I didn't know you were an auction fan."

"I'm not." April kept the smile frozen on her face. She

suddenly felt sick, nauseated, and she wondered with a distant curiosity if she would vomit there on the lawn, in front of Ann, in front of the old ladies on their lawn chairs, eyeing them both, glancing up through their thick bifocals.

"It's great fun, you'll see," Ann said, turning around, scanning the lawn crowd, "and a nice way to kill a summer afternoon. Lynn and I are old hands. And you won't believe the prices. I mean, compared to the City. Everything's a steal. I don't see your husband, April," she added, still scanning the crowd.

"I'm right here," Marshall said, striding up. "Hello, I'm Marshall Benard." He extended his hand.

"Ann O'Malley, honey," April said quickly. "We met at the bus stop. And this is Greta Benard," April added, including Marshall's daughter.

"Oh, yes, Ann. I remember you." Marshall said coolly, "You were wearing a navy blue skirt yesterday."

"Yes, I was. Why, aren't you observant." Ann was staring up at Marshall, her eyes wide with surprise.

"I never forget a pretty... navy blue skirt."

He was smiling down at Ann, charming her, April knew, as if she were a juror.

"I was suggesting to April that we should have a party at our place, show it off a little." Marshall kept smiling, filling Ann with his deliberate attention.

"Why, that would be marvelous," Ann answered back, matching his flirtatiousness.

"Daddy, let's go," Greta whispered. She was clinging to her father, had both her arms wrapped about his waist, as she tried to draw his attention back to her.

"In a second, sweetheart." Marshall tousled her hair. He said to April, "Why don't you get on the phone and set up the party?"

April nodded, her lips pressed together. She hated it when Marshall got dictatorial in front of other people, and started to give orders. It was the only one of his personal habits that enraged her, yet she knew it came naturally to him. At the office he had endless junior lawyers and secretaries just waiting to respond to his wishes.

"Well, Ann O'Malley, what have we got here? An estate

sale?'' He stepped past his wife, blocking her view of the auction, as he listened to Ann explain what was for sale.

From across the lawn, April could hear the auctioneer shouting out, ''I have an opening bid of 175 on this fine Colonial desk, Aunt Anita's favorite piece. Many of you folks might recall having seen it in her front parlor. Do I have 180? Yes, I do! I'm looking for 185. See the woodwork on the legs, folks? A thing of beauty. Real beauty. I have 185 on my right. Now 190.''

Timmy tugged on April's skirt and she reached down and lifted her son up, needing to embrace him, needing to have him in her arms.

''Mommy?'' he whispered.

''Yes, sweetheart?'' She kissed his smooth cheek and he nuzzled down next to her, pressed his warm face against hers. ''I see Luke!'' he cried out, twisting in her arms and pointing off across the lawn. ''I want to go see Luke,'' he cried.

She couldn't hold him. ''All right! All right!''

''April, are you coming with us?'' Marshall asked, walking off with Ann O'Malley. Greta held her father's hand.

April slowly shook her head, staring coolly back at him.

''It will just be a few minutes, okay, kiddo? And then we'll get to town and do the shopping.'' He kept smiling, kept watching and waiting for her to nod okay.

He knew she was upset, she realized, and that gave her some satisfaction. Still, he didn't break off from Ann O'Malley, or come back to where she stood in the shade of the thick maple trees.

And then he winked, as if everything was all right between them and he knew why she was upset. Often his charm did work with her and she would acquiesce, go along, begin to laugh in spite of herself. But not today. Not now. She wondered whether it was just because he was flirting openly with Ann O'Malley, or that, having been upstate without him all week, she was now angry that he wasn't spending all his time with her. But she wouldn't tag after him like his daughter, holding onto his hand while he went off with another woman.

Instead, in a spontaneous show of defiance, she followed

after Timmy, leaving the little old ladies and the shade of the maple trees, and walked across the lawn to where Luke stood by himself, watching the crowd of people, as if he, too, were an outsider at the auction.

"You're not buying?" she asked, coming up to him.

Luke shook his head, looking away. He was holding Timmy as if to protect him, wrapping his arms around the small boy's body.

"You knew this Miss Rotherham?" April asked, reading the name off the auction sign.

"Everyone knew her."

"Why? Was she the town gossip?"

"She was the midwife."

"Really? I thought midwifery wasn't common in this area."

"Oh, back in these hills we don't have much of a chance at getting a real doctor. Aunt Anita delivered most of the children up on Mad River Mountain."

"Really?" If only April had known that a few months ago. A few hours with Anita Rotherham would have saved her weeks of research in the county records. Now it was too late.

"When did she die?"

"This winter. Are you buying any furniture?"

"No, I'm afraid to even bid on her things." She told Luke then what had happened to her on the lawn.

"Cindy and Ralph didn't have the time of day for their aunt," Luke answered back.

April waited for some explanation. Every time she mentioned someone, the name pricked a person and gave her a tiny piece of further information.

"Yes?" she asked.

Luke shook his head, still not looking at her. He was letting Timmy wrestle with him as he finally answered.

"They wouldn't have anything to do with her because of us."

"Us?"

"Yes, the mountain people. The Tassels and Holts, Elys, Granges. The other families from Mad River."

"You're one of them?" April asked, hoping he would acknowledge it.

He glanced at her and she saw that his brown eyes momentarily lost their softness. She had pressed too quickly.

"In the mountains, Mrs. Benard, everyone is kin," he said softly, "and kin of kin, and next of kin, and double kin." He stared back at her. The hard edge was gone from his eyes, and again they looked sad. Then he finally admitted it. "Yes, I'm one of them."

"And this midwife, she was your friend?"

Luke nodded. "She was the only friend we had in this town. They don't like us much. They think we're bad for tourists." He smiled wryly. "God knows why any tourist would want to visit this end of the world."

"Well, I met some people the other day at the bus stop—city people—and they told me how helpful all the Hill People were."

"They get us cheap, that's why they like us." Luke straightened up, as if preparing to leave, then swung Timmy easily up onto his shoulders. April's son began to laugh, thrilled by the piggyback ride. "I want to show Timmy the tree house out behind. Okay?"

April nodded.

"I'll be right back," he added, walking off, and then broke into a slow jog as he carried Timmy away, making him giggle with excitement.

April walked across the lawn, dizzy and unfocused. Luke had talked to her openly, and she wondered why. Was it just because they were off her property and they felt like equals? Or was it being here, at the midwife's estate sale, that had made him want to open up?

She aimlessly walked among the furniture set out on the lawn—the pine cupboards and oak tables, the rocking chairs and old flowered sofas, the dozens and dozens of pieces that had filled the enormous Victorian mansion. She let her fingers slide across the fine oak tabletops, paused to open and close a desk drawer, stooped to examine the base of a standing lamp. She should be looking for pieces for the farmhouse, she thought, but she couldn't concentrate. Luke's confession had unraveled her.

She stopped at a tall pine hutch and opened the top drawer. There were still linen napkins in the drawers, all pressed and folded away. They had simply carted the heavy pieces onto the lawn. No one had even taken inventory. Cindy and Ralph were just distant cousins, she realized, selling off the property to make a quick buck.

She closed one drawer and opened another, full of old kitchen silver. She closed the drawer and moved on, curious now about the dead woman's possessions. She stopped at a cherry night table and opened the top drawer. There was a thick ledger tucked away in the narrow drawer and carefully, using her body to clock anyone's view, she pulled it out and opened it at random, flipped idly through the stiff pages.

There were dozens of references to names she recognized—names in her data file, all the offspring of the incestuous marriages. April took a long, deep breath to calm herself. This had to be the midwife's birth ledger. Slowly, casually, she glanced around, half expecting to be found out, but saw that no one was even aware of her.

She looked down at the thick ledger and fanned the pages. Each page, she saw, was given over to an individual year and there were in some years as many as a dozen births. She paused at 1984 and read the list.

Joe Tassel		
Betty Sue Holt	Boy	Stillborn
Clive Ely		
Cindy Gordon	Girl	Normal
Mark Tassel		
Mary Gurr	Girl	Brain Deformity

And beneath that, scribbled in the shaky script of an old woman, was a further notation: "People have always wished the Hill People weren't about. They have called their deformed children God's judgment for their sinful incest. A child is a child, I tell them. And a woman in her labor needs me. But, by God, I have never seen the likes of this birth on

Mad River Mountain, not in fifty years, I haven't. It isn't human. It isn't half human.''

April heard Timmy calling for her and she glanced around to see him running across the lawn, shouting that daddy wanted her. April slipped the Anita Rotherham's birth ledger back into the drawer and, stepping into the bright midday sun, swept Timmy up into her arms and walked over to where her husband was standing with Ann O'Malley.

"Darling, I don't want to leave just yet."

"Why? I thought you'd be bored by now."

"No, I found a lovely cherry night table I want for our bedroom," and without waiting for his reply, April turned toward the auctioneer, and moved closer to the wooden porch.

Nineteen

It was hot and humid. April opened the French doors and let the guests move out onto the deck. It was nine o'clock and the party had developed a life of its own. For the first time in hours, April started to relax.

She could hear the children upstairs, running back and forth between rooms, and wondered whether to check on them. Both Lynn and Ann had brought along their teenage daughters, and April prayed that Greta would like them.

She was glad she had taken Ann's advice to cast a broad net for the party, inviting people she did not know, friends of friends, city people who owned country places. For a moment, glancing around the crowd, April actually thought she was back in the City, at an art gallery opening or a fund-raiser. Everything looked so New York, she thought. It made her feel better, more confident.

One difference: In the country, men didn't dress for

parties. Or rather, they dressed in their country costumes: cord pants and jeans, denim and short-sleeved polo shirts, bush shoes. There were no ties, an occasional scarf knotted at the neck, safari jackets, and Banana Republic shirts.

The women did dress, however, though less than they would have in the City. It was a sexist thing, she realized, but it didn't upset her, as it once might have, when she was younger. She always hated it that women were expected to be decked out. Perhaps after a long week isolated in the country, the women just felt like fussing. That was it, she decided, giving everyone the benefit of the doubt. Perhaps they were just trying to reclaim their husbands' attention.

She knew how they felt. She had dressed, too, in a bright blue, hand-painted dress by Yves Saint Laurent which she had bought one year in Paris. But she had felt self-conscious, and soon after everyone arrived, she had slipped into the bedroom, changed into a plain white sheath, and removed her jewelry before reappearing.

Only Luke seemed to notice that she had changed. As she crossed the room, he said, "You look nice in blue."

"Pardon me?" She was not sure what he had said.

"That blue silk dress goes nice with your eyes." He sipped his white wine as he watched her over the rim of the glass.

"Thank you," she whispered, looking away, not sure of how to take his remark. Marshall had not wanted to invite Luke to the party, but she had insisted. Not only did she want to maintain good relations, she wanted to see how the New Yorkers would react to being at a party with this mountain person.

"Do you know any of these people?" Luke asked. He gestured toward the guests, but at the same time, he sandwiched April into one corner of the dining room.

"Yes," she said, and then faltering, added, "Some." April searched for Marshall in the crowded room. "Do you know anyone?"

"I know the wives," he said casually.

When his eyes were off her, she studied Luke. He was wearing a coarse white cotton shirt with an open neck and doeskin leather pants that were out of style, belted with an

Indian bead belt. He had combed his long blond hair into a
ponytail, knotting it with a brightly woven Indian band. She
thought he looked cute.

"Luke, please move," she said, "I have other guests."
As she spoke she spotted Lynn Grossman across the room.
The woman was talking to a cluster of people, but was
looking past them, staring across the long dining room table
and smiling coyly at April.

"You do like me, don't you?" Luke asked next.

The innocence of his question caught her off guard. She
stepped back so she could look up into his face, realizing as
she did that he had further blocked her view of the room,
isolated her in the corner.

"Whether I like you or not is irrelevant. The fact is that
you have squatter's rights on this property."

"My family has always lived here."

"Yes, I know. Marshall explained the covenant."

"Are you sorry I live here?"

"Luke, I haven't thought about it," April lied. She was
beginning to fathom how Luke operated. Once, in the year
after Tom was killed, there had been a young man, the
oldest son of a college colleague, who had come on to her
with the same boy/man routine, appealing first to her moth-
erly instincts, appearing misunderstood and fragile, a victim
of too worldly a world.

"I'd like to be your friend, April," he said, leaning
forward. She could feel his warm breath on her cheek.

"And I'd like you to be my employee," she answered
back. "Excuse me." Edging around him, she escaped from
the corner.

Lynn was signaling her to join them, but April, motioning
that she had work to do in the kitchen, veered away. She
didn't want Lynn quizzing her about Luke. Going into the
kitchen, she found Helen Smythe Ely, the realtor who had
found them the house, blocking the pantry passageway.

"Oh Helen, I've been looking for you!"

"Well, I must say, I don't think I'm hard to find." The
overweight woman answered, laughing. She had a teenager's high, nervous giggle.

"Come with me into the kitchen, please," April asked.

"I have to see about more ice," she added as an excuse and went ahead into the empty kitchen. "Do you need to freshen your drink?"

"Oh, I'll take care of it myself. You go ahead with what you need to do. My, it's a warm June. . . ." Helen fluttered her arms, as if fanning her body. She was wearing a loose flowery kimono and too much jewelry. April saw the spreading perspiration marks under the woman's arms and looked away, embarrassed for her.

"I think it's this oven. I had it turned on earlier to heat the pasta." April reached over the sink and opened the two windows. "I've been cold at night, but I think summer has finally reached the Catskills."

"That linguine of yours was just marvelous," Helen Ely remarked, digging her fingers into the bowl of ice cubes. "You New Yorkers, I swear, you are such wonderful cooks. How do you do it? Living in that city. Rushing about all day. The city makes me nervous, just being there among so many people. Why, I don't think I've been in Manhattan in decades."

"Tell me," April asked quickly, wanting to surprise the realtor, "what do you know about these Hill People?" April had opened the freezer to take out another ice tray, but she stopped to watch Helen Ely and hear her reply.

"I try not to know about them." The realtor tumbled the cubes into her tall glass. "They're an odd lot, the whole bunch."

"Luke Grange is related to them," April added.

"Oh, I suppose he is. Everyone is related some way to everyone else in these mountains. Even me!" She laughed.

"Yes, I know. 'Kin of kin, next of kin, and double kin.' " April dropped ice cubes into the bowl. "Did you know Anita Rotherham?"

"April, of course! Aunt Anita lived her whole life down there in the hollow."

"And she was the midwife of the Hill People."

"She was kind, that woman. A grand woman."

"Who's a grand woman?" Lynn Grossman asked, coming into the kitchen with her empty glass. Without waiting for April to ask, she dug her hand into the bucket of ice and pulled out three cubes. "Where's the vodka?" she asked next, glancing around the cluttered kitchen.

April nodded to the cupboard, annoyed by Lynn's attitude. It was the casualness of summer living, she reasoned, that brought out such bad manners.

"Who's a grand woman?" Lynn asked again.

"Anita Rotherham. From the estate sale," April replied coolly.

Lynn was shaking her head before April finished her comment.

"I knew her myself." Lynn stopped filling her glass to look over at April. "She came to me once. This would have been two years ago, at least, and asked about helping these people. You know, the inbreds," Lynn whispered. "She wanted help to get some federal aid, I think, into Mad River Mountain. Well, I told her, I didn't know anything about the government. Besides, it seems to me those people have done well enough without us."

"They like being by themselves. It suits them, really," Helen Ely agreed. She nodded knowingly at April.

Lynn laughed, whispered back to Helen, "Besides, it's too late to help that lot."

They both had had too much to drink, April realized then, and she picked up the ice bucket, stepped around them, and walked into the dining room.

For a moment she stood away from the crowd and took in her party, sizing up the guests again. She saw immediately that everyone was drinking too much. Was there nothing to do in the Catskills after dark but drink? Perhaps it was only the mountain altitude that caused the excess.

It all made her lonely for Marshall and she scanned the group again, this time looking for her husband. He was not in the dining room, nor sitting in the living room, where several of the guests had found the soft chairs. She spotted Luke. He was in the hall at the foot of the stairs, leaning against the wall and talking to two women. He was bent slightly forward, listening, but April saw that he was really focused on her, was watching her across two rooms. His insolence made her furious again, and she promised herself that this was the last time Luke Grange would be invited to her home.

April walked onto the side deck. There were a few people sitting on the railing.

"Come here, April," Betty Banks said, waving her over. "I want you to talk to Nancy and Hank. They're also academics, like yourself. Hank is chairman of the English department of the SUNY branch up here. And an amateur biologist. He can tell you more than you'll ever want to know about the flora and fauna of Ulster County."

"No, no! Now our lovely hostess will never talk to me," he protested, laughing. Then he smiled grandly at April, saying, "We were just about to read love poems to each other. We do it every year, it's our pagan way of communing with nature. Do you know any Cummings? e. e. cummings? I have a lovely Cummings to read you," he went on, staggering a bit, spilling his drink before he caught himself. His wife told him to sit down, and Betty Banks, giggling, reached up and pulled the bearded bear of a man down next to her on the narrow railing.

He'll tumble over backward and kill himself, April thought. But the big man steadied himself, and April, keeping her distance, asked, "Have you seen my husband?"

"Oh, I think Ann O'Malley finally landed him," Betty said matter-of-factly, then laughed, as if sharing a joke.

"What?"

Betty waved vaguely toward the dark lawn and pond.

"Follow at thy own risk!" the English professor shouted out.

April moved away from her guests. Who were these people? she asked herself. Why in the world had she let herself get carried away, invite all these obnoxious people? At home she would have been more selective. In New York no one invited strangers into their home.

She stood at the edge of the deck, peering out across the lawn, resisting an urge to call for Marshall, resisting the need to run down and find him somewhere in the darkness.

Then she saw their faint silhouette. He and Ann O'Malley were standing at the edge of the pond, Ann pointing upward, as if picking out stars and constellations. The woman was leaning against her husband, April saw. And Marshall had his arm protectively on her shoulder.

"They're contemptible." Luke emerged from a shadow.

"What?" April turned to Luke, alarmed by his sudden and silent appearance.

"Summer people. They come up to the Catskills, drink all weekend, make fools of themselves, sleep with each other's wives and husbands."

"I beg your pardon?" April took a step back, separating herself from the caretaker.

"They think right manners and morality don't count, not in the mountains. They come up here to do their sinning. In a little while, watch, they'll all be stripping naked and diving into the pond. You're not like them, April," he said next. He gestured toward Marshall down by the pond. "You're not like him."

"Would you please leave," April answered back, speaking softly so the others on the deck wouldn't overhear.

"He'll only hurt you, April."

"Get out of here!" This time she could not control her voice, and she was aware at once that the conversations across the deck had ceased.

Slowly and carefully, Luke set down his glass of spring water. April stepped back further, giving him more room to pass her and go down the deck steps, back to his cabin. He moved slowly and carefully without rushing, without concern for the attention they had attracted.

He paused at the bottom and said quietly, "They're watching you." Then he bounced lightly onto the lawn and disappeared into the darkness.

April didn't turn around, didn't face the guests. Slowly they picked up their conversations, like bits and pieces of broken bric-a-brac. She could wait them out, April thought, stand there, looking toward Mad River Valley. She'd wait until her guests were engrossed before she turned around. She thought Luke had meant them, her guests: that they were watching her.

But she was wrong.

In the woods, hiding in the thick underbrush, hiding in the high branches of trees, the Hill People watched. They listened to the tinkling of glass, the bursts of music, and all the bright and happy laughter of the city people. They waited and they watched.

But it was not April who held their attention. They were looking across the pond at Marshall. They saw him go off with the city woman, and when he and the woman stripped down for a midnight swim they glanced at each other, giggled, and quickly covered their mouths to keep from being found out. It was too soon, they knew. Too soon to go and get him.

Timmy sat up in his dark bedroom, startled by the laughing and shouting from down on the lawn. He had fallen asleep in his clothes, and in his sleep had half-covered himself with the quilts. Now he sat at the edge of the bed, yawning, rubbing his eyes. He could hear the girls down the hallway in Greta's bedroom. They were giggling among themselves, whispering.

Timmy stood and went to the window, stumbling in his grogginess and the darkness of the small bedroom. He could see people on the lawn below him running across the grass, and heard the water splash as they dove into the pond. He wondered where his mom was, and wondered if he would get into trouble if he went downstairs. It frightened him suddenly, not knowing where she was.

Then he saw the creatures.

Beyond the dark lawn, beyond the stillness of the pond water there was movement in the woods, movement here, more there. They had crept closer to the tree line, crouched behind shadbushes, climbed into the crab apple trees, perched there in the crooks of branches, crawled onto a slab of shale rock and stared silently across the lawn to the lighted deck where April Benard stood, staring after Luke Grange.

They were in the valley all the time, Timmy knew, hiding in the dark woods during the day, sleeping in caves and hollow trees, waiting for night when they came out to play. Luke had told him.

Timmy smiled and turned away from the window, went running out of his bedroom and down the hall. He would go out and play with them, he thought. He would go out into the woods and play with the Wild Things.

Twenty

April was dressed and in the woods by daybreak. She had slipped quietly out before her husband could wake up and want to make love. The night before, as Luke had predicted, the guests had gone skinny-dipping in the pond. And Ann O'Malley had been first. Stripping down to her panties and bra, she dove into the shallow waters and called back to Marshall, teasing and coaxing him to join her. Marshall had stood a moment at the edge, grinning like an adolescent at her exhibitionism, glancing back at April and the others on the deck. Then he set his drink on a tree stump and stripped down, plunging nude into the cold mountain water.

Seeing them, the other guests had come rushing out onto the deck to watch, then one by one, encouraging each other, shrieking, a dozen more ran down to join the frolic.

April had turned away then and gone back into the now-quiet house. From inside, the nude guests were only shadowy figures on the lower lawn. April was grateful for that, thinking of the teenage girls upstairs. She was sure they were all in the dark of Greta's room, glued to the windows.

"It happens every year," Helen Smythe Ely said, seeing April's annoyance. The heavy woman was standing by the dining room windows, peering out. "Up here, I guess everyone feels a little less reserved." Helen smiled.

"It's not my idea of a good time," April answered, making her position clear.

"Oh, you'll loosen up," Helen said. Then she added softly, as if she knew many secrets about the mountains, "All you folks loosen up when you come up here. You'll see.'' She glanced back at April, nodded. The smile had gone from her fat, jowly face.

April had no idea how to respond, but then she didn't have to. Timmy came running downstairs wanting to go out into the woods. He was talking about the wild things again, wanting to go play with them. The only way she could keep him inside was to go upstairs and lie down with him. Once he was asleep again, she couldn't bear to leave his room, to return to the party below.

She spent the night in Timmy's room. At dawn Marshall was still snoring as she went in for her clothes and dressed in the cold bathroom, wearing jeans, an old rugby shirt of Tom's that she had kept, and her own new safari jacket. She went into her office and got her camera, loading it with daylight black-and-white film, and carrying her heavy hiking boots went out onto the deck to lace them up.

It was a cold, cloudy dawn, with dew on the lawn and a chilly breeze coming up from the valley. Luke, she guessed, wouldn't be swimming this morning, and that made her feel better. She didn't want to run into him on the path, nor have him see the aftermath of her party. There were cocktail napkins scattered across the lawn, and several half empty glasses had been left on the tree stump near the pond's edge. In the pale morning light, the abandoned drinks looked like sewage.

Later, she planned to have it out with Luke, to tell him to quit telling Timmy folk stories. She could not go on like this, having the children waking at night, full of stories of wild creatures.

April stepped off the deck and started across the lawn, then stopped. Her footsteps in the early dew were leaving a trail and she did not want to be followed. Not by Marshall when he woke, nor even Timmy. She needed a few hours off by herself. She needed time to think, she realized, about her new marriage. She turned away from the pond and went out onto the country road, walked away from the farmhouse and down the slight slope. When she found a break in the crumbling stone wall, she went into the woods and followed a deep path. Within a few yards she was going downhill into Mad River Valley. Even in the early morning sunlight the

woods were damp and dark. Large bluebirds greeted her,
flapping out of the thick stands of evergreens and sailing
above her, as if they were marking her way.

It was peaceful on the path. She stopped in the midst of a
thick patch of maples, chestnuts and black walnut trees and
listened to the woods. She heard water running nearby, and
birds rustling in the higher branches of the trees. She felt the
dampness of the ground, felt it even through her clothes. It
chilled her suddenly, like a fright.

Yet the woods were not oppressive, nor bleak. The air
was clear and sharp, smelling of evergreens and the wet
moss that carpeted sections of the forest floor. She walked
for several hundred yards through the trees, feeling that she
was seeing the valley with an almost supernatural clarity.

She listened to her heart pulsing, felt the cold breeze on
her face, felt again her own fatigue from having been up so
late, having been so distraught by her husband's midnight
behavior. When she heard a rustling she glanced about and
spotted two squirrels a dozen yards away scampering around
the thick base of a tree, chasing each other in last year's
leaves. April smiled.

Then she spotted the golden deer and the sudden sight of
him so close to her almost made her cry out. He had come
up from the valley, was fifty yards ahead of her in a
clearing. He paused on the path, lifted his head and sniffed
the wind.

April stood perfectly still. Deer, she knew, had poor
eyesight and saw only shadows. If she could keep down-
wind of him, he would not notice her. Then he began
walking toward her. His head was up, balancing a full set of
antlers. She saw his damp black quivering nostrils. He was
watching her, she knew, as he came forward. There was no
nervousness or shyness in his steady gait. It was as if he
knew her, and was waiting for her there at the mouth of the
valley. She felt her heart race.

April held her breath, fought to calm herself, to keep
from panicking before this wild animal. He was close
enough for her to see his liquid brown eyes. She felt as if he
recognized her. He stopped then within her arms' reach. She
could touch him, April realized.

The buck snorted and jerked up his antlers.

April slowly raised her hand and extended an open palm, made a simple gesture of submission. Tentatively, and carefully, as if building up trust, the deer stepped even closer and nudged her palm with his damp nostrils.

April was in control now. Her heart had stopped racing. It was unbelievable, she knew, that this animal had come this close to her, had put his trust in her. The deer, she saw again, was golden. His silky fur was a soft metallic yellow, the color of gold.

The buck took another step forward and, lifting his head, looked into her eyes. April stared back, felt his hot breath on her face, smelled the sweat of the wild animal. He smelled of the woods and moss and dry leaves. He smelled of wherever in the valley he had slept that night, of his nest in the dark woods.

The deer leaned closer. She stood frozen, thrilled and still frightened by the buck's closeness. He touched her again, nuzzled her face with the flank of his snout. She felt his damp nostril trace across her cheek, like a kiss, a gesture of peace. She wanted to wrap her arms around his thick muscular neck, to tell him he was forgiven.

"April! Hey, kiddo, where are you?" Marshall shouted from the woods. He was behind her in the trees, thrashing through the underbrush.

The golden deer reared away, his brown eyes flaming with fear. His sharp hoofs bit into the ground, tore out the soft soil as he spun away from her and bolted into the woods. His hind legs kicked up as he leapt away, dodging one way, then the other, slipping between trees, and then jumping into a thicket of sumac bushes and disappearing from sight.

"Christ! Did you see that?" Marshall came running up, out of breath.

"What?" April asked coolly.

"That goddamn deer! It looked golden."

"It wasn't golden."

"It was golden, I tell you. Not buckskin like most. Goddamn honey gold! Did you see that buck?"

"I saw him." April turned to look at her husband. "But

he was no different from any other you'll see this time of year. Their color changes with the season.''

"Oh." Her confidence momentarily dispelled his certainty. "Are you sure?" He kept looking after the animal.

"Yes." April started up the path, back to the country road. "What do you want?" she asked, letting her anger show through her voice.

"Nothing. I got up. You were gone. I just came looking for you."

"I went for a walk."

"I can see that, for Chrissake! What are you so bitchy about?"

April kept quiet. She didn't want to start arguing with him. She wanted first to think through her own feelings and to understand why she was so angry.

"Are the children awake?" she asked.

"I don't know." He came after her on the path. "Don't go running off!" He held her arm.

"Let go, Marshall."

"Not unless you tell me what's bothering you."

"I went for a walk. I want to be alone. And you come charging after me, frightening away the animals. That's what's bothering me." She turned from him.

"I wanted to talk to you, that's all." He sounded chagrined. "I thought you were put off by last night."

"I am put off by last night." She walked away.

"It was a lot of goddamn fun, April. Everyone was having a good time. Don't be so tight-assed." He came after her.

"I don't appreciate other women making a play for my husband. And I don't appreciate my husband letting it happen right in front of me, as if I don't exist. It makes me feel cheap and look like a fool."

They had reached the gravel road and April stopped walking. The farmhouse was ahead of them, at the top of a slight rise. Now that they were talking about the party—now that Marshall had forced her into speaking—she wanted to get everything off her mind, and say it quickly, while they were away from the house. She didn't want to fight in front of the children.

"You're mad because we went skinny-dipping. What's a country house for if you can't let loose, have some fun?" Marshall did not look at his wife.

"Ann O'Malley did a little striptease for you, and you just lapped it up."

"For Chrissake, I can't believe it. You're a prude, April!" Now he was angry. "I didn't do anything! I didn't fuck the woman on the lawn. Everyone went swimming, that's all."

"Not everyone!"

"You and a few of the other old farts didn't go, but everyone else did."

April didn't answer her husband, but she didn't walk away either. Timmy had come out onto the back deck and was calling for her. She spoke quickly before he ran to her.

"I want you to talk to Luke."

"What about now?"

"He's frightening the children with his stories."

April was watching her son. He had climbed up on the railing and was teetering there at the edge of the deck.

"April, hey, all kids like to be frightened."

April could not answer. Her heart was caught in her mouth. Greta had followed Timmy onto the porch, and stepped up behind him.

"Greta!" April shouted.

"Jesus! What's the matter?" He looked from his wife to the porch, saw his daughter reach and steady Timmy on the deck railing, then help the child off the ledge. "Greta isn't going to hurt Timmy," Marshall whispered. "Pull yourself together, kiddo."

"I don't know that Greta isn't going to hurt Timmy," April answered back. She walked off then, up the road toward the house.

"That's a terrible thing to say, just because you're mad at me."

"She has been edgy and hostile to me all week."

"And?" He followed after April.

"She's carrying around a lot of hostility."

"Come on, don't give me that psychobabble."

April stopped talking. She didn't know how far she could

press Marshall about Greta; she knew that she would be upset if he tried to tell her how to raise Timmy.

"Why do you say that?" he finally asked, calming.

"It's a difficult period for her, the divorce, becoming a woman. She could use someone to talk to, that's all."

"She can talk to me."

"No, she can't. You're her father. And she won't talk to me. I've tried. She sees me as the wicked stepmother."

"She has her mother."

"Her mother is in California."

Marshall stopped walking and sighed. "Christ."

"I don't think there is anything wrong, but it would help if Greta could talk to a child psychologist. I know a wonderful one on the West Side she might see this summer. Let me give her a call."

Marshall nodded. He was watching his daughter. Both of the children had left the deck and were down on the lawn, chasing after each other.

"Why don't you and the kids come down with me this afternoon. You can see about the shrink."

April nodded, but didn't look at him. She watched Greta, who was now chasing after Timmy, tickling him as he tried to race ahead of her. He was screeching with delight.

Greta seemed perfectly warm and wonderful now, April thought. Perhaps having her father around improved her mood. April felt a tug of sympathy, thinking how difficult the divorce must be for her, having to shuttle back and forth between the parents on all holidays and vacations. April was thankful again that she hadn't caused the separation, that she hadn't been the other woman.

Instead, she had taken Marshall away from the woman who had been the culprit in his divorce. But it didn't matter. It didn't matter whether anyone was married or not. She had stolen Marshall away from another woman, and somehow, in the bottom of her heart, April held a secret fear that someday she'd have to pay for it.

"Okay," she told him. "It is a good idea. I need to have some additional computer work done by my student. But before we leave this afternoon I want you to speak to Luke about the folktales. Okay?"

"Okay."

"And I want another promise from you," April said, looking up at him directly to make sure he understood.

"What?" He kept smiling.

"I don't want you sleeping with Ann O'Malley."

"Hey, kiddo!" He sounded offended.

"I'm serious, Marshall. If you have an affair with her, I'll leave you." And then she did leave him, to go down onto the lawn and greet their approaching children.

Twenty-one

April was purposely early for lunch with Marshall. She had spent the first few hours of Monday morning getting herself and the children organized. She got Sara to come in and care for Timmy, and she set up Greta's appointment with the child psychologist. Then she telephoned James Galvin and arranged to meet him later that day at Columbia. She needed him to enter the information from Anita Rotherham's birth ledger into her data base.

By eleven she was out of the loft, free and on her own. She felt like a kid again, with no responsibilities and nothing pressing to do. She was amused at herself for feeling wonderful about being on the city streets, in the midst of downtown traffic.

She dropped off clothes at the cleaners, then picked up the film that Marshall had left the week before. There were photos she had taken on the first weekend in the country. It was only three weeks ago, but it seemed like a lifetime.

She turned up early at the Museum Cafe, across from the Victorian turrets of the Museum of Natural History, so she could get a front table and have a drink by herself before Marshall arrived. She was feeling guilty about their squab-

ble, and she wanted this lunch alone with him to patch
things up.

All day Sunday, and on the ride down to the city, he had
been distant with her. She knew his ways and how he
behaved when he felt offended. Now she would have to do
some coaxing and flirting to get back on his good side.

She ordered a glass of white wine and looked out onto
Columbus Avenue. This had been their restaurant—Tom's
and hers. They had met there in 1980 when she was
finishing her Ph.D. and he had just arrived from Idaho. It
had been one of the last warm fall afternoons and she had
been sitting with Mark Simon, her college boyfriend. Mark
had been reading aloud a poem in the new collection of
Auden's poetry, and she looked up and saw Tom crossing
Columbus Avenue, striding toward her. He had a bookbag
slung over his shoulder, was wearing khaki shorts, hiking
boots and a widebrimmed safari hat. Her strongest recollec-
tion was of his thick dark beard, and his beautiful long legs.
When he reached the sidewalk and came into focus, she
realized that he had been watching her as he crossed the
intersection.

He did not even break stride, but smiled and winked at
her as he passed. It was as if he had just returned from the
far reaches of the world for that chance meeting on the West
Side. Her heart dropped away as he strode off, but they
would meet by chance the next day in the Museum and be
married before the end of the year.

April realized she was crying and quickly wiped the tears
off her cheeks and checked her reflection in the front
windows. She hadn't thought that being back here would
upset her so much, and she didn't want to explain why to
Marshall. Then, to distract herself, she glanced through the
photos she had taken upstate.

There were a half dozen snapshots of them on the
mountaintop, others taken of the property from the back
deck of the farmhouse, and a few more from a morning
when she and Timmy had gone for a hike in the valley, past
where the trees had been cut and stacked for firewood and
down to the tiny pond of water Luke called Secret Lake.

She pulled the photos of Secret Lake from the other

snapshots and looked at them a second time, trying to find a spot where she might string a hammock between two shade trees, and then she noticed some strange shapes. For an instant she thought she was mistaken and tilted the print to catch more of the light from the window. In the bright sunlight it was even more obvious—there were odd shapes in the underbrush. She shuffled the photos, glanced quickly at the other photos, all shots of Timmy standing at the water's edge, smiling at her, waving. April didn't look at her son, but beyond him, across the small pond, where in the thick brush it appeared a weaselly figure was crouched and hiding.

"Hi, kiddo." Marshall appeared beside her, paused to kiss the top of her head, and then slipped into the chair across the small table. As she sat down, he glanced around the restaurant, took in the room. It was his habit, April knew. His way of checking that no one he knew was sitting close to him.

"Look!" April demanded, "What do you see?" She handed him the pond photos one at a time, talking quickly as she did. "Do you see anything in the bushes, the trees?"

Marshall placed the photos on the tabletop as he settled into the chair and loosened his tie.

"Nope," he said picking up a glass of water and looking off, out the window and across Columbus as he announced, "I'm going to L.A. tonight."

"L.A.? Marshall!" Her empty stomach turned.

"I have to file a brief in the appeals court on this RamDisk case. I need to talk to the firm out there, get their thinking." He took a pad and a silver pen from his breast pocket and began to scribble down names.

"Can't you telephone these people? You promised Greta that you'd take her to see *Cats*."

"She'll rain check me."

"What about me?"

"You've got the car. Drive up tomorrow, or wait until Wednesday. I'll be back by Friday."

"Greta will be terribly disappointed."

"I'll make it up to her," he answered, as if that was enough of a solution. The waitress appeared with the drinks, and Marshall asked, "What's good today?" He was smiling, making this waitress think for that moment that she was the only person in his life.

"I'm afraid to be there all alone," April told him once their orders had been taken.

"You're not alone. The kids are with you. And you have some new friends."

"Marshall, you know what I mean! I'm all alone at the end of Mad River Valley. You've seen how dark that place is at night. And those people are hardly my friends."

"I'll telephone Luke and make sure he stays close to the property."

"I don't want Luke Grange taking care of me."

"Did you get Greta to see that shrink?" Marshall asked, deliberately changing the subject.

April nodded, suddenly feeling very tired. She hadn't meant for this to happen, this arguing, getting upset. She had wanted them to have a lovely lunch together, alone, and free of the children.

"I'll give Greta's mother a call when I'm on the coast," he added off-handedly, his mouth full of bread.

April waited for him to continue, to say what he had on his mind.

"I've been thinking. Perhaps it would be better if Greta went back to California. As you say, I'm in and out of New York. And you're up there all alone. Besides, you have your hands full with Timmy."

"What are you going to do, tell Cindy I can't handle two children?"

Marshall sat back in the chair and stared at his wife, surprised by her objection. "I'm just trying to help you."

The waitress returned with their plates of food and April waited until the woman walked away before she replied, speaking softly, but with anger building in her voice.

"I've agreed to having Greta with us this summer. I'll stick by my bargain. I'm sure Cindy has vacation plans of her own." April glanced over at Marshall, and when he ducked his head and began to concentrate on his food, she realized what he was doing. "Marshall, you can't do that to Greta. Use your child to get at your ex-wife."

"What are you talking about?" He frowned at April as if confused by her remark.

He always assumed a look of innocence, she had begun to realize, when he was guilty. His pale blue eyes would widen; he'd look surprised and shocked, and then gradually appear hurt, as if she had failed him in some way by misunderstanding and doubting him.

"You know what I mean." April dug into her food, trying not to let herself get drawn into his chain of denials.

"I'm doing this for you, sweetheart," he whispered, and reaching over, covered her wrist with his hand.

"Marshall, please." She tried to pull free and he held her hand.

"You've misunderstood."

"No, I haven't." Now she stared at her husband, let him see how angry she was, and how well she understood his game. "Don't treat me like a hostile witness, someone you have to coax and connive. I'm your wife, Marshall. Greta is your child. We're not to be used like part of a deal, as negotiable pawns in your relationship with Cindy. It isn't fair to Greta. It isn't fair to me. You'll ruin it for everyone."

"Okay, okay." He picked up his knife and fork.

"I'm sorry," she said, feeling guilty and backing off.

"It's not your fault. To be honest, I don't think I was consciously doing that, you know, sending Greta to L.A. just to throw a wrench into Cindy's plans."

April said nothing. She hated to fight with Marshall, and she was suddenly aware that they had lately been getting on each other's nerves.

"It is okay then that Greta stays with us?" He asked innocently, cutting into the filet of sole.

For a moment she realized that once she agreed, she could never complain about Greta, even if Marshall disappeared for half the summer. But she wouldn't be a partner to Marshall's scheming, nor did she want Cindy to think she couldn't handle the child.

"Yes, we'll manage." April looked at her food and realized that she had lost her appetite.

"I'll try and cut this trip down to a couple of days," Marshall said, speaking quickly. "If I get the Red Eye, I could be up by Thursday, midday.'' He forked the sole, saying, ''This fish is very fresh. How do you know about this place? From your museum days?'' He glanced over at April. ''Aren't you hungry?''

She shook her head, said quietly, ''Don't kill yourself rushing back from California. I can survive a week without you.''

''Look, once I draft the brief, the L.A. office can handle the Monday morning filing. And I promise you, April, I'll get out of the city and take some time off. How about a trip? Do you want to fly over to London for a long weekend? See some plays?'' He reached out and patted her hands. He was smiling, being nice.

April shook her head.

''Okay, then, we'll just hang around the farmhouse. I kinda want to get into the country house anyway. You know, get to know the crazy locals. Oh, that reminds me. I want to show you the new buck knife I just bought. It's a beauty! A piece of art.''

April did not respond. She knew he would not be done with the RamDisk case for weeks. It was not his fault. Wall Street was not the academic world where classes ran on schedule and the calendars were planned a year in advance.

But at the moment, April was not bothered by what her husband did for a living. What upset her was the fear that Marshall had not been totally honest, that he had manipulated the conversation so she was committed again into taking care of his daughter for the whole summer vacation.

He was using her, April thought. Using her to help cover his responsibilities as a father. Of course Greta couldn't go home to Los Angeles. Her mother was going to Europe. Was probably there already. Greta had told them both.

April wondered if she really did know her husband.

''Are you okay, kiddo?'' Marshall asked, reaching for the bread.

''Marshall, please do me a favor,'' April asked, not looking up.

''Name it.'' He grinned, feeling good, now that his plans for the next few weeks were set.

''Stop calling me kiddo.''

Twenty-two

April spent Wednesday morning upstate on the telephone, calling Columbia University, making final arrangements for her fall leave, and then talking to James Galvin. He had finished the research, he told her, and the information would be on the university's computer by the end of the next week.

"And if you want," he went on, "I could search through the county records for you."

"Well, thank you, Jim."

"I actually tried to find Mad River Mountain on the map, and couldn't," he went on. "You'll have to give me directions."

April smiled to herself. The less outsiders knew about the area, the better it was for her. She needed time to finish her work. At the back of her mind there was always the fear that some other anthropologist might discover the Hill People in a dated journal and come up to investigate. Finding a new, unstudied society was a rarity, a tremendous gift to one's career.

"Call me when you have the information all in the computer," April said. "And I'll be in touch with you by phone."

When her morning telephone chores were done, she went out to the kitchen and made coffee, then stepped out onto the deck to check on the children.

Greta she saw at once. The teenager was floating in the pond, stretched out on an old innertube. She was wearing her Walkman and reading a magazine as she sunbathed in her bikini. Timmy was further away, on the farm tractor with Luke, riding between the man's legs as Luke mowed the back lawn. When Timmy saw her, he waved, grinning with pleasure.

April turned reluctantly from the peaceful scene and went back into the farmhouse. It was cooler inside. She had kept the shades down to block out the hot summer sun, and opened the cellar door, so that the air trapped in the stone foundation rose up and cooled the first floor like five thousand BTUs.

It was a lovely place, she thought, noting again how beautifully her pine and cherry antiques fitted into the natural look of the rooms. She had used only throw rugs in the downstairs rooms to expose the polished barnboard floors, and painted the walls in traditional Colonial colors, keeping everything simple, with an almost Shaker feeling. Her one regret was that Marshall didn't appreciate how she had decorated the house. But she had come to know his ways. He was simply oblivious of his surroundings. He could live out of a suitcase, he told her, and never be bothered.

She was different; she needed to feel a place was her own, and in the first few weeks she had worked at getting the farmhouse in order. Now, she knew, she could do her work, surrounded with familiar things, possessions she loved.

She was still doing background reading on the area, pulling up files that mentioned Mad River Mountain. It was from the research that James Galvin had done that winter. She had decided she had to look at everything Jim had found during the winter before she began to approach the local people and start doing her own interviews.

Most of the journal articles and book references Galvin had found dealt with the Catskills before the turn of the century, and the references to Mad River Mountain were made just in passing. Still, she remembered, she had found the name Grange mentioned as far back as 1820. There was more here in these lost books that would help her, she knew, remembering what she always told her students: "Glance at the obscure, but study the obvious."

April hooked up her telephone modem and turned on her computer, then tapped in the access code of Columbia

University's library computer. She brought up the menu for her research and selected a document at random, then opened the file and brought up the description of the book.

Item 432.
AUTHOR   Ludlum, Annie
TITLE   Exploring The Kaatsberg, by
              W. T. Ludlum.
              With intro. and notes by
              Paul F. Barber.
              [4th ed.]
PUBLICATION   Syracuse, N.Y.: Syracuse
              University Press, 1923.
DESCRIPTION   xi, 164 p. illus. 24 cm.
SUBJECTS   1. Catskill Mountains—Social
              life and customs.
CALL NUMBER   IRM (Catskills) 74-823

April went directly to the book's index and scanned it quickly, looking for mention of Mad River Mountain. It was in the last chapter of the old book. She typed in the page number. And the first page of the chapter flashed onto the green screen.

A MOUNTAIN FUNERAL

One of the lovely and simple-hearted customs of these mountain families, which still holds fast in this remote place, is the strewing of flowers before a funeral, and gracing the grave of a lost one. This custom, it is said, is from the primitive period of civilization, but it is also from the higher antiquity, for the Greeks and Romans, it is written, followed a similar rite. It comes then, we can surely say, from the age before song and the written verse. And, today, in this glen of tranquility, the rite remains true, connecting this small corner of an obscure world with the ancients themselves! And how lovely a sight it is, the strewing of flowers before the departed.

I came upon such a rural funeral here in the
backwoods of New York, on a ridge of Mad River
Mountain. Being a stranger, I stepped aside as the
mourning train approached, with uncovered heads,
and let the small group go by on the mountain
pass.

The small corpse was of a child, or perhaps a
young virgin. To my mind came a few lines from
that poem, "Corydon's Doleful Knell," where
the lover laments his lost love, saying,

> I'll deck her tomb with flowers,
> The rarest ever seen;
> And with my tears as showers,
> I'll keep them fresh and green.

And then I saw the faces of these hill people,
the gothic heads and hunchbacked bodies of the
deformed. I had heard tales of such people, and
seen crude drawings of the odd ones, but there,
high in the glen, on the sparkling bright summer
afternoon, I was astounded to see the shapes and
shades of such gross deformation.

I stood in silent reverence of the dearly departed, but secretly happy that this unfortunate creature would find, in another life, joy and freedom
from her godless body. For surely God Almighty
would not punish this young soul!

I reflected then—watching the procession silently
march off up the path—of what my old gentleman
friend, Diedrich Knickerbocker, once remarked at
a Corporation meeting, that "the sorrow for the
dead is the only sorrow from which we refuse to
be divorced."

Yet I am "divorced" from the sorrow of this
poor wretch. Let God's deformity pass from this
earth, and let pass away also the incestuous parents who coupled and gave this creature its brief
existence.

May they all, I privately prayed, be plagued

> from this good earth, these rich hills of the
> Kaatsberg. I did not follow after to see if they
> "decked with flowers" the tombs of this abnor-
> mality.

April stopped reading, went back to the directory, and
switched files. She had had enough, for a while, of travel
journals and personal diaries. She pulled up a file on
unpublished manuscripts on folklife and incest taboos and
searched what had been written recently by research psychologists at the Socioenvironmental Studies Lab of the
National Institute of Mental Health in Bethesda, Maryland.

She typed "Hill People" in at the Global Search com-
mand and hit the enter key.

Only five page references appeared on the screen. That
was a good sign, she thought, taking a deep breath. It
meant, as she had suspected, that even at the National
Institute of Health in Bethesda very little work had been
done on Mad River Mountain.

She scanned the material until one paragraph caught her
eye. It was from a talk on folk theory and incest taboo.

> Careful research may suggest that a folk theory
> for intrafamilial stability not be rejected. I suggest
> that in cross-cultural research a folk explanation is
> often the correct answer. We tend to wish away
> such "simple" explanations, wanting the comfort
> of a more modern scientific response. Resist this
> urge! Notice the obscure. Study the obvious.

April smiled and glancing down the page, read the footnote
and saw with satisfaction that she had been correctly quoted.
It was from a talk that she had given at the Museum of
Natural History in November on "Consanguineous Inbreeding: Is There Room for You?" The talk was one of a series
at the Museum on new careers for young professionals.

It was at this lecture she had told a group of doctors that
no one fully understood incest, telling them, "Oedipus and
his mother came first. We still don't know why he slept with
his mother. Freud said it was guilt. His scenario, as I am

sure you know, is that any ruler might keep all the women to himself until the young males attacked and killed him. Then, overwhelmed by guilt, they gave away their women to other bands, and the idea of no sexual contact with the females of one's own group came about.

"The anthropologist Robin Fox believes that young men in any band avoid their females because the dominant male would kill them, fight them off. We see this largely in the wild. Look at the relationships of a pride of lions in Central Africa.

"And Levi-Strauss simply believes that early man made a rational decision to form alliances with other warring bands as a way of giving away their women, and taking the other females in return. You've heard of the old tribal saying, 'We marry our enemies.'

"Given all this, what are some other reasons for the banning of sexual intercourse and marriage among primitive peoples?"

April had waited for some young doctor in the lecture hall to venture an answer.

"Well," said a young woman, speaking slowly, developing her ideas as she answered, "First, the current evidence on incest shows that the taboo on such unions was developed to prevent disruptions within the nuclear family because of sexual competition. And, second, intrafamilial stability is necessary because very young children need protection in order to mature." She looked up at April on the stage, waited for confirmation.

"You're right on both counts. But there is a third reason for the incest taboo. The ethnotheory based on genetic evidence is that incestuous unions produce defective children. Even societies that lack an understanding of genetics will soon see that defective infants are born of women who have had sex with their fathers, brothers, or sons. It might lead to or create the belief that the gods were punishing that behavior. A belief in the supernatural would indicate that this defective offspring was some kind of punishment.

"Given all that, we still find isolated communities in India, the Middle East, Africa, and here in New York State where consanguinity is allowed."

The young psychologists had waited for her to continue her reply, but instead April walked to the blackboard and quickly wrote out:

Freud	1918
Malinowski	1927
Levi-Strauss	1949
Murdock	1949
Parsons	1954
Seemanova	1971

"All of these people have faced the problem of incest. All of them have come up with reasons why societies forbid kinship relationships.

"What happens in a society where there are high degrees of close consanguineous unions is that for a while simple mutations caused by recessive genes appear. But after one generation of congenital deafness, another of muscular dystrophy or albinism, increased stillbirths, higher sterility, congenital malformations, the gene pool becomes so limited that virtually only recessive genes are present."

She glanced out at the lecture hall full of young doctors.

"Each of us carries three bad recessive genes. You all know that from your medical classes. But what happens when, because of generations of incestuous marriages, you have twice that number. What happens to your genetic make up? Who are you? What are you?"

"You have a genetic defect."

"No," April replied softly, "you're worse. You're a mutation. You're a genetic time bomb waiting to go off."

April reached out to type in Global Search and suddenly the screen blinked off. Her hand froze in space.

"Shit!" she shouted, thinking she had lost the information on the disk. "Shit! Shit! Shit!" She stood up and banged the top of the machine, then flipped the reset button. Nothing happened. "Shit again!" she shouted in the silent, empty house. She had done nothing wrong. The disk had crashed because the lights were out, the electric power was gone.

April pushed away from the desk, rushed through the house, and stormed onto the back porch. Luke was still up on the tractor, mowing the grass around the pool. She shouted to him, but he couldn't hear her over the engine, so she ran down across the lawn, waving for his attention, motioning him to stop.

"The lights, Luke," April shouted up to him. "The damn power went and I've lost my disk."

Luke nodded, then shouted back, "It happens."

"It happens! What do you mean, 'It happens'?"

Luke reached down and throttled down the roaring engine. The sudden silence was disquieting. April moved closer to the big machine.

"Mommy, Luke let me drive!" Timmy grinned. He had both his small hands on the steering wheel.

"The power company cuts off the electricity some days, when they're doing repairs." Luke shrugged.

"And I've lost a disk full of research because of those idiots." She stamped her foot, then began to pace, still raging. Last week the pump had broken and they had spent most of the day without water while Luke repaired it. Damn country living, April thought, fuming.

"I'll see what I can do," Luke said, pulling himself up.

"What's happening?" Greta called from the middle of the pond.

April waved that everything was okay, then she turned to Luke, asking, "What can you do?"

"The disk might not have crashed. I'll see if I can save it." He stood brushing the grass off his pants legs.

"You know about computers?"

"Some." Luke grinned, seeing April's surprise. "I took a few classes in computer repair when I was up at SUNY Albany." He turned around and lifted Timmy off the tractor, saying, "Come on, Tim, I need your help."

"Okay! Okay! I'll help." The small boy beamed as Luke swung him to the ground.

April sighed, touched by Luke's gesture. She felt immediately relieved, knowing that Luke would fix the computer, just as last week he had fixed the broken pump.

"What can I do?" April asked. The three of them had started walking up toward the house.

"Nothing. Why don't you go for a swim. You haven't relaxed since you got up here. Aren't country houses for rest and recreation?"

"I'm beginning to think they're nothing but trouble."

"Go swim," he repeated.

"No, but I think I might go for a walk." She thought of the golden deer then, wondered if he were somewhere in the deep wood.

"Good! You own all this land, you should use it."

"I do use it," April replied. "I look at it." She waved at the valley, laughing.

They had reached the deck and Luke stopped. "You're not afraid of going for a walk in the valley, are you?"

"No, of course not."

"Good. There's nothing to worry about." He smiled, encouraging her.

"I know," April replied defensively. "I know." Now, she realized, she had to go, if only to show Luke that she wasn't afraid.

"I mean, no wildlife will hurt you."

"And no brother?"

Luke shook his head. "No brother. He's gone." Then from the deck, he too glanced at the deep valley, and added, "You have nothing to fear in Mad River Mountain."

April glanced over at Luke and saw he was watching her, still smiling, and she nodded, as if she did agree with him, and then wondered once again if she could really trust this man.

Twenty-three

In the shade of the trees, hidden in the woods, April relaxed. She was surprised that the cool woods calmed her. From a distance the valley overwhelmed her. The vastness, all the miles of treetops, the ridge of mountains behind the house, all seemed impregnable, too dense and hostile. Yet once she had stepped on a valley path, she was quickly swallowed up and hidden in the green trees, the hugeness of the forest, and the woods made her feel safe.

She kept walking, plunging forward, deeper and deeper, taking each branch of the path that turned further downward. It would be lovely, she thought wistfully, to be lost forever in the valley, to never have any responsibilities or worries. And then she thought of Timmy, little Timmy, grinning as he ran after Luke, eager to help out, to be included, and her heart melted with joy.

April stopped walking.

She had come to a clearing, where a tiny pool of water lay magically in front of her. She heard birds, the wonderful loud chatter of dozens of birds, all living together in their peaceable kingdom.

She held her breath and slowly looked. It was like a picture in one of Timmy's storybooks, full of magic and adventure. What a wonderful place this valley was. No wonder Luke would never leave it. No wonder he kept it all to himself. She smiled, pleased that she had discovered it on her own. She could take Timmy here and share the spot with him, and she was immediately sorry that she hadn't paid more attention to how she had found the hidden pool in the first place.

She stepped closer and slowly sat down, still half expecting the sight to vanish, but it was real, all real, a tiny jewel of a garden deep in the woods. Everything was in bloom in this deep moist spot. The raspberry bushes sported white blossoms, the elderberry had flat-topped white flowers. There were clusters of daisies, and brassy, golden, black-eyed Susans, and, on the still pond water, brilliant purple lilies.

April could smell the lush bouquet around her. This is why city people drive hundreds of miles into the hills, she thought. She began to reproach herself for taking it all for granted. If the summer had only started differently. If only Marshall had stayed with her as he had promised and not kept flying off to the coast.

She moved over to the pool's edge slowly, quietly, as if she were in a church, and sat down on a dry boulder above the water. She could see her reflection mirrored in the deep water. The heat of the day hit her then, and made her suddenly dizzy and weak. She shouldn't have run through the woods. She could feel the perspiration beneath her arms, at the base of her neck, between her thighs. Her whole body was damp with sweat.

She unbuttoned her blouse and felt a moment's relief as the air swept across her breasts, then leaned forward and let the coolness of the deep mountain pool chill her chest.

April glanced around. There was no sound beyond the constant buzz of bees in the thick clusters of wildflowers. She cocked her head and listened harder. She could hear a brook somewhere deeper in the woods. It was running swiftly over pebbles and bedrock. It was so silent in this hidden grove of the woods, so still, that she could hear far-off birds, and the rustle of small animals, crawling through dry dogwood leaves.

April stepped out of her Reeboks, stripped off her blouse, pulled down her jeans and white panties, and stood naked on the high, dry rock. She knelt then, felt the water. Its intense coldness surprised her.

And then, before she lost her courage, she dove. It was even colder beneath the surface, and deeper than she had guessed. She opened her eyes at the end of her dive, was surprised that she could see so clearly, then realized it was a quarry pool, and the bright sunlight filtered down and reflected off the bedrock. She flipped over and kicked up to the water's surface, shouted with pleasure as she burst into the sun. Her whole body felt wonderfully alive, chilled and tingling in the cold water. She rolled over, like a dolphin at play, then came up and floated on the surface, looking up through the high arbor of green leafy trees, smiled at her own pleasure, the silence of the woods, this peaceful moment.

April raised her head and looked down at her floating body, the twin islands of her breasts, with her nipples erect in the chilly water, the slight bubble of her stomach, and the dark patch of pubic hair, curly and dripping wet. She turned and dove deep into the crystal water, down to the sheer quarry wall, touched its hardness with the palm of her hands, and like an Olympic swimmer, kicked off, and sailed straight to the surface, popped into the sunlight in a spray of foam.

Then she saw the snake. The thick brown ribbon twisted past her, its tiny, triangular head above water level. April kicked off. The snake turned in the water. She lost it in the wake of her swimming stroke, then saw that it was coming at her, its cottony white mouth hissing open. She flipped over and frantically swam for shore, touched the muddy bank and scrambled out of the water.

From the corner of her eye, she spotted the man. He came out of the trees, and with his bare hand, he reached down into the water, seized the snake and tossed it onto the bank. Then, just as quickly, he came down on its head with the thick heel of his boot.

April dove again into the water, shielding her nakedness. "Who are you?" she demanded. "This is private property!"

"Ain't nothing but an ol' pygmy rattler," the man said, picking up the snake and throwing its twisting body into the underbrush. He turned, grinning, to April, saying, "You see this one, Nick boy?"

April spotted another small man in the foliage of the shoreline. He was squatting on the smooth dome of a boulder, a white-haired and fully bearded dwarf, dressed oddly in a black suit, with a white shirt and black tie.

Involuntarily, April curled her feet up in the water and lost her balance, tilting her small breasts into the warm air.

She shielded her body with her hands and glanced over at her clothes, tried to guess how fast she could be, leaving the water, scooping up her clothes, and running for home.

"Don't be so shy, lady. We've seen many a maiden in our day, haven't we, Nick?" He was squatting on the muddy bank now, staring at her. He was another dwarf and deformed in the way of the Hill People. He was worse than the other, April saw. His whole face was whacked out of shape. She couldn't take her eyes off him.

"Who are you?" April demanded, using the question as a way of keeping the men at bay.

"Who are we?" the wild-haired one retorted. "Now that's an odd question. Well, I'm a dwarf! You can see that well enough." He stood up, threw open his arms.

"Are you Tassels?" April glanced back and forth between them, still wary, keeping as much water as she could between herself and the small men.

"Indeed I'm not. They're scumbags, those Tassels," the man said, grinning.

"Please leave!" April shrieked, glancing around the pond, watching for the slithering wave of another snake.

"And leave such a pretty lass here in the pool? Now why don't you come here and Nick and I will have some fun."

He kept circling, moving, April realized, for her small pile of clothes. She was terrified of them now. They had not taken their eyes off her body. Both of them had small blue bullet-hole eyes, and kept her in sight, like telescopes. She was freezing, chilled to the bone.

"Please," she begged, "I'm freezing."

The white-haired dwarf jumped off the boulder, landing in the soft muddy bank.

"Where's that husband of yours?"

"He's coming to take a swim," April said quickly.

"We saw you up around your place by yourself," the second man said. All the fun was gone from his voice. He had crept closer on the muddy bank, and as she watched, he pulled off his thick shoes, saying, "But we'll come join you, lassie." He was grinning, and the smile sliced across the width of his pink face like a badly made jack-o'-lantern.

"No!" April shouted.

She was crying now, swearing at herself for letting this happen. "Please," she begged. As he continued to strip off his clothes, she saw that his small chest was matted with black hair, all curly and thick, like a baboon's.

"Come out then, lassie!" the old dwarf shouted, then hopped back onto the dome rock, "Let us have a look at your loveliness."

"No! No!" April shouted as she frantically paddled. Her legs were numb from the cold water. She had to get out, she realized, searching the shore again for her pile of clothes. She would grab her things, run up the path. They couldn't keep up with her, she thought, not these deformed creatures.

"Is it cold in that water?" The old man kept grinning as he reached down with the tiny fingers of both hands and pulled out his penis. "I'll warm up the water for you."

"Oh, dear God, no!"

"Don't piss in my pool, Nick!" the other man shouted, throwing down his shirt. "I'll get her! I'll get the little bitch. Wait! Wait!" He was dancing on the muddy bank, pulling at his jeans. "I want her! I want her first! It's my turn. My turn!" Naked, he was even more grotesque, with short rickety arms and legs, a skinny torso, and the heavy, pumpkin-shaped head.

She'd let him get into the water first, April thought, forcing herself to keep calm. She could outswim him, she knew, and the older one was on the opposite side, away from the path.

As the younger dwarf eased into the water, April kicked for shore. As her feet touched the muddy slope and she began to stumble up the bank, they started shouting, and the older one started toward her. She tried to run, but her legs, numbed by the water, gave way, and she fell forward into the shallows. Several frogs and toads hidden in the stiff cattails and pond-weed leapt past her, and splashed into the pond.

The naked, pumpkin-head dwarf was on April then, seizing her from behind as she tried to scramble forward. She swung at him, smashing his face with her forearm.

He slid down and seized her leg like an angry child. April bent over and banged the top of his head. She could feel her clenched fist dig into his flesh as if it were rotten fruit.

"Hold the bitch! Hold the bitch!" the old man shouted. He came around the pool, thrashing through the thick underbrush.

The dwarf jerked up April's leg and tumbled her over. She kicked out at him with her bare feet, swearing now herself, and trying to roll away. He had his pants down; she could see his hairy genitals. They would rape her, she realized; she couldn't fight the two of them. She kicked and caught the pumpkin-head in his flat face, knocking him back. He fell into the shallow water, cursing and yelling for the old man to hurry.

April felt another pair of hands on her shoulders, pulling her up. There were more of them, she realized, and still enraged, she wrestled herself free.

"Easy!" Luke said quickly, pulling her into his arms.

"Oh, Luke! Thank God." The strength went out of her, and she let her whole body go limp. Safe, she began to cry.

Luke carried her to the mossy patch at the edge of the path, then went and collected her clothes. She nodded her thanks when he came to her, too exhausted to talk or be embarrassed that she was naked.

The dwarfs were gone, fled into the woods when Luke appeared.

"Who were they?" she asked, when she found her voice.

"Holts. The white-haired one was Nick Holt. The other guy was a cousin, they call him Beer Mouth."

"God, they're disgusting." She stood to slip on her jeans. "I can't stand this any longer!" she said out loud, more to herself than to Luke. "This place is a nightmare."

"I'm sorry, I should have warned you."

"Warned me?" She paused in her dressing to look at him. "You told me I was safe here!"

"Yes, I know. I'm sorry. It won't happen again."

She sat down on the boulder and pulled on her Reeboks. She could still feel the slimy hands on her body, still smell his foul odor. They all smelled gamey, as if they never washed and slept with livestock. "Get me out of here, please," she said.

"This way," Luke said softly. He pointed off into a patch of white birch, and she saw there was a thin deer path there through the lovely trees.

April nodded and followed. After several minutes of uphill walking they emerged onto the sunny green lawn of

April's property. The pure, pale blue summer sky of the Catskills framed the scene as if it were a Norman Rockwell painting: the swimming hole, the old white farmhouse, and her little Timmy sitting on the back deck, grinning at her, his face and hands blue from berry juice.

April waved to Timmy, immensely relieved that she was free of the woods.

"Thank you," she finally said to Luke, "for saving me. How did you know where I was?"

"We were out picking blueberries and I heard your screams."

"I screamed?"

Luke nodded.

"And you could tell where I was out there?"

He nodded again. "I've lived in these woods all my life, April. I can find you anywhere you go." And then he led her across the green lawn to the farmhouse.

Twenty-four

It was a mountain night without moon or stars. But the farmhouse was well lit. He could see that the woman had all the first floor lights turned on, and had not drawn the blinds. He saw her move from room to room, busy with dinner, setting the dining room table. She had changed from the jeans she had been wearing. Now she wore a yellow skirt and a white shirt. It was a man's shirt, he saw, and she had unbuttoned the top half. She was wearing lengths of pearls. She had washed her hair, too, and left it loose. The hair was longer than he had thought, and now that it was wet, and had been shampooed, it glistened in the light. She finished setting the table and turned away from the windows, went back through the pantry and into the kitchen. He could no longer see her.

He circled the farmhouse. He was far enough away so that he couldn't be seen from the windows, but he moved carefully, slowly, his footsteps rustling the dead leaves at the edge of the woods. He liked it better after a rain; he could move soundlessly then, in wet leaves and soil.

The second-floor hallway light was on, as well as the light in the upstairs bedroom. There were curtains there, but they weren't drawn. The girl had taken a bath, and now she stood in her room at the mirror naked, drying and combing her hair. When she lifted her arms to comb out her blond hair, her small breasts disappeared. He swallowed hard.

There at the edge of the woods, he could hear her radio. She was playing music loudly, and it had frightened away the small animals that lived close by the house. There were usually deer grazing on the mowed lawn. But not tonight. He was the only one out after dark. He saw the boy in his bedroom. He was in pajamas sitting up in bed and had a large book propped against his knees. He could not see the boy's face, but he smiled anyway, pleased by what he saw.

He looked away from the boy then to again watch the naked young girl. But she had finished with her hair, and now slipped on a bright yellow nightgown. That disappointed him. She turned from the mirror and flipped off the light, disappearing from sight.

He gave up on the children and concentrated on the woman. She was standing at the sink in the brightly lit kitchen, and he moved closer to the house so that when she looked up from washing vegetables she stared, without knowing it, directly at him. Outside on the lawn Luke smiled into the dark night.

April shut off the faucets and placed the lettuce leaves in the colander, then she turned away from the sink and put some of the children's lunch dishes in the dishwasher. There were few things that pleased her more than having a clean kitchen. And now living with both children, it seemed she was continually cleaning up after them. Timmy she didn't mind. He was really just a baby. Greta, however, knew better. She wasn't a child any longer.

The doorbell startled April. She had never heard it be-

fore, hadn't even known it worked. April wiped her hands
on her apron, then pulled it off as she walked through the
pantry. Going through the dining room, she glanced at
herself in the mirror, paused to fix her head, reset the silver
clip which pulled her hair back and away from her face. She
had not put it up, knowing that wearing it loose made her
look younger.

As she walked by the stairway, Greta called down, "Who's
that?"

"My dinner guest."

"I'm coming down to say hello." Greta announced.

April paused at the bottom of the stairs, thinking how she
might phrase her answer, then stepped into the well of the
staircase. Greta was at the top of the stairs. She was
wearing just a short nightie, no panties or bra. April could
see through the thin yellow fabric.

"All right," she said. "You can come down to say hello,
but not like that. Put some clothes on. I don't want you
parading around half naked."

"He's seen me in less," she added smugly.

"Greta, you're being outrageous! Put on clothes if you're
coming downstairs."

"Oh, April, you're such a prude! Where were you in the
sixties? A convent? My mother, thank God, isn't hung up
like you." She turned away from the top of the stairs as if to
dismiss April's objections.

I don't even want to know what your mother lets you do,
April thought, crossing the room to answer the front door.
Marshall had already told her enough about Cindy's kinky
sexual games, her strange kicks. They grew up fast in L.A.,
she reminded herself, but she wasn't letting this girl be
compromised while she was in charge. Then she opened the
door and said cheerily to Luke Grange, as if everything was
perfectly all right, and he was always welcome into her
home, "Why, don't you look handsome this evening!"

And he did. Secretly, she was surprised by how good he
did look. He was wearing jeans, a blue shirt open at the
neck, and a soft green suede jacket. He had also washed his
hair and pulled it back into a tight ponytail, tied up with a
bright beaded Indian belt.

"It's getting cold," he said, following her inside. "I'll set a fire, if you'd like."

"Thank you. That would be nice. I feel a little foolish having a fire this late in June, but I am cold. Would you like a drink?" She paused at the entrance to the pantry and glanced back.

He was standing between the dining room and the front room, standing with his legs slightly apart. She saw now he was wearing Top-Siders and no socks, and she smiled.

"What?" he asked, grinning back, but unsure of what pleased her.

April shook her head.

"Hey? Are you laughing at me?" He started to laugh, growing embarrassed. He did seem softer, shyer, when he was in the house, off his turf. She'd have to remember that, dealing with him.

"I'm not. I'm sorry. I'm amused by myself really, not you."

"Don't I get some explanation?" He came closer, the smile softened into a slight pout.

"It's just that every time I think I have you categorized, you know, as this sort of a person or that, well, then you surprise me," she explained. "Look at you tonight! You could be a photo spread in *GQ*."

He nodded, then asked, "What's *GQ*?"

April laughed, shook her head, and turning toward the kitchen, said, "Never mind. Make the fire."

The phone rang as April reached the kitchen. From upstairs she heard Greta shout, "It's Daddy! I'll get it." April could hear her pounding down the stairs.

It would be Marshall, April realized, glancing at the clock. It was six o'clock in L.A. Perhaps he was already on his way to the airport. That made her feel better, thinking he'd soon be back with her. She'd never understood the need for these endless business trips. Why didn't they just do their work on the telephone, instead of wasting all their time and money flying back and forth across the country just to have lunch, to be seen. It was all silly. Adults playing office, she thought. And lawyers were taken so seriously, when what she did for a living, teaching, was so little appreciated by others. "It's because you deal with children," Marshall said once, when she complained about how little college professors were paid.

Reaching up to the top cupboard, where she had stored her large bowls, April stopped. It had been a week since she had opened that cupboard and maybe rats, or worse, had come to nest there. She could get Luke, she thought, tell him the shelf was too high for her. She wouldn't have to admit she was afraid to open the door.

No, she told herself, she couldn't do that. She couldn't be so dependent on others, men especially. She had been that way with Tom, so totally involved with him that when he was killed, she, too, had been shattered. It was only because of Timmy that she was able to put herself back together, and she had promised herself then, in the depth of her depression, that she would not ever again become so dependent on another person. She'd carve out a corner of the world that was hers alone, and always keep part of her heart just for herself and Timmy.

April reached up and opened the cupboard, took out the large clay bowl. Nothing slithered out or fell into her face.

She arranged the salad in the bowl and carried it into the dining room. She could hear Greta in the small office off the living room, chatting away to her father, asking him if he had picked up clothes and books she had requested. Then her voice rose shrilly. "Daddy! You said you'd talk to her about the Hawaii trip!"

April glanced over at her stepdaughter. Greta was standing in the doorway to the office, wearing the same thin shift she'd had on before. And the light was behind her. It highlighted her slight body, her small breasts, the dark web of her sex. She kept talking, being demanding and dramatic on the telephone while she turned about, paced in the bright open doorway, giving Luke every opportunity to watch her.

April was momentarily dizzy with rage. She seized the back of a dining room chair and squeezed it, checking her anger. Greta was telling her father, "Yes, she's here. Yes! Yes! And Luke, too. She invited him for dinner, but Timmy and I can't come. She said she wants a 'quiet dinner.'"

"Greta, I want to talk to your father," April said quietly,

walking over to her. Out of the corner of her eye, she saw Luke. He was still crouched before the fireplace, still fussing with the kindling, but she knew he wasn't as absorbed as he pretended. April was angry at him, too.

"Yes, Daddy, I love you. But I won't love you if you don't get Cindy's okay for Hawaii."

April took the phone out of Greta's hands and, covering the mouthpiece, said coolly to the teenager, "Go up to your room!"

Greta stared back. For a moment she met April's gaze without moving, testing her. April did not look away, nor did she speak. She let the girl know how angry she was just by her voice, the look on her face. The child did not know what she was doing. No, April thought again, Greta knew exactly what she was doing. What she didn't understand was how dangerous it might be for her.

April raised the phone and said sweetly to her husband, "How are you, darling? How did the trip go?" She went into the office, closing the door slowly and firmly behind her.

"I've run into a fucking buzzsaw here, sweetheart," Marshall was saying.

April could hear conversations in the background and the clinking of glassware. She hated it when he phoned her from a public place, the Polo Lounge, or wherever it was that lawyers gathered to drink and make deals.

"I can't get back by the end of the week. We have to have a meeting with these people here on Saturday."

"When are you coming home?" she asked, knowing as soon as she asked him what he would say.

"Maybe Monday. I can't promise you." He didn't sound sorry.

"Fine," April answered. She would not argue with Marshall over the telephone, and not with Luke in the next room.

"So, how you getting on? Greta said you went swimming with Luke today."

"Not exactly."

"And you invited him over for dinner?" He was merely curious, not upset.

"Yes." April had stepped over to the window. All she

could see was her face reflected in the glass, and she saw that she was crying.

"That's good. I'm glad you two are getting on better," Marshall commented, then he called for a waitress, ordering a dry martini with a twist.

"I'd better let you go," April said. "I can see you're busy." If she stayed on the telephone much longer April knew she would start fighting no matter who was in the house with her.

"I'll call you tomorrow night, sweetheart. And I promise, as soon as I can get this appeal back on track, I'll be home. I'm sorry about all this, April. I owe you. Maybe in the fall we can get away for a few days."

"I teach in the fall, Marshall. I can't fly off somewhere, once the semester begins."

"I thought you were taking a sabbatical."

"I changed my mind."

"That's news. When was that decided?"

"About five seconds ago."

Marshall fell silent.

"Can we talk about this when I get back home?"

"Yes, we can talk."

"Honey, I've got to go," Marshall responded abruptly. "Oakland just walked into the lounge."

"Fine."

"Give my love to Timmy. Tell him I got him a present from L.A. You know, one of those dogs. I spotted it at the airport."

"Surprise him."

"Honey?"

"Yes?"

"I love you."

April paused before replying, then said swiftly, "Have a safe trip home," and hung up the receiver.

April stood perfectly still as she tested her reactions. She was surprised she was not trembling, nor near tears. Yet all she felt was cold. She wondered if it was just the house cooling down at night, or in some mysterious way, had her anger toward her husband chilled her to the bone?

She started to turn away from the window and something

outside caught her attention. Realizing she was spotlighted, she reached over and flipped off the lamp, stood still in the dark room.

Greta was in the living room. April heard her flirting, going on about all the television stars she knew in Beverly Hills. Then April was distracted again by movement on the lawn. She leaned closer to the window, felt the night's coldness on the glass. She waited a moment, staring into the darkness, waiting for her eyes to adjust to the blackness. There was nothing. The lawn was bare. Not even the deer had come up to graze on the new grass.

In the living room, Greta was giggling. A high, silly, uncontrollable adolescent screech. It sent a shiver the length of April's spine.

April pulled open the office door and went back inside. Luke was sitting in the blue wing chair close to the fire; Greta was standing in front of the hearth, as if to warm herself in the flame, presenting herself to the caretaker as if she were a porn queen.

"Greta! Go to bed!" April interrupted the child's hysterics.

"I don't want to!"

"I don't care what you want." April kept walking through the room, heading for the kitchen. She had not opened the wine and now she very much wanted something to drink.

"You treat me like a child!"

"You are a child." This was all wrong, April knew. This was not the way to handle her stepdaughter, but she couldn't stop herself.

"I'm talking to Luke."

"You're going to bed!" April stopped at the entrance to the pantry. "And you're not being clever or cute parading around with no clothes on."

"I am not . . ."

April didn't wait for Greta to speak. She went into the kitchen, took the chilled white wine out of the refrigerator and quickly, noisily, opened the bottle, filled half a wine glass and still standing at the butcher-block counter with her back to the doorway, took a long swallow.

"I sent her off to bed," Luke said softly.

April nodded.

"You're being a little rough on her," Luke said, still speaking gently. He had stepped into the kitchen and moved over to April.

"Please, let me handle my stepdaughter in my own way."

"You're not handling her; she's handling you." Now he was standing close.

"I won't have her acting this way. The child isn't sixteen and she has no shame!" April stopped speaking before she burst into tears. This was all Marshall's fault, leaving her alone to run everything, including his wild teenage daughter.

"I don't want Greta."

April could feel his warm breath on her neck. She had to move, she realized, walk across the kitchen and put space between them.

Luke touched her. His hand slowly crossed her back and began to gently massage her tense shoulders.

"Don't," she said.

"Yes."

She was tired. So tired from the long day, so tired of dealing with Greta, taking care of Timmy, and now Marshall, telephoning to say he wasn't coming home. She felt used and abandoned. Luke kept softly massaging her back muscles, then he moved his fingers up her neck. His hands were strong. Stronger than Marshall's. Stronger even than Tom's. She could feel his body. She could smell the man. She wanted to turn from the counter and fall into his arms, disappear from sight and everyone's demands on her. What Luke wanted of her was nothing. She could give it as a present for all his kindness, for being with her in the middle of nowhere, for not flying off and leaving her alone.

She leaned against him, slipped into the cradle of his arms. Holding her easily against the strength of his body, he raised his hands and began to massage her forehead with the tips of his fingers. She kept her eyes closed, moaned softly with pleasure. She was so tired. In his arms, leaning against his strong chest, she felt safe. So safe. Wasn't it strange, she thought, knowing what would happen, what she wanted now to happen, that here at this moment she was where she wanted to be.

Her heart was pounding in her chest. If he touched her

breast, her heart would tear through her shirt. She had not worn a bra, and now she knew why. It was funny, she thought next, how the heart conceals secrets from the mind. She knew what she wanted from him. Why she had badgered and argued so with him. She knew it now, had known it from the very first moments when she saw him standing in the misty morning, looking wild and dangerous, as he held up the roaring chainsaw. Now she realized she had wanted him, and nothing else mattered in her life.

She wanted the moment to last forever, to have him softly stroking her body, taking this simple pleasure from what he was doing to her. She also wanted him to take her. She wanted him not to be considerate or kind. She wanted to fight with him, struggle, and beat back with her fists his first advances. She wanted him to be a wild man, to rape her on the barnwood floor.

He touched both her breasts with the hardness of his palms and her knees buckled.

"Please," she asked, not knowing what she meant.

"I can't stop," he answered.

Giving themselves up to their passions freed them both, made everything that followed seem wonderfully natural and right.

She turned and embraced him, burrowing her face into the folds of his cotton shirt. She could smell his sweat as he lifted her into his arms. Her eyes were closed, her arms draped loosely around his neck. Again, his strength surprised her. She had never been with a man this strong, whose body was so rippled with muscles.

He carried her through the rooms. She felt the draft of the dining room, the heat of the fire, then it was cool again in the bedroom. When he softly lay her on the quilted double bed, she came back to her senses, opened her eyes, and shook her head, begging him to listen.

"Luke, we can't," she told him, trying to sit up. She had children upstairs, awake in the house. She couldn't now sleep with this man in her husband's bed. And Greta might be poised at the top of the stairs, watching, listening.

He took her shoulders and pressed her back into the soft bed. She looked up at him, saw the rage in his eyes. A

moment before her fantasy of being taken by him had
seemed daring and wild. Now she realized she couldn't
make love to this strange man. It was dishonest; it was
beneath her.

"Stop!" she demanded, trying to resist as he unbuttoned
her blouse. Ignoring her struggles, he bent forward and took
her right breast into his mouth. Her heart swelled.

"Oh, dear God," she whispered, "please stop." She
tried to grab his arms, to keep him from slipping off her
skirt. His hand went under her panties and pulled them
down. He touched her and she moaned, kept struggling, but
now she could no longer fight. It was as if he had seized her
heart in his fingers, and pumped the life out of her.

He possessed her, she realized. She wanted him to pos-
sess her. Her mind blocked out any common sense and the
realization that Timmy and Greta might hear them.

All she heard was his breath. His face was pinned against
her cheek, his mouth to her ear. He was panting, snorting
like an animal. She caught his wave of excitement. And
then he was making love to her, the way Tom had made love
to her, as if nothing else mattered in the world but her body.

"The door," she finally managed to say. "Please."
When he stepped across the room to close the door, she
slipped under the quilts. It made her feel immediately safe,
snug in the warmth of the bed.

Her heart had stopped pounding. She lay still in the
darkened room and watched him. He stripped to his jeans
and pulled them off, and she realized he wasn't wearing
shorts. That excited her even more.

He came silently through the shadows and back to the
bed, moving with the quickness and smooth grace of an
animal. She could not take a step in the old house without
the floor squeaking, but his steps were soundless, and the
wide double bed did not move when he slipped under the
blankets and touched her flesh. She was shivering from her
fear and excitement, but when his hands, as warm as the
inside of kid gloves, felt her breasts, she warmed at once,
and came to him, tumbled onto his body, dove at him, while
she told herself:

I will make love to this man. I will kill this desire by

having it done with and over. Once I have made love to him, he will cease to be important.

"Hurry," she asked.

He did not hurry. It was her bed. Her adultery. He would make love his way, she realized, and she loved him for it.

She seized his shoulders and dug her nails into his smooth flesh. She wanted to hurt him, to claim him in some way by drawing blood.

Her fingernails scored his body. She felt the warm blood on her fingers.

Luke stretched away from her, moved his mouth along the flank of her body, nuzzled her, explored her crevices.

"Darling," she whispered, reaching for him, wanting him inside her. She dug her fingers into his blond hair, grabbed hold of him, and sitting up, tried to embrace her lover. She was dizzy with excitement.

They were both sitting up. She had straddled him, had wrapped her arms around his strong body. And gently, naturally, wonderfully, he had slipped inside her, claiming her. She arched her back, leaned away, so that his penis might rise and penetrate, giving him the chance, and her the pleasure, of having him lick the warm salt sweat off her breasts.

Then she came, surprisingly, unexpectedly, with a swiftness and urgency that amazed her. She seized him again, rolled her hips into his, began to seek her pleasure again and find the final edge of her desire.

He slipped his hands into her hair and buried his head in her neck as she came, wave after wave, cresting and falling away, cresting and falling away. She kept gasping for breath, crying with pleasure.

His eyes were open and he was smiling in the dark bedroom. He was pleased with her pleasure, knowing that now she was his, now and forever, and he raised his head. All he could see in the window glass was his own reflection, but he nodded to the others he knew were crouched in the darkness beyond the bedroom wall.

Twenty-five

Luke slept, his breath soft against her face. April smiled, closing her eyes. She would not sleep, she told herself. She wanted to enjoy this feeling of him in her arms. She kissed his cheek, kissed the lids of his eyes, tasted his salty skin. He didn't stir. She closed her eyes in the silent house, and against her will and common sense, she too slept, exhausted by her labor of love.

In her dream, in the deep dream of her exhaustion, she was once again with Tom, speeding through the rain to the heavy beat of the windshield wipers, peering out at the dense foggy night.

She heard a cry. She was crying, she thought, watching the foggy road and spotting the golden deer at the edge of the forest. Then she realized it wasn't her cry. She looked down at Timmy, bundled in her embrace, and opened her blouse to feed him. She pulled the blanket away from his face.

His lovely cheeks were blotched with red, bleeding sores, his lips and eyes distorted out of shape. He looked like a baby pig nursing at her breast. She screamed, screamed for Tom.

But Tom didn't answer her. She looked into the black night and saw the golden deer pinpointed by the high beams. Then April remembered it all. She screamed, but there was no sound.

She sat up abruptly in the dark room. Her husband's side of the bed was empty. Luke was gone. She reached over and felt for the warmth of the sheets, trying to verify that she had been with Luke, that he had made love to her there moments before. The sheets were cold.

Someone was crying.

148

Deep in the house she heard it, and it took her a moment to understand it was Timmy. He was crying in his bedroom, far from her.

She leapt from bed and rushed for him, reaching her bedroom door before she realized she was naked, feeling the draft between her thighs. She pulled her heavy nightgown off the door peg and kept running, through the dark living room and hallway upstairs, running for her son.

"Timmy? What is it?" She knelt beside his bed.

"I hurt," he whispered.

"Your tummy hurts, darling?" she said soothingly, fully awake now and wondering what might have upset him.

"I hurt. My skin hurts."

April turned on the small bedside lamp and saw red blotches on his face, arms, and neck.

"Dear God."

"It hurts, Mommy," he cried, pulling his hand free from April's tight grip. "It hurts all over me." There were tears on his puffy red cheeks.

"You'll be all right, sweetheart. You'll be all right. Mommy will take care of you."

April stood. She'd have to wake Greta, take her with them to the hospital. Where was the hospital? She had meant to find out when they first arrived, but Marshall had told her he'd check. She was seized with a rush of anger at her husband for not being there, and at her own helplessness.

"Timmy has been affected with a poison sumac," Luke said behind her. "It's from that swamp sumac." He stepped into the child's room. He was dressed and wearing his suede jacket.

"Here." Luke pulled back the blanket, reached down and picked up a small branch, hidden in the folds of the blankets. "Timmy, where did this come from?"

Timmy shook his head, began to wipe his eyes.

"Honey, don't!" She grabbed his wrist, afraid he would spread the poison into his eyes. "Where's the hospital, Luke?" she asked next, reaching for Timmy's clothes.

"That's not necessary," Luke answered. "I have a home-made ointment down in the cabin. He'll be okay."

"Luke, I don't want to take chances. If I don't treat this the right way, he could be disfigured."

"He can't be harmed by swamp sumac." Luke touched her shoulder. "We've always used our own ointment. I'll fetch the jar."

At the doorway he paused, glanced down the dark hallway before he said quietly, "That branch of sumac was put in the bed, April. I warned Greta and Timmy to watch out for it."

"Greta?"

"You might want to talk to her."

"That little brat!"

"Easy, April." Luke nodded to Timmy. "Maybe he brought it in himself."

April grabbed the top sheet and jerked it completely off the bed. There were other clusters of sumac at the bottom of the bed, out of sight, but where Timmy could touch them with his bare feet.

"That bitch!" April whispered.

"I'll talk to her if you want," Luke offered. "I don't think she knew how much harm she could do."

"She knew," April answered, and then said to Luke, taking charge, "Please go get the medicine. I'll speak to her."

"April, remember, she's a kid."

"I'll handle her, Luke."

"Wait 'til morning, okay?"

"Get the medicine," she told him, and started to strip the bed. She was angry at him now for defending the girl. She would wait until he left the house, then wake Greta. She wouldn't wait until morning. She didn't want her anger to cool.

April began to whisper to Timmy, trying to soothe him. Everything, she realized, all his clothes and the bedding, would have to be washed separately.

When she glanced back at the doorway, Luke was gone and Greta was in his place. She was wearing black panties and a baggy T-shirt with a picture of Prince on it.

"You!" April said. "See what you've done?"

"What?" Greta asked, yawning.

"You know what I mean. Stop smiling or I'll slap you."

"Go ahead. I'll tell Daddy you've abused me."

"You put that sumac in Timmy's bed."

"I did not!"

"Well, who did?"

"Ask Luke."

"What are you talking about?" She felt as if she was standing in sand.

"Why he was up here, creeping around."

"He was not!"

"April, I saw him," Greta insisted. She turned and ran angrily down the hall, slamming the door.

April stood very still. Perhaps by not moving she could stop this rush of events. She knew better than to bicker with Greta. She remembered her friend Susan warning her about young girls' attachments to their fathers, their possessiveness.

"Mommy?"

"Yes, darling?" April knelt beside him, but she could not bring herself to look at the blotchy red marks that covered his body.

"It hurts, Mommy." He began to cry again.

"Yes, I know, sweetheart," April whispered, slipping off his cotton pajamas. "Honey, did you see anyone in your room before?" she asked, trying to sound casual.

"Anyone?" He looked up, puzzled by her question.

"Yes. Did Greta come say good night to you?"

He shook his head.

"Did you see Luke? Did Luke come to see you?" She winced as she studied her little boy's limbs. Both his legs were welted with red marks. How could the rash have spread so quickly?

"Luke said good night to me."

"He did? When?"

Timmy shrugged. "It was dark."

Of course, Timmy wouldn't know when. Had it been early, before they had made love, or after she had fallen asleep and given Luke a chance to roam free in the dark house? Had he also gone upstairs to see Greta? Had he been locked away with her when Timmy began to scream?

The thought of Luke having made love to her, and then going upstairs to Greta's bed, made her shiver. She blocked that thought from her mind and studied Timmy for a moment, tried to think of how to dislodge an answer.

"Did Luke say good night to Greta, too?" April asked.

Downstairs, the deck door opened and closed. Luke had returned with the ointment.

"Luke came because of him," Timmy said, pointing to the other upstairs bedroom.

April spun around, looked toward the dark doorway. She could hear her heart pounding. "Who, honey?" she asked gently.

"He's there, Mommy."

"No one is there, honey. Remember how you used to think alligators slept in your dresser drawers?"

From deep in the dark room, April heard a chair move on the creaky barnboard floor. She should go over there, flip on the light. She was only scaring herself. But kneeling beside Timmy, she couldn't move.

The chair moved again and she heard scraping feet on the hardwood floor.

"Oh, God!" April seized Timmy.

"Mommy! Mommy!" Timmy cried, frightened by his mother's fear.

It was an animal, she kept telling herself; a woodchuck, perhaps, that had gotten caught in the house.

Taking a deep breath she stood up, crossed the hallway, reached into the darkened room, and flipped on the overhead light.

He cried out, frightened by the brightness. It wasn't a wild animal at all, but one of the inbreds, a small and grotesque man cowering in the far corner of the bare room. He had the same wrinkled face and small eyes as the two dwarfs who had attacked her in the woods.

"I'll get him," Luke said, stepping past her, talking softly to the deformed creature. His arms were open, his palms up, as if he was trying to show the small man that he meant him no harm.

April turned around and grabbed Timmy, lifting him protectively into her arms.

The dwarf backed away, skirting the wall. He was growling as Luke closed in.

"What's going on?" Greta demanded, reappearing at her bedroom door.

"Go back in there, Greta, and shut the door," April ordered.

Luke had dropped into a squat as he advanced on the little man, coaxing softly.

The dwarf sprang at Luke.

April screamed. Timmy screamed.

"What is it?" Greta yelled, running toward her stepmother.

The dwarf clipped Luke in the jaw, knocking him off his feet. April stumbled out of the way as he pushed by her, and he knocked Greta over as he went for the stairs. April heard his feet scurry on the bare floors as he fled into the night, leaving that foul, animal stench in his wake.

Twenty-six

"How did he get into the house?" April asked Luke after they had treated Timmy with the ointment and put him back to bed.

"I don't know. I heard him, that's all."

"Heard him?"

"Well, I didn't hear him. I smelled him."

April nodded. "I'll say." She had opened both windows in the small bedroom before coming downstairs, but she could still smell the dwarf's musky odor in the upstairs hallway.

"He must have come up through the cellar," Luke said. "But when I went upstairs, I couldn't find him. I guess he had crawled into that small space behind the chimney."

"What did he want?" April asked, watching Luke pace the room. His nervousness surprised her. She was usually the nervous one, he cool and detached.

"You wouldn't understand," he said'.

"Don't put me off like that! I'll have that man arrested and thrown into jail for trespassing." She heard her voice rise dramatically and she stopped talking. She didn't want to wake the children, not after the time it had taken to calm them down and get them both back to sleep.

"You're not going to do anything," Luke replied.

"Watch me."

"April, you don't understand what's happening here." He stopped pacing and came over to where she sat in an armchair, hugging her knees. He stood with his back to the fire, and talked to her as if she were a child, or a foreigner who needed help with the strange customs of this country.

"You don't want to upset these people. You don't want to get the police involved or draw attention to them. It will only cause trouble for you here on the mountain. Let it go."

"Luke, that creature—who was he anyway?"

"He's called Willy the Weeper because of the way his eyes droop. He always looks like he's crying."

"Well, this Willy breaks into my house, and seeds my child's bed with poison sumac. And you tell me to let it go." She grew more enraged as she thought of Timmy's puffy, blotched skin.

Luke raised his hand, motioned April to calm down. He knelt beside her chair, whispering now, as if what he had to tell her was secret and obscene.

"We don't know that he put the swamp sumac in Timmy's bed. Don't forget I pointed out the plant to Greta, told her the sap was poisonous and she had to keep Timmy away from it."

"But why?"

Luke shrugged. "Maybe she thought it was just a joke."

"Maybe she thought she could hurt him," April said, considering that possibility; but then, unconvinced, murmured, "No, Greta wouldn't hurt Timmy."

"Well, you know how kids play. They can be malicious without meaning to be. I'll talk to her," Luke offered.

"I'll talk to her!" He was so presumptuous. That's how some men were. Once they had slept with a woman they assumed proprietorship. "That still doesn't explain why your Willy the Weeper was in this house, hiding. What did he want?'' She stared back at Luke, angry again, and showing it.

''They used this place last year, the Tassels and Holts.''

''Used it?''

''Yes used it!'' Luke answered, as if unwilling to explain more.

''How?'' April asked, the confidence slipping from her voice.

''Well, I'm not sure.''

''Luke, you live here! You're the caretaker! What do you mean, you don't know?''

''They'd come and go, slip in through the cellar. Every once in a while when I came up to check on the place, I'd notice, you know, that there was someone in the house. I couldn't keep them out.''

''You mean, you wouldn't.'' For a moment, both of them were silent. April could imagine just what had gone on in the empty house. ''Christ,'' she said out loud. She did not want to begin thinking there was something dirty about the old farmhouse, something obscene and filthy.

''I cleaned the place before the realtors brought people around,'' Luke said, guessing her thoughts.

April nodded. When she and Marshall looked at the house over the winter, the rooms had been swept clean.

''All right,'' she said, wanting to put it all behind her. ''Tomorrow, please, Luke, I'd like new locks on whatever doors or windows they might have used to get in. I don't want to be surprised again.''

''I'll have a word with them.'' Luke paused, watching April closely.

''Yes,'' April said slowly, as an idea formed in her mind. ''I want to see these people, too. Is it possible?''

Luke studied April a moment his eyes narrowing. ''Why?'' he asked.

''I want to talk to them, let them see I'm a nice person. They don't have to feel hostile to me or the kids. I want to make peace with them.''

Slowly Luke nodded. ''When?''

''Tomorrow morning, first thing.'' April said quickly. ''I

think I can trust Greta to take care of Timmy for a few hours. We won't be gone much longer, will we?''

Luke shook his head and then leaned closer. His eyes had softened. She felt as if she were swimming in the warmth of his gaze.

''April?''

''Go home, Luke,'' she ordered.

''No.''

''Yes.'' She was in control now. He couldn't sweep her off her feet a second time. ''I know what I'm doing.'' She was smiling at him, enjoying the pleasure of him within reach, pleased by his sudden docility. It made her feel smug and secure.

''Will we make love again?'' he asked.

''I don't know.''

''Why not?''

''Don't press me, Luke. Okay?'' She moved to stand and he placed his hand on her arm, holding her in the chair.

''Are you afraid of me?'' he asked.

''No, why should I be?''

''Because of my being related to them.''

''I slept with you, didn't I?''

And then she kissed him good night.

BOOK TWO

Twenty-seven

They came out of the trees halfway up a ravine and April sat down at once on an outcrop of shale, exhausted by the half hour walk across the top of Mad River Mountain. Below her in the hollow she saw a wide creek, running wild after the summer rains.

The creek divided the sheer wall of the hidden ravine and the woods beyond. Across the creek, and cut out of the trees, was the settlement, a half-dozen tar-paper cabins built together at the edge of the water.

From the distance of several hundred yards, the small village looked picturesque, clustered there in the clearing and in strange harmony with the evergreen forest that encircled it.

"How do we get down there?" April asked, still gasping.

"There." Luke pointed to a footbridge.

"There!" A jab of fear cut her heart. The footbridge was chained to oak trees on both ledges, and swayed high over the creek waters.

"Yes." He sounded annoyed, as if she were failing him. "You wanted to meet them," he reminded her, and then pushed ahead, striding down the sloping path to the swaying bridge.

April pulled herself up and went after him. Yes, it had been her idea. She also realized that Luke's sudden sullenness

meant that he was having second thoughts about taking her
to the families' homestead.

She needed to appear simply interested, nothing more.
And she was thankful again that in the intimate aftermath of
their lovemaking, she hadn't confessed to him what she was
really doing in the Catskills.

"Don't look down," Luke advised, stepping onto the
narrow bridge.

April couldn't help herself. The rushing creek water
immediately made her dizzy. She grabbed the rope guards to
steady herself and focused her attention on the opposite
shore, where seven stripped and abandoned cars lay smashed
against the rocky creek bank.

There were other vehicles filling the edge of the woods,
stripped of salvageable parts and discarded. Sassafras bushes,
cattails, and sedge plants grew through the broken windows.

She concentrated on the junked cars as she moved slowly
across the bridge. Luke was nearly at the end, and when he
stepped off, the swing bridge rolled and April lost her
balance. She tightly gripped the old ropes until the swaying
stopped, then inched herself forward again, furious at him
for not waiting. Several small children had come running
from the dark interiors of the box-shaped houses, and now
they stopped and stood back, silently watching.

When April stumbled off the footbridge onto hard ground,
her legs went weak. She leaned against the oak tree to
steady herself, enormously relieved that she had made it
safely. It would be easier from now on, she told herself.

She saw a few sullen, rail-thin women down by the high
water creek. One, wearing a thin summer dress, stood
beside a scorched washtub, slowly rubbing clothes against a
galvanized board. A small boy, smudgy-faced and barefoot,
clung to her dress.

There were other children in the yard as well: older boys
wearing corduroy overalls, girls in summer dresses and
embroidered skirts. Some of the children were wearing
elbowless argyle sweaters and denim pants. Others had on
heavy, hand-me-down shoes. All were dirty-faced with mucus dripping from their noses. But not all were deformed.

There were a few normal children—even one or two pretty faces—and seeing them made her feel immensely better.

So not every one of the clan was a monster. Like Luke, some had escaped the curse of abnormal genes. But why? Scanning the group, she knew at once that the answer was there, hidden in the backwater settlement.

Luke had kept walking, moving through the clusters of children, and several of them spoke to him as he went ahead.

"Luke, I gotta me a deck o'cyards," one boy said, holding up a fistful of playing cards.

"I don't doubt hit none a-tall," Luke answered back, smiling and slipping easily into the mountain dialect. "Looks like a real good'n." He reached out and rubbed the head of the little boy.

April smiled at the exchange, pleased by the attention they paid him. Luke was clearly their hero.

He stopped at the porch steps of the first tar-paper shack and she came up beside him, stepping close, needing to feel the man beside her. An old man was sitting on the porch in an old upholstered chair.

"How ya doing, Luke-boy?" he asked. He did not move in the chair.

"Pretty good, I reckon. Ya mind if I ask ya fer a favor?" Luke said, speaking hesitantly.

"Naw, if hit's not going to cost too much." The old man kept grinning, displaying his dark toothless gums. His face was pinched and wrinkled, like the funny dried-apple dolls she had seen for sale at craft fairs in the City.

"This here his my friend," Luke began again, gesturing toward April. Then, in the same slow, clipped speech, he explained who she was. April could only understand an occasional word as Luke spoke.

"Hit don't make no differ," the old man said finally, not moving.

"Tell him," Luke said to April, stepping away to sit on the rock porch steps.

"What?" she said, confused.

"About the pond! About the house!" Luke snapped. "He said okay." Again he was short with her.

"Luke, I don't want to talk out here," she whispered.

"Why? There are no secrets, April. No confidentiality," he answered back.

"Luke, I can't," April insisted. "Suppose Nick or Weeping Willy came along?"

"Tyler, 'is here lady liken to pass hers time inside. Mind you, Tyler?"

The old man shook his head and sat forward. "Betty Sue, where ya girl?"

Out of the crowd of thin children a young girl jumped onto the wooden porch and helped the old man from the deep chair. It was then that April realized he was blind. She followed him and Luke into the tar-paper shack.

For a moment, in the darkness, April could not see at all. Then she made out the contours of the single room, with a loft reached by a ladder. There was a stove, some pieces of pine furniture, a table and two chairs. In the dark corner she saw a narrow bed. Someone—a child perhaps—was asleep under a small quilt.

The old man, led by the little girl, eased down into a battered sofa. The other children and adults silently followed April, slipping through the door, and circled the room.

Luke had been right, April realized. There were no secrets here. She couldn't keep the others out. She walked over to the table, to where Luke had already sat down in a cane-bottomed chair. "You want anything?" he asked nicely, "Tea or coffee?" He glanced around. "Sara-girl?"

"No. No, thank you," April whispered. "I'm fine." She took out her notepad, and to compose herself, to decide how to proceed, she looked around at the grimy interior.

Clothes hung from wall pegs and nails, alongside strings of dried apples, peppers, bunches of herbs, twists of tobacco, and a few advertisements and pictures torn from magazines and nailed to the rough-hewn walls. Nothing was square, April realized. The shack had been built with green timber and now there were shrinks, warps and sags in all the boards. There wasn't a square joint or a neat fit in the room.

"Are you ready?" Luke asked again.

April was angered by his attitude, and she let him know it with one quick look. Then she asked, "Will you help me?"

"Help you?"

"Yes. I'm not understanding everything he's saying."

"What are you looking for? What's the notepad for?" Luke sat back, as if alarmed by what April might be up to.

"These are my neighbors, Luke, and I'd like to know something about them," she answered vaguely. "There might be something I can do for them."

"None of you city people cares 'bout these people," he said, in dialect.

"I care about you," she said quietly, looking back at him, and she meant it. It was illogical and foolish of her, a married woman with a child and a professional career, but she did care. She realized it even more when she told him.

"What can you do?" he asked, curious now.

"Perhaps I can help them."

"Help them?" He snorted and started shaking his head. "Look around yourself. There's no helping these bastards. That's why I brought you back here, April. Seeing Willy the Weeper at your place, that was nothing. But look around you. You got a whole village of them." The anger had returned to his voice, coupled with contempt. April saw the self-hate in his eyes as he surveyed the silent room; she saw their soft brown harden like burnt clay.

"We can talk about this later," she said, nervous with the crowd of people filling the small shack. They would have as much trouble understanding her as she did them, but surely they'd be following some of the talk.

"We can talk about it now," he answered. "I know what you want. I know why you're here."

April stared at him, holding her breath, but she could feel her heart pounding. He couldn't know, she kept telling herself.

"I fixed your computer when the power went out, remember? I saw what you were researching. All those files."

For a moment, April was too stunned to reply. Then she asked, "Then why did you agree to bring me here?"

"Because I had something myself I wanted to show you." He stood up and motioned to her to follow him across the room.

April followed, aware that the others were watching her, tracking her as she went after Luke.

He approached the narrow bed and leaned over to whisper to the shrouded figure.

As April stepped closer, she smelled the same foul stench that the dwarf had left in the house.

"Here," Luke said, turning to her. "Come look and see yourself a real inbred."

He jerked back the old quilt.

April swallowed hard at the sight of the small creature, the strange alabaster girl-child lying on the dirty sheets. Yet she couldn't look away. The child repelled and fascinated her. This was the same figure of her dreams, the one that swam at her through the murky waters of the farm pond. This was the child of her nightmares. The girl was sucking her thumb and she looked up at April, her wet pale eyes set deep in a tiny, hollow face.

"Who is she?" April asked, recovering.

"She's my sister."

Twenty-eight

April stopped walking to take in the view. They had come out of the woods again, and were high above the tree line. From where they stood, she could see for miles. It was a breathtaking sight. In all directions the sky was cloudless blue. How wonderful the land was when seen from a distance, she thought, and how terrifying it became once she stepped into the woods and came closer to nature.

He came up beside her on the path and after a moment, said quietly, "Let me tell you a story."

"No more, please." She shook her head. He told stories

the way a grandfather would, to entertain and to baffle, to make a mystery of his life.

He went ahead anyway. "This land here, all of Mad River, was once farmed by Indians. They were a branch of the Onondaga, a small tribe. They grew corn in this valley, and pumpkins, a few crops, and hunted in the hills. Then in the eighteenth century settlers came, Dutch and Scottish farmers. They came up from the Hudson River like my family, and they farmed wheat and flax on the slopes of the valley, in the bottom land, and in time they overfarmed and destroyed the soil and overcut the trees.

"There was an outcry then by the Indians. They attacked the settlers, burned them out, killed most of the men, raped the women, and kept some of them—married them, as it were. They became known locally as the Hill People, and their children were all half-caste, and closely related.

"This valley went fallow once the soil was gone. But in time a forest grew back. Oak and pine trees on the limestone, and chestnut, oak, and sumac bushes up on this ridge. That's what we have here today, mostly.

"The few people, descendants of the original settlers, survivors of the massacre, stayed in the valley and during the 1840s and 1850s a village developed where the river makes a pool."

"Secret Lake," April said, needing to speak.

Luke nodded. "Secret Lake, that's right. The town was called Secret because it was locked in down there at the bottom of the valley. It was a pretty little place. I've seen tinplate photographs of it taken at the time of the Civil War.

"One year—1868—there was a hard winter. That spring the water washed down off the mountain and flooded the valley and wiped away the town. Villagers were swept away in their sleep, whole families were lost, and everything in Secret—the houses, stores, the church—was destroyed. Some bodies were never found; others washed ashore twenty miles away, got caught up in the branches of smaller tributaries.

"They say—I mean, the old people on the Hill tell me—that the pastor of the Dutch Reform Church was not killed. He had been down in Kingston during the storm, and when he reached Mad River Valley and found his family was dead, the town gone, he cursed the valley. He blamed everything on the godlessness of the Hill People, the half-breeds as he called them, and he told them it was God's anger. God was angry at him, God was giving him a sign for his failings, for having gone up on the ridge and trying to convert the Hill People. He swore then that never again would any outsider be allowed to have congress—that was the word he used—with the Hill People.

"He went into the hills on a dark night—a summer night, with a ghost of a moon—and armed with an axe, he went from shack to shack killing people. He murdered women and children along with the men. But he killed only the normal children, the healthy ones, and then he stopped."

Luke moved away from her, kept staring off across the valley. When he spoke again, his voice was full of sadness. "So that's why we are the way we are, April. It would have been better if all of us had been killed, but you see what that mad preacher wanted, don't you?"

April nodded, too shocked to speak.

"He wanted a legacy on Mad River Mountain. He wanted the half-wits and retards, the feeble-minded and the abnormal, all the mutants to stay alive, to breed with each other, to produce more of their own kind, until this whole mountain-top would be as it is now, populated by monsters."

"Luke, stop it! You're not a monster!"

"You've seen my sister! What do you call her?"

"Luke, don't."

"She's a freak. She can't take care of herself. None of them can. Let 'em die. Let them all die."

"Luke, please." April paused a moment. "We can help them. Together."

She moved closer to him. "If you help me. My . . . our research will bring attention to Mad River Mountain . . . all of these people . . . you."

"We're not interested in being some research topic," he said, moving off.

"Don't you want to help your sister?" she asked, struggling to keep pace on the path.

He laughed at that, dismissing the suggestion. "How would you suggest we help that creature?"

"I don't know. I'm not a geneticist. But certainly you could make her life more comfortable if you got her out of that hovel."

"Who'd pay for it?"

"Well, the government for one. There are state agencies, federal money. There's welfare—public assistance. You know that as well as I do. You've been to college! Why are you being so obstinate?"

He stopped and turned abruptly on the path, seizing her shoulders with both hands. "No agencies."

"Why not? They can help all of those people."

"I'll tell you why, April. If the government sets in here to 'help us,' they'll destroy us. They'll take my little sister away from here. They'll mess up all our lives. Don't interfere with my family, April. They're happy. They've got each other. And they've got me. I look out for them."

"You've lost the midwife, Luke. Who is going to come up here now to deliver the children?"

"We have our women. We'll just go on as we are."

"That doesn't have to be." She reached out and took his hand. "This is a very special place, Luke. A scientific phenomenon. Don't you understand?" She saw his eyes blink, but he didn't pull away, and she kept whispering, afraid he would interrupt. "If you help me. If I can do the research, now, before it's too late, we can make Mad River Mountain a field laboratory. A research center."

"A game park."

"Yes, okay. A game park. Like Jane Goodall's chimp park in Tanzania, if you want, but it will save your people."

"How will it save them?"

"With money. I can get funding from Columbia University, or the Museum of Natural History, or maybe the Smithsonian. We own the only piece of property below the mountain, so we can block other people's access. It's possible to keep the way of life of your relatives. To keep them safe."

"But you'll write about them?"

"Yes. I'll do scientific articles in journals, and maybe a book." April knew she could not fool him. "And I'll be able to prove that people like you—a healthy and accomplished person—can be produced from a negative scorecard of inbreeding. That a double dose of abnormal genes does not necessarily produce monsters.''

''What about my sister?''

''What about you?''

''I may be the exception that proves the rule.''

''Well, my research will show if that's so.'' She grew excited at the thought of what lay ahead of her.

Luke stepped away again. She kept very still, not following him.

''How do you do this? I mean, how do you start?''

''Well, I have to collect the data first, exactly what the relationships are. You said everyone on Mad River was kin, next of kin, and double kin. I need to know the marriage contracts and the offspring. I need the records of births as far back as your people have documentation, or at least some sort of oral history. That old man I met, for example, and the people of his generation—they'll have the best recollections. I do have some documentation from the county office, but I need to know more about the births. Even the children who died, who were stillborn, who never lived beyond one or two years of age. All of that is important to establish a family tree, a composite picture of the clan. I want to find out if the gene flow is entirely centrifugal. Do people ever leave the Hill? Does anyone new come onto the mountain and marry? If no one does, well, that increases the coefficient of inbreeding—the rate of it, in other words, from one generation to the next.''

''How do I find that out?''

''Well,'' April went on, ''people often used their bibles as the place where they record such happenings. Events of the family. If you could find those old bibles, that would help.''

''Okay,'' he said slowly, ''I'll help you.''

''Thank you.''

''I'll get you all the information you need. All the marriages and births, that stuff, but you need to know something else.'' He stared at her, locking his eyes on hers, as if he wanted to be sure to see her reaction.

''Yes?'' April said, realizing she was holding her breath.

''That girl we just saw, that little monster . . . ?''

April nodded slowly.

"Her name is Cindy Sue. She's not my sister," he said quickly. "She's my daughter. My only child."

Twenty-nine

Marshall set the handsome hardwood case on the bed beside April and snapped it open, revealing the green velvet interior and the disassembled rifle.

"It's enormous," April said, touching the carved gunstock. "What is it?"

"A .25-06 Browning A-Bolt." Marshall lifted the barrel from the case and began to assemble the rifle.

"Marshall, why did you buy it?"

"For killing vermin."

"Vermin! What are you talking about?" April sat up in the bed, alarmed now.

"Greta told me after I got here last night about that dwarf breaking into the house," Marshall answered, shooting a glance at his wife.

"There's no need to bring guns into the house because of them," she answered back. "Luke promised me . . ."

Marshall snapped the twenty-four-inch barrel into the stock.

"If you had had a rifle like this you could have blown a few holes in that freak."

"Please, Marshall, don't talk like that."

"What is it? Trying to protect those precious inbreds of yours? Make all of Mad River Valley a wilderness for them?"

She hadn't told him anything when he had arrived upstate. He was only guessing.

"Marshall, that's enough!" April kept her voice low. She

didn't want the children to hear them fighting. "Did Greta also tell you that she put a branch of swamp sumac in Timmy's bed? The poor child was covered with red blotches. Thank God Luke was around. He had a local remedy that cleared it right up."

"She told me the pumpkin-heads did it, not her." He set the Browning on the bed and started dressing, putting on a new pair of khaki pants and a blue denim shirt.

"Where are you going?"

"Target practice." He lifted the rifle off the bed.

"Marshall!"

He glanced over, scowling at her from under his hat.

"Be careful," she pleaded. "The kids." But she was thinking of Luke.

"I'll set up a sight beyond the pond and fire over the valley. No one will be hurt, not even your friend." He pulled open the door.

"Marshall!" she shouted. "What are you implying?" He stared coldly back at her, not answering. April continued calmly, trying to weigh her words with sincerity and gloss them with truth. "You're wrong. There is nothing going on between us." She stared back at her husband.

He nodded once and then walked out of their bedroom. She listened to his boots on the bare barnboard, listened to him slamming open the deck door, going off to shoot, preparing to kill.

She sat perfectly still in the wide bed, then pulled the quilt up against her breasts, feeling chilled and abandoned.

The night before she had gone out onto the deck and sat alone in the dark drinking a glass of wine and watching the starry night. She had fallen off to sleep at some point and woke to the touch of a hand on her shoulder.

"Don't, Luke, please," she had whispered into the dark, and then Marshall had moved out from behind her chair.

"Is it Luke that you're expecting?" he had said, breaking the stillness of the night. "Well, then maybe I made a big goddamn mistake rushing my ass back from L.A. and renting a car to be up here with you tonight." She could only see the shadow of him, hovering above her.

"I'm not expecting Luke," she had said, "but he plays these silly games." She spoke quickly, forcing out the lie.

"I bet he plays silly games. Lots of silly games with my goddamn wife."

"Oh, Marshall, don't be ridiculous!" She tried to tell him that Luke liked to play games to frighten the children, but she knew Marshall knew she was lying. She had committed adultery and now her husband was going to make her pay for it.

The memory of that conversation came back to her now, as a rifle shot rang out. April had been waiting for it, but still the report startled her. The roar rebounded across the valley, echoing away. There would be no wildlife left in the valley. She thought of the golden deer, of how terrifying the sound must be to an animal.

She got up and put on a robe. Timmy would wake up frightened by the rapid firing. As she hurried to the stairs, she glanced out the window and saw Marshall standing by the pond. He had stopped shooting and was talking to Luke Grange.

April went out onto the deck, into the cool morning. The sun had not yet reached that side of the house and the wooden boards were damp with morning dew. She went to the far end where a thin edge of sun had cleared the mountain and warmed the corner.

"Marshall!" she shouted down to him, wanting to interrupt but having no idea of what to say.

Luke glanced up and smiled. She was wearing just her nightgown, and she realized that the slanting sun was silhouetting her. She did not move. She wanted Luke to see her body, to be distracted by her, to leave her husband and walk away before there was trouble between them.

Marshall followed Luke's gaze. She knew that he, too, could see the curve of her breasts, the shape of her thighs. Then he looked back at Luke.

"Do you hunt?" She heard him ask Luke as he reloaded the Browning.

"Nope, I'm not keen on guns."

"I thought all you good old boys were born with rifles shoved up your butts."

"I guess I'm not one of your good old boys," Luke said softly.

"Well, let me show you how it's done, boy," Marshall answered deliberately. He picked up four empty cans and walked them over to the edge of the cliff and spaced them on tree stumps.

"You know you're only living on this property at my invitation," he said, returning to where Luke waited at the edge of the pool. "I don't care what that goddamn covenant says. If I want you off this property, you're off. I can break that clause you've got wedged into that old deed. I make my living as a lawyer, remember?"

Marshall shoved the rifle into Luke's hands, saying, "Go ahead and shoot!" Then he tilted up his ivory snap-brim jungle hat.

"I don't hunt, Mr. Benard. I don't kill." Luke handed the Browning back to Marshall.

"You mountain hippies are all alike. Nothing but candy-asses."

Marshall turned quickly, raised the deer rifle, and fired rapidly, missing the cans on the flat tree stumps.

"Shit!" He broke open the smoking chamber. "The sight's off."

"You're jerking the trigger," Luke said softly. "Pull it slowly and let the rifle recoil."

He stood back with his hands in his pockets and glanced sideways at Marshall. Up on the deck, April stood mesmerized.

"Is that so? Smart-ass talk from someone who doesn't shoot."

"You pick up things, living in the woods."

Marshall tossed the rifle at Luke. "Show me!"

"What load are you shooting?"

"Load?"

"Yes, cartridges. One hundred grains or less? In an A-Bolt like this," Luke added, examining the new rifle, "I'd use eighty- or ninety-grain."

"They just gave me these at the store," Marshall admitted, handing Luke a fistful of cartridges.

"The load depends on what you're hunting," Luke commented casually as he loaded the deer rifle. Then he turned toward the cans and squeezed off three rapid shots, scattering the thin aluminum cans across the edge of the valley.

"Your sight is just fine, Mr. Benard." Luke tossed the rifle back at Marshall and stepped around him, moved up toward the farmhouse where April stood with her arms crossed and clutched to her trembling body.

"Wait!" Marshall shouted. "Where are you going?"

Luke halted and looked around at him.

"I'm headed to get the power mower. It's time to cut the grass, Mr. Benard." Then he turned and continued across the lawn.

He would kill him now, April thought. He would raise the rifle and blow Luke Grange away as he strode toward the barn. Who would blame him? He could tell the sheriff that Luke was fucking his wife. In the mountains, she guessed, that was reason enough to kill a man.

But Marshall didn't turn the rifle on her lover. Instead, he looked away from the house, spotted a huge black crow perched on the tip of a bare maple tree, steadied himself, took aim as Luke had advised, and gently squeezed the trigger.

The shot recoiled across the hills. The black bird plunged down, its feathers scattering, before its wide wings caught the breeze and it floated into the safe coverage of greener trees. Marshall had missed his prey.

"Marshall!" April shouted to her husband, wanting to get her husband into the house before he did kill something.

Marshall glanced at her as he quickly reloaded, and April waved, beckoned him to the deck, but instead he turned away from the house and strode off.

"Where's Daddy going?" Timmy asked.

"I don't know, sweetheart. I don't know what he's doing," April whispered, and not knowing suddenly made her very afraid.

Thirty

"Do you want to talk about this?" April asked her husband as soon as they had driven away from the farmhouse.

The night was warm and April had rolled down her window and turned sideways in the front seat so she could lean back and catch the cool breeze. Sitting that way, she could look directly at her husband.

"Talk about what?" he asked.

"Why you are being so difficult? You're gone for a whole week and when you come back you're impossible. You haven't said a nice word to me all day."

"Maybe it's because I'm not sure you're interested in me any longer."

"Marshall, you're not being fair."

"What about you? Greta tells me . . ."

"Is your daughter spying on me?"

"You know what I mean."

"No I don't!"

"I think you're spending too much time with Grange."

"How would you know?" She sat up. "You haven't spent more than two consecutive days here at the house."

"April, it was your idea to buy this place. You wanted to do your goddamn research."

"And you said you wanted a country house!" she shot back.

"I didn't say the Catskills. I wanted a place out on Long Island, on the water." For a moment he was silent, staring ahead at the dark road. Then he asked, "Who are these people having this party, anyway?"

"Their name is McNulty. Grace and Chuck McNulty. I met her at Lynn's one afternoon when I took the children

174

swimming. She babbles, but she seems okay. Anyway, it was your suggestion that I try to get to know some of the other New Yorkers here. They live in the village."

"What does he do?"

"I don't know. The same as all the rest, I guess, an investment banker."

There was a pause. Then Marshall spoke abruptly.

"Well, are you?" he asked.

"Am I what?" she asked back, knowing what he wanted to know, and stalling for time.

"Are you sleeping with the goddamn caretaker?" he shouted, turning on her. In his anger, he raced the car and she said quickly, "Marshall! Please."

When he slowed the car, she spoke deliberately and calmly. "No, I'm not. I'm not sleeping with Luke." She stopped herself from saying more. Liars, she knew, always made the mistake of going on too long, of protesting too much.

"Greta says . . ."

"Greta is a fourteen-year-old impressionable teenager who doesn't like her stepmother. And, in case you haven't noticed, she's also got a crush on Luke."

"I noticed you this morning, out there on the deck. If any of my women have a crush on him it's you, April."

April did not respond. She knew that she had behaved like Greta that morning, flaunting herself. None of this, she realized, would have happened in the City. It was only because they were living away from civilization that she lost her common sense.

They reached an intersection and Marshall stopped the car.

"Which way? Do you know? Where the fuck are the road signs?" He flipped on his high beams and leaning forward, peered out at the dark.

"Turn left. I know the way. It's not far." He was so volatile, she thought. Everything seemed to ignite his anger. She wondered if it was his work, or her, or just being in the Catskills.

When the car picked up speed again, she said, "Don't rush. I want to talk," and then she went on quickly. "I admit I am attracted to Luke. He's handsome, and I've flirted with him. I think Greta has seen that, but not even that much would have happened if you'd been around.''

"April, please. I've got responsibilities. . . .''

"You told me you'd cut back so we could enjoy the summer together.''

"Look, April! I didn't plan this mess out in L.A. It happens, you know. The best-laid plans and all that crap!'' He leaned over and glared at her. April could see his face and flashes of the dashboard lights in his eyes. "I don't operate in the hushed halls of academia where nothing ever goes out of whack, and you can take all fucking year to move your ass.''

"Stop it! Please! Stop yelling at me.'' Her hands were trembling.

Marshall jerked the Volvo to a stop in the middle of the dark road.

"I'm sorry,'' he said quietly.

"And I'm sorry I ever heard of this place. I'm sorry that I even suggested that we buy the property. I don't want any of this to come between us.'' She was crying now and she bent forward, burying her hands in her face.

"Hey, kid. Hey!'' Marshall moved over and pulled her into his arms. "It's all right. It's all right.'' He was whispering.

"No, it isn't. We're fighting. I'm picking on you for not being around when I need you.'' She started to choke on her tears and stopped talking. "And you're never in a good mood these days.''

He kissed the top of her head, squeezed her tighter in his arms, whispered back, "It's my fault, I know. But when the appeal blew up out in California, I thought you'd be busy with your work, and you'd like the time alone, not having to take care of me.''

"I want to take care of you, Marshall. I'm your wife.''

"Yeah, but you have your career. You know.'' He let her slip out of his embrace and sit up. "Maybe if you weren't saddled with Greta,'' he said, momentarily sounding guilty.

Another car was coming up behind them. Marshall started

the car and turned off toward the McNulty house. The lights of the house were visible, ahead and through the trees.

"I'm sorry I got you so upset," Marshall offered.

"Oh, it's not you," she answered, thankful that he was again nice to her, and then she thought how volatile Marshall's moods were of late. He was nice to her one moment, terrible the next. It was his sudden rages that were upsetting her the most.

"This place is out in the middle of nowhere," Marshall commented, an edge of annoyance returning to his voice.

"No worse than ours."

"Yeah, but you have Luke."

"Marshall!" April took a deep breath. He had done it again, flipped from being gentle and caring to insulting her.

"Forget it. I didn't mean anything." He pulled the station wagon in behind another car at the edge of the gravel road. "This place, all these goddamn woods and shit. It gives me the creeps." He ran his hand nervously through his hair.

"Leave us enough room to get out of this parking space in case we want to leave early," April suggested.

"Hey, it's Friday night, April. Party night."

"We have two young children at home alone."

"They'll be okay. They've got . . ."

"Yes, I know. They've got Luke." She wondered suddenly if it had been wise to leave Greta at home.

"I spoke to her, you know," Marshall said, as if reading her thought.

"What?"

"Greta and I had a father-daughter talk about Luke. She's okay. She's still a virgin, in case you were wondering."

"Are you sure?"

"I'm sure," he snapped. "So let up on her, okay? Stop thinking of her as some kind of teenage slut."

"I never said that!"

"You don't have to say anything, April. You know how to make your point." He pushed open the car door and stepped outside before she could answer.

As April followed after him into the house, she decided

she needed a drink. Marshall hadn't waited for her. He had gone ahead into the house, leaving her to make her own way. This lack of courtesy was so unlike him. He was a different person in the Catskills.

"Oh, April, hi! I just saw your husband," Grace McNulty said, coming to greet her.

"Which way was he heading?" April asked, smiling. She tried to act as if entering the party on her own was a matter of complete unconcern.

"Chuck corralled him. They know people in common, I think, from the City. Chuckie said, your husband's firm had done work for his company. Or something!" She laughed and her full mouth of bright teeth flashed. "I can't keep track of all this wheeling and dealing, and keep up with my own work."

"Oh, you work?" April brightened. At last, she thought, another career woman.

"Well, I call it my 'work'; I'm a potter. Ceramics. I've taken some courses at Parsons, and I just love it. I mean, it's so satisfying to make something artistic. Now, you teach, right?"

"Yes," April replied quietly, "I teach."

"Do you like it? I mean, do you find it satisfying?" Her hands fluttered like quail startled by a sudden sound.

"Yes," April said, keeping up her level tone. "Very satisfying."

"That's exactly how I feel about my ceramics. I mean, it's so satisfying to sit down at the wheel and turn out a bowl or a mug. It's given me a whole new dimension to my life. I mean, we don't have children. I don't, that is. Chuckie has two children by his ex, but they're both off at college, and we . . . well." She shrugged, then went on quickly, "Also it gives me something to do. Gets me out of the apartment." She kept talking compulsively. "I never see Chuckie during the week. I mean, the poor dear. Flying off here. Flying off there. I imagine it's the same with you, another Catskills widow. Are you glad you have your little job?"

"Yes, quite," April whispered, and kept scanning the crowd, looking for a familiar face. She knew them all. All city people. There was no one from town, no locals. The two cultures didn't mix.

"Grace, have you seen Stephen?" a young woman asked, appearing at their side.

"Oh, no, Debbie, I haven't," Grace said, turning to the other woman, and then asked, "April, have you met Debbie? Debbie Kinlin. Did you look by the barbecue, Debbie? I heard him tell Chuckie that he'd help with the chicken." The doorbell rang and she looked up over their heads, and added, "Excuse me, gals, those nice people who bought the old Howard place on Rabbit Hop Road just arrived." She slipped passed April, leaving the two women alone.

"I have to find Stephen," Debbie said at once, smiling apologetically to April. She was a tiny, timid woman with a small frightened face.

"Oh, I'm looking for my husband as well." April peered across the room. She could see through the windows that floodlights were lit, and that the party had already moved onto the deck and the back lawn.

"He's not exactly my husband. More my 'significant other.' " The woman giggled.

"Well, aren't they all," April replied. Excusing herself, she veered off and stepped up to a counter laden with liquor bottles. Out of the corner of her eye, she saw Debbie Kinlin continue through the kitchen. April took a deep breath and reached for the gin. It was going to be a long evening.

She took her gin and tonic outside onto the deck, into the cool of the evening, and for a moment stood off by herself and took in the party. In the few weeks she had been upstate she had become shy and tentative with people. She had lost her city edge, her aggressiveness, and that surprised her. She wondered if a whole year in the Catskills would turn her into a vegetable? Already she was having trouble remembering just what day of the week it was. But it would be different once she started working full time on her research.

It was time to do some mixing. With a sigh, she left the corner of the deck and walked across to a group of women, plunging herself into their midst, and saying lightheartedly, "Has anyone seen my significant other?"

"Oh, April," Betty Banks chimed, "you don't need Marshall, not with Luke Grange back at the ranch."

It was meant to be a joke, April realized, but she answered coolly, "I do need my husband."

"He's out by the barbecue," Lynn said quietly. "See! With Chuck McNulty."

As April glanced in the direction of the back lawn, she saw Marshall move away from several men standing by the pit. He walked off to the edge of the lawn and stood alone, sipping a drink, and stared into the woods.

"He seems preoccupied," Lynn added nicely, still trying to make amends for Betty's comment.

"Yes, he is." April smiled over at her gratefully. "He's involved with a time-consuming case, and he has to keep flying back and forth between L.A. and New York."

"Oh, they've all got work excuses," Betty said bluntly, "as long as they can park us and the kids here for the summer, they can damn well do what they please in the City."

April turned on her. "Betty, I don't know what your husband does, but Marshall is a partner at a law firm that never closes. And he has major responsibilities." It made April feel suddenly better to defend her husband.

Betty Banks smiled back condescendingly. Then, nodding toward Marshall, she replied, "Well, I can see he doesn't keep his working ways here in the Catskills."

April glanced down at the lawn and saw that Ann O'Malley had moved over to join Marshall. As April and the other women watched, her husband slipped his arm around Ann's shoulder, pulling her closer.

"Excuse me," she said firmly and, setting down her drink, walked off the deck and down across the lawn.

"Marshall," she said calmly, approaching the shadowy figures. "I'd like to go home."

"April, hi!" Ann pulled away from Marshall. "Your hubby was just telling me . . ."

April silenced her with a quick glance, then looked again at her husband. "Marshall, I want to leave."

"Fine." He stared back at her. "I want to stay."

She paused a moment, then told him, "I'm taking the car."

"Fine." He sipped his drink, watching her, his eyes narrowing.

"I better see about freshening my drink," Ann put in, edging herself around April.

"Don't leave, Ann," Marshall said, not taking his eyes off April.

But Ann O'Malley kept walking, hurrying back to the main party, and April waited until she was out of hearing before she whispered, "You've embarrassed me, Marshall. And you're making a fool of yourself."

"Fuck off!"

"Don't you dare talk to me like that."

"Get off your goddam high horse. You don't think I know what you and Grange have been doing all summer? Shit! You piss me off." He turned away from her to look again at the woods.

"Marshall," she whispered. "Stop it. Don't do this to us." She had to bite her lip to keep from crying.

"Leave me alone, will you. I'm having a good time."

"Marshall, please."

He spun around and her heart leapt to her throat. She stumbled back, expecting to be hit.

Marshall grinned. "I'm not going to hit you, kiddo. Not now."

"Darling, what's wrong?" She reached out to touch him, but he pulled away.

April dropped her arm. She knew they were being watched, and that they had already given the women on the deck a week's worth of gossip.

"Go home," he told her.

"Please come with me. I'm worried about you."

"Fuck off!"

April turned around and walked back across the lawn. She did not go up onto the porch, but circled the house. Once in the darkness on the other side, she ran along the gravel road to where they had parked the car. She pulled the extra ignition key from beneath the rubber floor mat, started the car, turned it around, and headed back to Mad River Mountain. She was crying uncontrollably before she was off Pearl Peak.

Thirty-one

"Bitch," Marshall yelled after her. He finished off his drink, tossed the ice cubes onto the grass, and then, enraged, threw the heavy whiskey glass into the trees. He heard it thump against a tree. "Fuck!" he said next, and walked quickly toward the house.

"Is something wrong at home with the children?" Ann O'Malley cut him off as he approached the porch. "I just saw April rushing off." She smiled up sweetly at Marshall, blocking his way to the house with her body.

"What?" he asked, staring down at her.

"Do you feel all right, Marshall?" she asked, reaching out and touching his arm.

"Don't touch me!"

"Sorry! Jesus!" She backed away. "Excuse me."

"Fucking woman!"

"Hey, listen, you!" Ann answered back. "Don't you speak that way to me. I'm not your wife."

"Piss off!" Marshall said. Pushing past her, he went around the house, and down the road to his parked car. It was only when he reached the empty spot on the road that he realized it was gone, that April had really taken it.

"Shit!" He slammed his fist against the next car. Leaning against it, he pressed his forehead to the cold metal and spread his arms out across the roof. "Jesus, what is wrong?" he said out loud, breathing deeply and trying to pull himself under control. He couldn't catch his breath. There wasn't enough air. He grabbed his collar and ripped off a button, exposing his throat.

That was better, much better. He smiled and looked

182

around. Fuck them all, he said to himself, looking back at the brightly lit house. Fuck April. Fuck Ann O'Malley. Fuck all those women. He grinned, feeling better.

He pulled himself off the car and took a deep breath. Yes, much better. He felt as if the weight was off his neck, as if he were free of them all. He smiled. He looked around at the dark night, the deep, dark forest of trees. Yes, he wasn't afraid of the woods, or Luke Grange, or any of them. He grinned, thrilled by the discovery.

Then he bolted, like a wild deer into the woods, bolted for the thick coverage of trees and underbrush. Someone might drive up the road and see him there. He kept running into the trees that edged the lawn, circling the house until he had a clear view of the back porch, the barbecue pit, and the crowd of city people.

He listened to their voices, the tinkling of glasses, the bursts of laughter and sudden shouts, all drifting through the night air to where he stood, hiding at the edge of the woods. Who were these people? he asked himself. These strangers. Why were they here in the mountains bothering him?

They were getting drunk. All of them were getting drunk. Or stoned. He saw a few of them standing on the deck. Saw the sharp flicker of burning ash, the shadowy profiles.

He smiled, thinking of what he could do to them all.

What was that?

He heard a voice. A whispering, funny voice. He didn't move. Be a silent shadow, he told himself. Be a watcher in the night. He turned his head slowly. One way then the other. No one lurked beside him. No one was hiding in the trees.

He smiled.

The night was humid and dark and no one knew he was in the woods. He was in no hurry. He could kill them all, he thought. He could walk into their private lives, kill them whenever he wished. Pull off their limbs, one by one, cut their pale throats, poke out their blue eyes, jerk out their pink tongues.

He kept grinning.

Summer in the Catskills.

He slipped his hands into his pants and let his fingers find and gently stroke himself. This was the very best, he thought, being alone in the woods, being all alone and knowing what was going to happen next.

He lifted his head, sniffed the clear mountain air, smelled the charcoal.

He hated the smell of charcoal. Later, the raccoons, he knew, would come out of the trees and push over the pits, tear at the burning stone and eat the chunks of burnt food left in the ashes.

The porch door banged opened. A woman moved into the dim shadows. She stood on the open porch and sipped her drink, looking out into the dark. No one followed after. No man came to hold her, to lead her off the porch and down onto the dark lawn.

The woman stepped off the porch and walked slowly down toward the wood, away from the house and out of the arc of bright lights. One of the men standing at the barbecue pit said something to her, but she did not respond, just kept walking slowly, aimlessly, into the dark lawn, moving slowly toward where he stood, half hiding in a stand of maples.

He held his breath. She would not come too close, he knew. The woods would frighten her. The dark woods always frightened them. It was not time. It was not right. Not yet. No. Please.

"Stop!" he whispered. "Stop, you bitch!"

She had a glass in her hand. She sipped it as she walked. He could hear the clear click of ice against glass. She was drunk, he knew. Yes, she was drunk. She moved one way, then another, unsteady on her feet, yet still coming toward where he was. Did she know he was there, waiting for her?

He could not really see her clearly. Her thin body was simply a shadow, a dark smudge against the house lights.

He closed his eyes. Please, stop. Don't come to me. Don't see me.

He would run away. He would thrash through the woods. She would think it was a deer, some wild animal, and go back into the safety of the house, back with the others.

She stopped. She had heard him, he guessed. She was at the edge of the woods now, less than ten feet from him. He could rush her, seize and muzzle her mouth. He could grab her hair in his fingers and drag her deep into the trees, pull her along the forest path and the ravine, and then cut her up.

He could dismantle her, he thought. Dismantle her like a toy doll. And then stuff all the pieces up her vagina.

He smiled, pleased by that idea, imagining how it might look to have her stripped naked, her long fingers sticking out of her crotch.

She slowly turned her head and searched the trees, looking.

Goddammit! What did she want? Why didn't she go away? He wasn't ready. It was too soon.

"Who's there?" she said.

She wasn't afraid. He heard it in her voice. She wasn't afraid at all and that enraged him.

"Stephen? Stephen, is that you?" She stepped into the long grass and came at him, explaining as she approached.

"Honey, I'm sorry. It didn't mean anything. I love you. Peter just had too much to drink, that's all. You know how he gets on weekends. I didn't want to cause a scene in the house by fighting him off. There was no harm done. A little innocent necking, okay. I'm guilty! But please don't make a federal case out of it."

Marshall lunged from the brush and seized her by the throat. He held her with one hand, the way one might grab a barnyard chicken.

She tried to hit him, flailed at him ineffectively. Her eyes popped in her head. He backed her up against the rough bark of the maple and ripped off her blouse, ripped off her bra, snapping the straps as he threw her clothes away. With the same motion he pulled out his new Buck knife and snapped it open; then, catching her left nipple between the blade and his thumb, he snipped it off.

She screamed but the sound caught in her throat. He stepped closer, to wedge her squirting body against the tree, and quickly sliced off her right nipple and dropped it, too, into the weedy underbrush. Then he let her go. He wanted her alive. He wanted the others to see her bleeding breasts.

She crawled away, sobbing, bleeding. He stepped back, began to move, wiping the blood from his knife, keeping his eyes on her as he backed deeper into the trees. She reached the lawn and tried to stand up, to shout for help, then tumbled over in the grass.

Then he ran. He ran back through the white birch, ran out onto the gravel road, perspiring now, and chilled by the cold sweat on his body. As he kept running toward the house, hiding behind the line of parked cars, he saw men running toward the woman, racing to where she lay screaming in the grass.

He made himself slow down and calm himself. He took a dozen deep breaths as he always did before going into court. He walked up the front steps and into the McNulty house. No one was inside. The women were clutched together on the porch, and the men had run down onto the lawn, were huddled around the woman.

In the kitchen he slowly and calmly picked up another glass and dropped in two cubes of ice and added an inch of scotch, marveling at his calmness and control. His hands were no longer trembling, but in the kitchen light, he saw there was blood caked to his fingers and beneath his nails.

It wasn't him, he told himself. It was someone else, someone inside him, who had done this, who had cut that woman. He wondered why. He knew it had happened. He had seen himself doing it, but why? He could feel the sweat soaking his clothes.

Jesus, this wasn't right.

He turned on the faucet and dunked his head under a thick stream of cold water, then washed the blood off his hands.

It wasn't him, he told himself, trying to submerge the memory of slicing the girl's breasts. It was him. That little runt who always betrayed him, told on him, told his mother, told his teachers, told everyone whenever he didn't do it right.

His thoughts kept spinning, leaving him dizzy and breathless.

Okay, be calm, he told himself. He gripped the counter and saw that his hands were clean. There was no blood there, caked to his fingers. Of course not. He wasn't a fucking madman. He looked up, grinning, at the window, and caught sight of his smiling reflection.

Grace McNulty came into the kitchen and grabbed the telephone receiver off the wall.

"Please," she pleaded, seeing Marshall. "Do this for

me. Call the police! An ambulance!'' She shoved the receiver at him.

"What happened?" he asked, frowning.

"Debbie! Debbie Kinlin! She's been attacked by someone! Or something!"

Marshall grabbed the telephone receiver before it dropped from her hand.

"Is she alive?" He tried to sound alarmed.

"Unconscious. I saw her. He cut off her nipples," she whispered, and pressed her hand against her breast, spreading her fingers to cover her own breasts.

"I'll call," Marshall said as he dialed, and then whispered to Grace McNulty. "It's one of them, I'm sure." He pointed off into the woods. "One of those pumpkin-heads." At that moment he knew there was someone else, his other self, loose in the woods, and if he could get away from Mad River Mountain, he would be all right, they would never know. No one would know the truth about him, who he really was, and where he had come from.

Then he dialed the police.

Thirty-two

April slept with her son. She was afraid to be alone in her own bedroom, afraid to be there when Marshall came home. She had pulled the quilt over herself, hoping that when she woke, it would be morning. But she feared also that she'd dream again of the ghostly alabaster child, of Luke's daughter.

Asleep beside Timmy, she dreamed instead of the pumpkin-headed children. They kept swarming out of the trees, reaching for her with their dirty fingers. She was screaming as she ran, beating them off with her hands. She could feel her fists sinking into their soft flesh.

She woke and bolted up in Timmy's bed, confused for a moment about where she was, and then immediately she heard someone downstairs. Marshall was home.

April slipped out of bed and Timmy stirred. She covered him quickly and tucked him in, praying that he would stay asleep. Then she thought: It wasn't Marshall. The dwarf was back. Willy the Weeper had sneaked again into the farmhouse. Or one of the mountain kids. She pictured one running from room to room, his wet pink eyes dripping bubbly mucus on the barnwood floors, on all her beautiful possessions.

She glanced around for a weapon. Timmy's baseball bat was leaning against the dresser and she picked it up. Then she stepped slowly across the small room and out into the hall, closing the door behind her. At the entrance to Greta's room, she stopped again and glanced in. The child was asleep. The summer moonlight filled the bedroom, swept across her face and figure. Beneath the white sheet she looked ghostly.

She was driving herself crazy, April thought—hearing things, seeing things, dreaming of translucent alabaster creatures and pumpkin-headed children. Then again, and distinctly, she heard more sounds downstairs, heard a chair move, a door close. Marshall was trying to keep quiet, trying to walk across the living room. She would not go down, she told herself. She should huddle the children together in one bedroom, lock herself up until morning, until she had the safety of daylight.

Yet even as she thought of taking refuge, April knew she couldn't. Marshall might need her; in any case, she had to confront him. She couldn't let what had happened at the party just pass away unresolved.

Downstairs, a pine log still flickered in the fireplace. She stood in the middle of the living room and listened for more noise, something to tell her where Marshall was in the house. She held the bat in front of her with both hands, like a samurai. But it felt too light to really hurt someone. She was sorry that Timmy didn't have a full-size bat, a Louisville slugger like the ones her brothers had had years ago when they were children. That was a bat that could kill someone, she thought.

A movement in her bedroom caught April's eye, so she stepped cautiously to the door and pushed it open.

"Marshall?" she whispered, trying to spot him in the darkness.

"No, April, it's me," Luke whispered, stepping out of the shadow.

"Luke! Why are you here? Why are you sneaking around? Marshall will be coming home." She retreated into the living room.

"I was worried about you. I saw you came home alone, and I didn't know if you knew."

"Knew what?"

"A woman was attacked over on Pearl Peak, at the McNultys. I heard the sheriff's office on my CB."

"Luke, what are you talking about?" She could see his profile in the flickering fire light.

". . . with a knife. The report was that some woman was slashed. I was afraid for you, here alone with the children."

"Slashed? I was just there. . . . I just got home."

"Someone sliced off this woman's nipples—snipped them, you know, like if you were pruning a honeysuckle bush."

"Luke!" The strength went out of her and she grabbed the back of the armchair. "You don't think? I mean, that it was one of them . . . Willy the Weeper . . . ? But he wasn't violent." Her mind jumped like summer lightning from one thought to the next.

"It could be," he whispered.

"But that's way over on the other side of the mountain. . . ."

"Come here. Let me show you something." He took her arm and led her into the dining room, where he flipped on the light.

Luke opened the topographical map of Mad River Mountain and spread it out on the dining room table. "Look," he said, pointing to a thin line. "This is a firebreak road that cuts across the top of the mountain, and along this ridge." His forefinger drew the course. "It touches the top slopes of Slide Mountain, then crosses over here."

"Where?" April asked, not recognizing any landmarks.

"This is called Pearl Peak. The McNultys are located here." Luke pulled back and looked at April.

The one downstairs light hid them both in shadows. She could not see Luke's eyes.

"What are you saying?"

"That someone from Mad River Mountain could easily have walked the ridge; we're talking about maybe a mile total. Someone, one of us, could have done it."

"Beer Mouth?" April blurted out, remembering her encounter.

"Maybe." Luke folded the map.

"But why? I mean, who was this woman anyway? I mean, it could have been her husband, or boyfriend. Someone she knew, not one of the Hill People."

"Well, you're the one who keeps talking about all those fouled-up genes of ours."

"Luke, I never said all your people were dangerous. There is so little known about this clan, your ancestors. Perhaps, with the right data, I could pinpoint what geneticists call a 'bottleneck.' That's when the accumulated consanguineous marriages collide and produce a gross case of genetic default."

Almost automatically, April had retreated into her academic language. It made her feel safer to speak in code to Luke, as if what was happening on Mad River Mountain was only a laboratory experiment and not a threat to her life.

"When I was fixing your computer, I read part of one of the reports. This guy said that isolated, inbred groups could produce real psychopaths."

April nodded. She remembered the monograph.

"Well, what if they—the city people—begin to think it's one of us? That we knifed that woman?"

"Luke, you're the only one who's suggested that! You're the one with the map and the theory!" April said angrily.

He leaned across the table, his face in the light. "My brother may be the one, April. And if the cops find out, they'll have dogs up on the ridge."

"I won't tell anyone," April whispered.

"What about the kids who got into this house? Are you going to tell your husband?"

"It's not important. Greta already told him. He won't say anything."

Luke nodded slowly. "This is all between us," he said finally. "No one else. If the cops or anyone hears about this, I won't help you with your research."

April nodded.

"They'll accuse us anyway," he told her. "They always do. They just want an excuse to come into Mad River Mountain and go pumpkin hunting."

"I won't tell anyone," April promised again, whispering, letting him know with a look how much she did trust him, and how much she knew he trusted her. Leaning forward in the shadowy room, she found his lips to kiss.

Headlights swept through the dining room, panning the walls like searchlights. April jumped, frightened at being caught in Luke's arms.

"Just a car," Luke said soothingly.

"Yes," she answered, as she realized who it was. "My husband."

Thirty-three

"What's the matter?" April asked, following her husband into the downstairs bathroom. He had barged into the house, pulled off his shirt, and now was leaning over the tub rinsing the wine colored cotton in water.

"What does it look like I'm doing? I'm washing my shirt."

"I see that. But why?"

He lifted the garment from the water to inspect it and answered, "Because there's blood on it. A woman's blood."

"The woman who was knifed? But why do you have blood on you? Who was she?"

Marshall tossed the shirt over the towel rack and turned back to April.

"How do you know about it?"

"From Luke. He came up to see if I . . . we were okay. He heard about it on his CB."

"Someone called Kinlin. . . ."

"Debbie Kinlin?"

"Do you know her?"

"Yes . . . No. I mean, I met her. We were introduced at the party. She's young."

"She's got no tits now."

"Marshall! What's the matter with you?" April shouted after her husband as he walked into the bedroom. He had kicked off his shoes and was stripping off his pants.

"Come to bed," he told her.

"No! Tell me what happened."

"I want to make love." He reached over and pulled back the quilt and top sheet.

"Why is there blood on your shirt?" She stayed in the doorway, away from him. "Tell me!" she shouted.

"You'll wake the kids," Marshall said. Naked now, he was sitting on the edge of the bed.

"Tell me!"

"Your inbreds did a job on her; that's all there is to tell."

"How do you know?" April demanded.

"I guess she and her boyfriend had a fight or something earlier in the evening," he said, softening his voice so she had to come into the bedroom to hear what he was saying. "And someone—one of the inbreds, everyone said—attacked the poor girl out on the back lawn. I helped carry her to a car. No one wanted to wait for the police or an ambulance."

"She's dead?"

Marshall shook his head and slipped under the sheets. He lay for a moment staring up at the ceiling. "Tomorrow morning, she'll wish she was dead."

"I can't believe it! Here in the Catskills . . ."

"Her breasts were squirting . . ."

"Stop!" April reached down and seized his arm. His skin was cold. "Marshall, you're freezing." She rubbed his forearm, thinking of the woman she'd met earlier in the evening.

"Where was he . . . her boyfriend . . . Stephen?" April asked, seizing on his name. "Maybe he's the one who hurt her."

"He was in the house all the time."

"How does anyone know? It was dark."

Marshall rolled over on one side, tucking the pillow under his head. "He was upstairs in one of the bedrooms with Mel Blockman's wife. That's where they found them."

"I can't believe these people." April remembered what Luke had told her about how the city people behaved in the Catskills. It was all true.

"Are you coming to bed?"

April shook her head. "I can't, Marshall. Not now. Don't ask me, please."

"You blame me for being away too much, and then when I come back, you won't even have me. Hasn't Luke got you all warmed up?"

"Marshall, don't," April whispered. "Not now."

"Yes, now!" He grabbed her arm before she could move off the bed. "I'm your goddamn husband, remember?"

"Marshall, you're hurting me."

"I don't give a fuck. Do you think that little inbred cared that he was hurting Debbie Kinlin when he snipped off her tits?" He pulled April down beside him.

"Marshall, what's the matter with you?" She stared up at him. She had never seen this look on his face. His eyes had narrowed to small bullet holes and his cheeks were drawn.

"You didn't see what I saw," he hissed. "You didn't have to see the blood. Thick, warm blood pumping from her pink little breasts." He had the woman again in his arms. She was squirming, trying to get away. He saw the flash of fear in her eyes. It made them bright, like a raccoon's when you catch him near the garbage.

April tried to pull away but he blocked her with his forearm around her chest.

"She was crying hysterically," he continued. "Her blood was all over my goddamn shirt." He had loved that, he remembered, loved the warmth of the thick blood squirting, spraying his face. It had made him feel closer to her.

April caressed her husband's cheek and his face twitched at her touch. "Please," she whispered, trying to calm his rage. "It's all right. Everything is all right. You helped her. You got her to the hospital. You did what you could. It's not your fault."

"No, it's not my fault." He dropped back onto his own pillow. He was sweating again and suddenly too tired to struggle with April. Why had he done it, he wondered. Ever since he'd come onto Mad River Mountain, he'd known he would do something, but why?

"You did everything you could," April whispered. She reached over and touched him again, let her fingers gently massage his chest. He was trembling. She could feel his fear. "Everything will be all right." She spoke as if he were a child.

"She shouldn't have gone into the woods," he said out loud. She had sought him out. She had come to find him. It was her fault, he told himself. Not his. Let them leave us alone, he told himself.

"Of course not. It's dangerous after dark."

"Those fucking . . ."

"Okay, Marshall. Okay," April whispered, backing off. It must have been terrible for him to see Debbie Kinlin. She had never seen Marshall frightened, and it scared her. In the city he always was in control—of himself and everything else in their lives. "Try to sleep, honey. Try to get some rest."

"I want to make love." He turned to her.

"Honey, I don't want to, please. All this news. It's upsetting."

"No!" He swung himself over, pinning her to the bed.

"Mommy?" Timmy's small voice broke the silence.

"Yes, darling?" April slipped away from her husband and scrambled off the bed to go to her son.

"I heard something." He was standing in the doorway wiping the sleep from his eyes.

"Okay, I'll go lie down with you." April swept her son into her arms and took him out of the room.

"April!" Marshall called after her.

She didn't answer, but she knew that when she came back to bed he would be waiting for her.

"You sleep with me?" Timmy asked, hugging her.

"Yes darling," she whispered, thankful for that escape from her husband.

Thirty-four

"Now, that was a G and T, wasn't it?" Lynn Grossman asked, returning to the pool.

"Yes, thank you." April said, not taking her eyes off Timmy. He was in the shallow end of the Grossmans' pool playing with Lynn's daughter, Alex. Greta and Ann O'Malley's twin girls were at the other end, diving into the deep water. All of the children were screaming with delight as they played. April was thankful, for that reason alone, that she had decided to drive over to Pearl Peak.

The pool was set away from the house and perched at the edge of the cliff, so that from where they sat under huge, bright red beach umbrellas, April could see across the valley floor and into the hills beyond. She could see where the road to her own property, the same dangerous gravel road, wound up the steep rise and then disappeared into the deep heart of Mad River Mountain.

April was feeling better. She knew she had done the right thing by getting away from Marshall for a few hours. And here, she would have a chance to talk to the women about the attack on Debbie Kinlin.

"April was just asking about Debbie," Ann O'Malley explained when Lynn returned with the second round of drinks. "She was wondering if it might have been someone else, someone from the city, you know, settling a score. Was Debbie into drugs, do you think?"

"No more than any of us," Lynn remarked, keeping her voice down. She glanced over at the children to see that they were out of hearing. "It's possible, I guess." And now she looked across the white table and asked, "You think Debbie owed drug money and some dealer paid her back by cutting her up?"

"They've done worse," April remarked.

"But why come up into the Catskills?" Ann asked. "They could have done the same to her in any dark hallway back in the City."

Lynn kept shaking her head while she reached for a cigarette. "It was one of the Hill People, I'm sure. The sheriff said as much last night."

"Why does he think so?" April asked at once.

"Oh, you know how the locals don't mix. They blame everything on the Hill People."

"And for good reason," Ann chimed.

April turned on her. "Have you had trouble with any of them?"

"I don't trust them. They all look like criminals to me. Last summer I took the twins to the county fair, you know, as a way of letting them get a little local 'culture.' You should have seen the riffraff! We don't realize it up here on the Peak, but we're surrounded by Neanderthals. Especially you, April, living cheek by jowl with them. Here you buy a wonderful old farmhouse and a perfectly nice woman is mutilated two miles away."

"Well, I won't say Debbie Kinlin is a 'perfectly nice woman,'" Lynn said wryly, then rushed to add, "No, but we have to realize that these things happen all the time in the mountains. These are violent people. You've seen the pickup trucks with those rifle racks. And just take a look at what hangs out at Bonnie and Clyde's Bar." She sighed. "I don't want to think about what this attack is going to do to real estate prices. Helen Smythe Ely must be pulling out her hair."

"The inbreds are not dangerous, Ann," April said sharply.

"Well, I hope not," Lynn broke in, wanting to make peace. "They are the only people I can get to do lawn work. And they're so . . ."

"Yes, we know, Lynn, 'cheap.'"

"Well, they are. They're also unreliable, of course. I

never know when they're going to show up. They have no phone.''

"They have a phone,'' April remarked.

"They do?'' both women said in unison.

"Yes. I saw it in one of the tar-paper shacks the other morning.'' April could see the surprise in the women's faces and it pleased her. She looked away, as if checking on her children.

"You've been into the houses?'' Ann sounded incredulous.

"Yes.'' April stood and moved her chair. It was almost four o'clock, and shadows were lengthening on the lawn.

"Why in the world would you do that? The children didn't go, did they?'' Lynn asked.

"Lynn, why are you so alarmed? You just said they worked for you.''

"Yes, but I don't let them into my house, near my Alex. They're freaks!''

"Yes, but they work cheap.'' April reached down and felt for her bag. It was time to go.

"Haven't you heard about Julia Stonequest?'' Lynn asked.

April shook her head and looked for her car keys. "Who is Julia Stonequest?''

"She was the daughter of friends of Ann's,'' Lynn answered, "local people who live on Possum Creek. That's across the interstate, about five miles below your place. Julia got in the family way, as they say up here, when she was just fifteen or sixteen.''

"Fourteen,'' Ann said, interrupting. "The poor girl had no idea what was happening.''

"Well,'' Lynn continued, lowering her voice, "the Stonequests are Catholics. Ann met them through the twins; you know, at one of those Catholic affairs, bingo or whatever, and when their little Julia became pregnant, they came to her.''

April looked over at Ann O'Malley.

"Someone raped her?'' she asked. Timmy was crossing the lawn and April called out to him, told him to get Greta and to collect his things.

"She was gang raped,'' Lynn whispered. "By Hill People. No one knew for sure how many. Julia wouldn't say.

She just took her father's deer rifle and blew a hole the size of Delaware through her chest."

"She said it was Hill People?" April pressed.

"Yes, but her parents did tell me Julia was disturbed. They had her on some medication, I know. She was seeing the local doctor, but . . ." Ann shrugged.

"It could have been anyone then, couldn't it," April said, and then saw Lynn calmly shake her head.

"The girl was nearly seven months pregnant when she died. They took her to the county hospital and delivered a stillborn male child. It had the same pumpkin-head as all those others."

April shivered. She was still sitting in the sun, but the story chilled her. She thought at once of Greta swimming alone and half-naked in their pond. She thought of the mountain kids creeping into the farmhouse.

"They're around your place, aren't they? Those inbred kids?" Lynn asked.

"I'd watch them, if I were you," Lynn warned.

"I can take care of myself, Lynn."

"It's not you I was thinking of, April," Lynn answered back. She nodded toward Greta, running across the lawn toward the umbrellas. "I was talking about her."

Thirty-five

Marshall was drunk. He had begun to drink that afternoon, when April and the kids were up at Pearl Peak, and now at dinner he didn't even touch his food. The Scotch made him belligerent, and his mood frightened the children.

"Daddy, you're drunk!" Greta told her father.

"Don't talk back to me, Greta!"

"Marshall, please," April whispered, not meeting his eyes.

"What?"

Oh, God, she thought, it had come to this, fighting in front of the children. It made her feel cheap. Had she set him off last night when she hadn't come back to bed, or was it the attack on Debbie Kinlin that was making him behave like this?

"Your friend drinks, doesn't he? White wine, isn't that right? White wine on the deck?" Marshall taunted April with his questions.

Greta glanced back and forth between her father and April, her eyes wide. No one was eating, not even Timmy.

"Mommy, I don't want this," he announced, pushing away his plate.

"Honey, but you like fried chicken!"

"No I don't. Luke says we shouldn't kill little animals and eat them."

"Sweetheart, it's okay to eat chicken. Luke didn't mean . . ."

"Your friend is just full of good ideas, isn't he, April?" Marshall sipped his Scotch, grinning.

April shot him a glance. She had to just get through the meal, she told herself.

"Okay, honey, eat your mashed potatoes and veggies, okay?" She coaxed him with a smile.

Timmy shook his head. "I'm not hungry."

"Timmy, you're hun . . ."

"Eat, Timmy!" Marshall shouted.

"Marshall, let me deal with this."

"You've not dealing with him. The kid is out of control." Marshall leaned forward across the table and, lowering his voice, demanded: "Eat your chicken, Timmy! Luke doesn't know shit. He couldn't make a buck for himself in the real world."

Timmy started crying and April reached for him, pulled him off the chair and into her arms, then walked with him away from the table.

"Eat your goddamn food!" Marshall shouted after them.

"Enough, Marshall! Enough!" Timmy was sobbing. His

head was buried in her shoulder and both his arms were wrapped tightly around her neck.

"Daddy! Daddy! What's the matter?" Greta, too, was shouting, frightened now by her father.

April carried her son upstairs into his room, closing the door behind her.

"Mommy, I'm scared." His small fingers clung to her sweater.

"You don't have to be scared. Look! You're in your own room. I'm with you. Nothing's going to happen."

"Daddy's mad at me," he whispered, still crying.

"No he isn't. Daddy loves you. Daddy feels sick, honey, that's all. Now, come on, how about a nice hot bath? That'll be fun, won't it?" She kept up her cheery banter as she slipped off his clothes. A bath always helped to get him into his routine.

"I'm hungry," Timmy announced.

"Yes, I know you're hungry. Let's get you into the tub and I'll bring you up a plate of food, okay?"

"I don't want chicken!" He looked up at her, his small face creased with worry.

"No chicken, darling. You don't have to eat chicken."

"Promise?"

"Promise."

Downstairs, there was a crash of furniture.

"What's that?" Timmy asked.

Marshall must have stumbled over something. Oh, dear God, she thought, it was getting worse.

"Timmy, honey, finish undressing. I'll be right back."

"No, Mommy, please. Stay here, please." He patted the bed beside him.

"I have to see if Daddy is okay. Don't worry. I'll be right back." She bent and kissed the top of his head.

Perhaps the sun had done it, April thought, rushing for the stairs. He had sat on the hot deck all afternoon. Sat and drank.

There was another crash and April ran for the stairs. Greta was still downstairs, alone with him. No, April told herself, racing. He won't hurt her, no matter how drunk he is.

She ran into the dining room. Marshall's chair at the head

of the table had been tossed aside. His glass of Scotch was still beside his plate, the ice cubes half-melted. All the settings were in order. The steam from the mashed potatoes rose, visible in the growing shadows.

The dining room was empty. April saw that the deck door was open.

"Marshall? Greta?" April shouted, going for the door.

"Is he gone?" Greta asked. She had followed April onto the porch and stood shivering in the early evening breeze.

"Yes. I don't know. Where were you?"

"In the bathroom. He got me all frightened. He was talking about Mommy. Calling her names and stuff." The girl was crying.

In an effort to seize control, April grasped Greta's shoulders. "Let's go back inside. Why don't you go upstairs and play with Timmy a little while before he takes a bath."

Greta kept nodding, shaking in April's grip.

"What's the matter with Daddy?"

"I don't know, honey. Something terrible happened at the party we went to last night. And your father had to . . . help out. It upset him, I think." She smiled at Greta, feeling better because she was telling her some of the truth. Greta was too old to try and fool.

"Where are you going?" Greta clung to April.

"I'm not sure. I think I should telephone Luke. Tell him Daddy is out there somewhere and ask him to find him."

"Why don't we go look? I'll get my coat." She turned to pull out of April's embrace.

"No!" April held her. "I don't want you going outside." Debbie Kinlin, she was thinking, had wandered off alone into the woods.

"But Daddy . . . he might need us."

"Please, Greta, don't argue with me."

"Why?" She pulled free of April and announced. "I'm going to find Daddy myself!"

"Greta, listen to me! At the party the other night a woman was attacked. She was knifed by someone when she went off alone into the woods." April had Greta's full attention, and she could see fear crossing the child's face as she told her what had happened. "The police don't know who did it. They say it might be one of the Hill People. I don't think it was, but I can't let you go out there alone tonight.''

"Is she dead?" Greta whispered.

"No. She was in shock. That's all I know." April stopped short of telling Greta how the woman had been cut.

"They'll kill Daddy!" Tears filled Greta's eyes. "They'll find him and kill him!" she shouted.

"Greta, they won't." April seized the teenager by the shoulder. "I'm going to call Luke. I'm going to get help, all right?"

Greta nodded slowly.

"I want you to go upstairs and stay with Timmy."

"I want to stay with you, please." She moved closer to April.

"Greta, you'll be all right with Timmy. And he needs someone with him."

"They'll come get us like before. They'll creep into the house and murder us." Her eyes had widened; they were brilliantly blue and glassy, as if she were running a fever.

"Greta, they won't! Please, you're making yourself hysterical. Go upstairs. Get Timmy dressed and we'll run over to Alex's house? Would you like to stay with her tonight?"

The young girl nodded slowly.

"Go upstairs and help Timmy with his bath. I'll be right back. Promise." April smiled.

"Where are you going?"

"To get Luke to help us," April answered, lying to her stepdaughter as she hurried off the deck. She had to keep Luke and Marshall away from each other, April knew. It made her nervous just to think what might happen between them, especially with Marshall being so irritable. Maybe they should go off to Paris for a short vacation when Greta returned to California. She had to do something, April realized, to help her husband through this appeals case, to help him relax. A house in the country obviously was not the answer.

April circled the pond and walked through the woods, down toward Luke's cabin. She saw Luke working in his small vegetable garden behind the log cabin and she debated a moment about asking if he had seen Marshall, but she didn't want to involve him in her problem with Marshall.

Also, Ann's story about Julia Stonequest had upset her. She would bring it up, she knew, and quiz him about the inbreds. She knew he would have a plausible explanation; he always did when it came to defending the Hill People.

She also didn't want to talk to Luke because of what Lynn had implied about him being interested in Greta. She knew Luke found Greta attractive, but she had refused to believe it meant anything more. Now, as she walked into the dark woods, she wondered if she had been simply fooling herself. She remembered how he'd said fourteen wasn't too young to marry in the mountains.

She walked past the patch of white birch trees that Luke had felled earlier in the summer and cut into firewood. Several cords were still stacked in the clearing, but he had not cut down more trees and she was thankful for that. At least he was now doing what Marshall told him.

Beyond the birch trees, the deer path dropped down suddenly, following the edge of a dry mountain stream. Ahead of her, April saw that the night had already closed off the valley, and the long lovely shadows that were stretched across the back lawn, here looked dark and dangerous. She stopped walking, and felt the edges of fear grabbing at her self-control.

She was being silly, April told herself. She had only told Greta about Debbie Kinlin because she didn't want the child going off into the woods and seeing her father when he had had too much to drink. But she had frightened herself, April realized.

And that was just being stupid. She knew where she was in the woods, and Luke was less than two thousand yards away. She could call for him, if she needed help. Determined now to keep from panicking, she forced herself to keep walking, to go down the path and into the darkening valley. She had to find Marshall before he hurt himself.

She came out of the woods at Secret Lake and the lost village. There were a few ruined walls of the old town close to the water, but the wildflowers and bushes had claimed them. April stopped at the edge of the trees and looked around, scanned the banks of the small lake that was not much bigger than their own pond on the ridge, but here in the cool, dark evening, was already shrouded with valley mist. It took her a moment, peering hard into the dark fog, before she realized that Marshall was there, too, ahead of her in the clearing.

He was sitting on one of the walls looking away from her. One leg was propped up on the rock wall, and he had hooked his arm around his knee. His head was bent forward, resting on his arm. She could not see his face and she wondered if his eyes were closed, if he were sleeping.

She thought of calling to him, or perhaps just walking over, but both gestures seemed like an intrusion. He was all right, she realized. She had been alarmed over nothing. Let him stay by himself for a little while and cool off, she thought, now that she knew he was safe.

She stepped quietly back from the clearing, not wanting to be found out. She turned toward the path, and then she realized Marshall wasn't alone. He was talking to someone hidden from her behind the ruins.

She moved away from the path and circled the clearing, keeping herself hidden in the trees, but stepping over to where she could see around the edge of the embankment and spot Marshall's companions. Nine of the inbreds were clustered there by the lakeside, looking up at her husband, talking to him. To April, they looked mean and vicious, like a pack of dogs when they have been starved and brutalized by keepers.

They were going to attack Marshall, she thought next. They had cornered him in the woods and were about to pounce on him. She started to scream, to alert Luke, to cry for help, when Marshall's voice suddenly rose above the others. He was shaking his fist at them, shouting.

"I tell you what to do and when. It's us against them. We'll blast the whole damn bunch!"

The dwarfs shouted back: "Kill them! Kill them!"

"You just leave Luke. I want him."

"Pearl Peak," one of the dwarfs shouted, and the others answered again, "Kill them. Kill them."

"Marshall!" April couldn't listen to any more. She ran to

her husband, ran through the long grass and the underbrush, ran out of the gathering mist.

Seeing her, the Hill People scattered. Marshall came at her, jumping through the grass, as if he wanted to stop her from getting too close, from finding out too much.

"What in God's name is happening?" she demanded, reaching him.

"Why are you following me?" He seized her shoulders as if she were an errant child, and she could smell the liquor on his breath.

"Marshall, stop!" April broke loose from his grip. "I wasn't following you; I was looking for you." She rubbed her arm muscles, teary from the pain. "You've had too much to drink. I was worried. . . ."

"Goddammit, I own half a mountainside in the Catskills and I can't even get away from you."

"I'm sorry. I didn't know you wanted to get away from me." She backed off, and then demanded. "Why were you talking to these people?"

Marshall came after her, hissing, "You didn't see anything."

"What do you mean?"

He seized her shoulders and stuck his face in hers. "You didn't see them! Don't you go telling your goddamn lover."

"You're hurting me, Marshall. Please," she whispered, crying, "let go of me."

"I wasn't talking to them, do you hear?"

"What's the matter with you?" She whimpered with pain.

He let go, shoving her away.

"Marshall? Talk to me, please," she begged. His face looked as it had the night of the party, after he'd seen Debbie Kinlin. His eyes had narrowed in his face, and his cheeks were drawn tight, as if he were trying to hold something inside himself. April forced herself to touch him, to make contact, and he jerked free of her, twisting from her fingers.

"Marshall, I'm going to leave you alone," she told him gently, afraid now to ask too many questions.

"Good! Don't come snooping after me." He stepped closer and she couldn't stop herself from backing off. She was afraid of him, she suddenly realized. She saw the rage in his eyes, saw the way his skin tightened and twisted his face out of shape. "Leave me alone," he told her. "Leave me alone."

"I will," she answered. "I will." She turned and started to walk away, then broke into a run, wanting to get out of the valley, wanting to get away from her husband.

As he watched her leave, Marshall felt a breeze, a cool breeze from deep in the dark valley. It cooled him and made him feel better. He stood alone on the deer path looking after his wife, remembering how he had just spoken to her, shouting at her.

What was the matter, he asked himself, as if thinking about a stranger, some madman that he might pass on a city street. Why was he doing this? Why was he upbraiding his wife. He didn't want to do it, but he couldn't help himself. It was because of them. They pushed him. They made him do it. He reached out with his arm as if to call her back, to comfort her, to tell her it was all wrong, all a mistake, but he couldn't speak, his words choked in his throat and he gasped. He could no longer stop himself, and he stared at his upraised arm, and saw that the buck knife was already open in his trembling fingers.

April ran all the way to the house, ran without glancing back to see if Marshall was chasing her, ran without seeing if Luke was still working in his garden, ran because she was afraid of being in the woods.

When she reached the deck, she stopped, put her hands on her hips and bent over, exhausted and out of breath. It took her a few minutes before she was able to talk, and then she went into her office and flipped on the desk light.

She saw Jim Galvin's letter on top of a stack of her mail. Marshall had not told her when she came back from Pearl Peak that she had mail, and as she dialed the Grossman number, she opened the envelope with her fingernail.

"Hello? Hello?"

April heard Lynn Grossman's voice, but she needed to take another deep breath before she could speak.

"Who's this?" Lynn asked, sounding annoyed.

"Lynn! It's me. April Benard. I'm sorry, I know it's

terribly late, but would it be possible to have Greta spend the night at your place, with Alex? I told her about Debbie Kinlin, and, well, it just freaked her out." She glanced again at Jim's note and scanned the first paragraph.

"Of course it's not too late. Alex would love having her. And bring that husband of yours. We'll all go for a swim."

"I don't know if I can get Marshall to break away," April said vaguely. "We'll see. But thank you for taking Greta. She'll feel much better with Alex. I'm thinking now that I'll take everyone down to the city tomorrow for a few days. Marshall has to fly back to the coast, and . . ." her voice trailed off. She could not think of what more to say to Lynn Grossman.

"April, are you okay?" Lynn asked, and then said quickly, "I'm sorry we upset you this afternoon, talking about Julia Stonequest. Look, I'm sure it'll turn out not to have been anyone local after all. Maybe it was a drifter. One of those people who come up here to pick fruit."

"Yes, I'm sure you're right. I'm not upset . . . just haggard from dealing with this teenager."

"Of course. Come on over, I'll take her off your hands. See you soon. 'Bye."

April replaced the telephone receiver but did not move from her chair. She was staring at her student's letter, reading it slowly and carefully, reading it for a second time, and concentrating on what her student had discovered in her computer files.

DATELINE NEW YORK CITY

Dear Professor,

Your humble and obedient serf has faithfully done your assignment of keyboarding the ledger material of one Ms Anita Rotherham as well as all those names from the county files. That giant conglomerate, known affectionately as Columbia University, now owes me a grand total of two hundred and twenty bucks! (Should I go harass them, or wait until you return to the bright lights of uptown Harlem?? Please advise.)

As for the material. You'll notice this note

comes sans printouts. I am having the box forwarded by UPS. First class would have cost an arm and a leg! So . . .

The big news—in case you can't wait—is that when I ran all the historical facts, i.e., county records dating from the 1830s, and the new names from Rotherham's ledger, the computer spit out a name that was new to our base collection. I went back into the files again—those you had gotten from the old Court House in the county—and found it recorded in those records. The surname is Boyd, and it just disappears from any of the county records around the 1900s.

What gives? I thought the Tassels, Holts and Granges were the key families among the inbreds. Maybe I made a mistake somewhere. Call me if you have questions. I'll be sunning myself in Weston until the end of the month.

Your most faithful servant,
James

P.S. If you need me, I can drive up to the Catskills in a couple hours. No problem. Just howl. Have computer, will travel!

Marshall's great-great-grandmother's name was Boyd. No, she told herself. It didn't mean anything. It didn't mean anything at all. The name had to be a mistake, she told herself. A computer glitch. She was being paranoid and irrational. After all, the Boyds had lived in White Plains, not upstate New York. The last Boyd had died two hundred miles from Mad River Mountain. She had to keep thinking like a scientist, and she tossed the letter aside and went to get the children.

Thirty-six

Lynn Grossman waited for her husband to fall asleep before she stripped off her clothes and went out to the pool to swim. If he saw her naked now, after he'd had too much to drink, she knew he'd want to make love, and she didn't want to. At least not with him. She stood poised at the deep edge of the pool and mentally drew up another list of possible lovers. She had several lists. One for the City—men she saw in Manhattan, men who worked with her husband. Another list was from television: Don Johnson, Dan Rather. And then she had her country list.

Luke Grange was at the top of that one. She wondered if April Benard was making it with him. It wasn't fair, she thought. It was all that blond hair and peachy skin. She hated April Benard for her assurance and poise.

Well, there was April's husband, Lynn thought next, trying to be positive. She hadn't made love to a real WASP since college. She'd have to move fast, though, or Ann O'Malley would have him in the sack before the end of the summer. That little hustler, Lynn thought, angry at the thought of her best friend getting the jump on her. She dove into the lighted turquoise pool.

The water froze her nipples and chilled her flesh, and she swam fast to warm up, doing two quick laps before she turned on her back and opened her eyes.

Often on summer nights like this one, when the sky was brilliant with stars, she'd float in the dark pool and remember summers in Vermont, when she would swim out into Lake Champlain to meet Tony Clark and smoke dope and make love on the barrel float.

Lynn smiled at the memory and then realized that she

hadn't yet taken Alex to the doctor's for her yearly checkup. She made a promise to herself to do it next week when they were back in the City. Then she turned again and with slow, steady strokes began to do her nightly laps.

He stood at the edge of the trees, waiting and watching. He wanted to be sure her husband didn't come out of the house and follow her into the pool. He had watched her strip naked, watched as she came across the lawn to the lighted pool, watched when she paused at the deep end, with the wavy blueish water lights fanning her body. He had smiled, thinking of what he would do to her. Anticipation was the best part, he thought, thinking again of how he had waited for Debbie Kinlin, then remembered with glee the terror in her eyes. He had to make sure he saw her eyes, this one's eyes, he told himself. He had to see the fright in her face.

He slipped out of his loafers, pulled off his pants and shorts, and was surprised to see he had an erection. Perhaps he should fuck her first, he thought. No, he didn't long to make love to the woman. All he wanted, he realized now in the hidden passion of his heart, was to see her fear, to know that this bitch was terrified by the sight of him, by what he was going to do to her.

She was in the middle of the pool when he reached the water and he carefully eased down, gasping at the shock of cold water on his naked body. Knowing what he was going to do was making his body temperature drop, and that puzzled him. He was not a hot-blooded killer then, he thought, grinning at the crazy notions that popped into his head.

He was having fun, he realized. For the first time in his life, he was really having fun, and he dove deep into the pool so he could come up from below and grab Lynn Grossman.

She felt his hand on her pubic hair.

"Sam!" she shouted, furious.

But it wasn't her husband.

"You! What a nice surprise." She grinned and seeing that he too was naked, swam into his arms, rubbed her body along the length of him, giving him the pleasure of all of her.

"Have you ever done it in a swimming pool?" he whispered, teasing.

She smiled, shaking her head, thrilled at how excited she had become when she realized it was him in her pool. "No," she said, and licked the inside of his ear as she linked her arms around his neck. "But I'd love to do it with you."

She was still grinning with anticipation when he slit her throat.

She never said a word. She couldn't even utter a scream. Her body jerked. Her legs kicked. She splashed in the water, gasping for air as her blood and breath mixed and bubbled out of her mouth and neck. Twisting and turning, she flipped over and sank in the deep pool, settled at the bottom for a few minutes until her lungs filled with chlorinated water, and then she rose swiftly to the top, and like a fishing bob, popped up into the cold night air.

He swam away from her, to the edge of the pool, and pulled himself out in a quick jerk. Then he glanced toward the woods and waved. The cousins came out of the trees, running across the freshly cut lawn and across the stone terrace, ran to the unlocked sliding back door and slipped inside the house.

They kept coming, a half dozen small, wiry men and boys, all fast on their feet. They carried knives and claw hammers, bits and pieces of old junk from abandoned cars and trucks, the wrecks of automobiles that had been driven into the hills and pushed over cliffs, left to rot in the woods. They swept through the house, finding Sam Grossman asleep in a drunken stupor in the living room. Someone hit the side of his head with an axe, smashing his brains against the arm of the blue upholstered wing chair.

Alex was next. She was in bed, listening to Madonna on her headphones, when her locked door gave way. She screamed for her parents, but her mother floated stone white in the family pool and her father lay slumped over in the living room chair, his bloated tongue sticking out of his mouth.

Swarming all over her, they fought among themselves for the first chance. They stripped her and tossed her back onto the water bed, bouncing up and down, laughing, delighting among themselves as they fucked her back and forth, two at a time, sodomizing her as if she were one of their farm animals.

Then they butchered her.

* * *

"Damn it!" April swore under her breath as she stopped the Volvo in the middle of the mountain road. She was lost, completely and totally. She should not have tried to take a short cut, not at night, not with the children, and not, she tried to keep herself from thinking, with an unknown slasher somewhere on Mad River Road.

"Are we lost?" Greta asked, peering into the darkness.

"I know where we are," Timmy said from the backseat. He jumped up and, leaning forward, pointed into the darkness. "Just go ahead, Mommy. We'll find it."

April flipped on the reading light to look at the map, trying to get her bearings. All the lines on the map were narrow and faint. She couldn't be sure if they were country roads or cross-country ski trails.

She looked up again and tried to see the lights of the house through the trees. Maybe Timmy was right. But she couldn't see anything.

"Damn it!" she said again, louder. And then she saw the men. They came out of the trees, down into the shallow ditch, and kept walking, crossing the road and disappearing into the trees and underbrush on the other side. They were not running exactly, but their movements were fast and deliberate. Fleeing seemed more like it, she thought.

There might have been a dozen of them, she guessed, men and boys. They crossed in front of the car, their pumpkin-heads shiny in the glaring headlights.

"Oh, God, look at them!" Greta cried.

April reached across the front seat to lock the car doors, and when she looked up again, they were gone. They had slipped into the dark woods, melting into the underbrush like animals.

She hit the gas pedal and the heavy Volvo skidded on the gravel and roared off. She reached a slight rise in the road before she brought the car back under her control. Ahead, she saw the lights of the Grossman house.

She took a deep breath and raced ahead, relieved that she was safe now.

"I want you two to stay here in the car, understand?" April said. "Greta, lock this door behind me."

"No, I don't want to stay," Greta cried and immediately Timmy tried to open the back door.

"Listen, both of you! Stay here. I'll be right back." Before they could protest more, she ran up to the house and knocked hard on the door. When no one answered, she edged over to the front windows and peered inside. Sam Grossman was sleeping in front of the fireplace.

April tapped the glass with her ring, then shouted, "Sam!" He didn't stir.

April stepped to the edge of the porch and looked across the yard. Lights from the back of the house made the lawn look wet. She could hear faint voices and she listened hard, straining to catch the sound. It was a radio, she realized with relief. Of course. Lynn was out back swimming. She jumped off the porch and walked around the side of the house.

The moon had cleared the mountain ridge, and the pool lights were on. The ghostly blue lights looked like a landing pad for a spaceship, April thought, hurrying to greet her friend.

"Hello, Lynn? We're here. Sorry to take so long. I got us lost." She spoke up as she approached, not wanting to shock Lynn by coming at her from out of the darkness.

Lynn turned over in the water as April reached the edge of the pool.

"I hope this isn't too much trouble, taking Greta in for the night...." April stopped talking and stood perfectly still, staring down at the water. The filter pump was gently pushing Lynn Grossman across the pool, edging her from one end to the next, as if even in death, she was doing laps in her own blood.

Thirty-seven

Ann O'Malley slipped to the bottom of the bed, wedged herself between Jim's legs and slowly, deliberately, began to work on him. She hated having him come like this, but it was the only way she knew to get him interested. They hadn't made love since the Benard's party, and then, she knew, it was only because Jim was enraged that she had gone off swimming nude with Marshall. Ann smiled in the bedroom darkness, thinking of Marshall and how he had reached for her in the deep water of the pond. She shivered with delight at the memory and plunged back into her task.

"Hey, what was that?" Jim said, pulling up.

"What was what?" Ann mumbled, annoyed.

"I heard something out back. Must be the damn raccoons." Jim shifted on the bed and hugged his puffed-up pillow.

"That's not raccoons," Ann whispered, sitting up herself. She was familiar with the noisy scuffle they made while scavenging in the trash cans. This sound was more subtle, as if someone were opening something carefully.

Ann slid up beside her husband and whispered in his ear, "Jim, someone's in the house!"

"No, they're not, Ann. Come on, aren't we going to have some fun here?" He rolled over on the bed and eyed her, but Ann was looking toward the closed bedroom door.

"I want you to go check the kitchen."

"Ann, give me a break, will you? I've been on my feet all day. I played eighteen holes, and I got a nine o'clock tee off tomorrow. Come on, if you don't want to do it, okay, then let's hit the sack."

"I can't sleep, Jim, not if I think someone's in the house."

"Maybe it's one of Nanci's boyfriends, that little jerk, what's-his-name." He was mumbling again, slipping off to sleep.

Ann lay perfectly still, listening. Nanci wouldn't try anything this risky, she told herself. She wouldn't dare. And then to relieve her tension, she slipped out of bed, cracked open the door, and listened.

Someone was in the kitchen. She heard footsteps on the tile floor, then whispering. That little brat, she thought, angry at her teenage daughter. Slipping on her silk nightgown, she walked quickly through the house, thankful that the hallway was carpeted, so she could sneak up on them without being heard.

She didn't see him at all when she came out of the downstairs hallway, just felt her arm being caught and then a palm over her mouth, muffling her voice. When she saw who it was, he took away his hand and smiled.

"Well, isn't this a surprise," she whispered, staying exactly where she was, with her breasts pressed against his wet shirt. "Is this a social visit, or do you have something naughty in mind?" Where could they go, she wondered. Where could they go and make love without waking her husband?

He kept smiling.

He was drunk. She could smell the liquor and his sweat, but she didn't mind. It was better with some men when they drank.

"Well?" she whispered, waiting. To encourage him, she nudged closer. "Do you want to go outside and play?"

"How about here," he whispered and, still smiling, he shifted his body slightly, as if to free his right hand. He jabbed the kitchen knife into the silk of her nightgown, catching her low in the abdomen, and pulled the long blade up, rending the sheer fabric and her soft flesh in one easy motion. She gasped at the shock of pain, staring up at him with the startled look of someone who realized she had just made a terrible mistake, then she slipped off the edge of the long kitchen knife and hit the deep pile carpet with a solid thud.

He stepped over her body, walking carelessly through the rush of blood that quickly soaked the rug, and went to the front door. He unlocked it to let the others in, snapping his fingers at Willy the Weeper and Beer Mouth as they rushed for the daughters' room. He waved them away. He wanted the girls himself. He hadn't had his chance with the Grossman girl. There had been nothing left of her when he reached the bedroom. There were all crazy, he knew, all the others. None of them were normal, not anymore, and he took a strange comfort in that fact, as if he were no longer responsible for what he was doing to these city people. He couldn't help himself. None of them could help themselves.

At the end of the hallway, he opened the door, stood

silently to make sure the teenagers were asleep, then stepped inside and closed the door behind him. The air conditioner was humming and that made it easier for him. He could walk across the room without a sound. He was glad they were like that, that they brought all their creature comforts to the country. It made it easier to kill them.

He stood above the bed, looking at them. The girls' breathing was deep and even. The thin mountain air made them all sleep soundly; it exhausted them to be out of doors and in the sun all day.

He waited, listening for a scream, some sound from downstairs, but the steady drone of the air conditioner concealed the house noises. He reached down to pull off the top sheet from one of the twins. She was wearing a white T-shirt that said in pink letters across her small chest, I'M A VILLAGE GIRL, and under that were Bloomingdale's pink panties. She had her legs curled up, hugging herself in the air-conditioned cold.

He grinned. She was so cute, he thought, watching her. She reminded him of Greta.

Her legs were not as long as Greta's, nor as lovely, and she was not as developed, but she was still a woman, a lovely young woman. He sat down softly on the edge of the bed so as not to disturb her or her sister. In the semidarkness he looked longingly at the girl, building up his desire, his lust, and trying to decide if he should kill her first, and then make love to her. It would be nice, he thought, to snuff out her life, to choke off her breath, and then to play with her body while she was still warm. He didn't know what to do, but then she woke up, reaching for the top sheet in the cold.

When she saw his dark shadow, she screamed and rolled away, desperately shouting for help. He smashed her face, breaking her jaw, and then as she tried to scurry away, he kicked out and caught her in the spine with the heel of his hiking boot, already soaked with her mother's blood. He broke her back. The child was dead before she hit the floor.

Then he grabbed her sister.

Thirty-eight

April unlocked the front door of the farmhouse and rushed the two children inside, then locked the door behind her. "Go upstairs, Greta, and lock Timmy and yourself inside your room."

"They'll come get me. Those pumpkin-heads," Greta said, crying.

"No they won't. I've locked all the doors. Please, Greta! I need your help." She maneuvered the girl toward the stairs. Timmy, too, had begun to cry, frightened by the urgency in his mother's voice. He clung to April's leg. "Stay with Greta," she said, peeling him loose from her leg. "Go lock yourselves in your room."

"Mommy, what's happening?"

"Please, Timmy. I don't have time. . . ." She needed to telephone the police, but she wanted to make the call from Luke's cabin so Greta wouldn't hear what she had to say.

April shut the stairway door and prayed that Greta would stay upstairs. Then she slipped out the side door and ran down off the deck. She had to get Luke.

On the path beyond the pond she ran out of breath and slowed to a walk, her heart pounding more from fear than from exertion. She heard everything in the woods. The squish of her rubber-soled Reeboks. The cracking of branches as the night cooled. Dry leaves rustling, being blown by gusts of wind, or small animals running from the sound of her on the deer path.

Once April moved beyond the lights of the house, her eyes adjusted to the blackness. But being able to see in the dark frightened her even more. The edge of the path was all

217

shadows. There was nothing to fear, she kept telling herself. Nothing to fear between the farmhouse and Luke's cabin. She had made the walk dozens of times before.

Of course she was lying to herself. The Hill People were out there, somewhere. They could be following her even now. She glanced around and imagined a dozen creatures hiding in the shadows, surrounding her on the thin deer path. Then, too frightened to look again, she burst into a mad run, spurred on by the strength of her fear.

She ran from the woods, down the slope and across the open front lawn. She ran to the lights of Luke's house and burst into the log cabin.

Luke was sitting reading in a deep armchair. Bob Dylan's raspy voice filled the room. It was all so peaceful that she felt she had stepped into another world.

"Luke," she said, out of breath from running. "They're killing people!" She leaned against a chair, exhausted.

Luke came to his feet.

"It's okay, April," he said at once, moving toward her, trying to calm her down. "Everything is okay," he whispered.

"The Hill People," April rushed on. "They killed Lynn Grossman . . . her husband. I just came from Pearl Peak." In bursts of sentences, she told him how she had seen a dozen of the Tassel and Holt boys on the road, and then found Lynn Grossman floating in her own blood.

"It's not just the Hill People," Luke said quietly, taking her into his arms.

April pulled back to look into Luke's eyes. She was afraid of what he was going to tell her.

"Marshall," Luke whispered.

"Oh, please, no," she cried, shaking her head. "Please don't tell me that."

"He's one of us. A kin." Luke slipped down into a kitchen chair and stared at her. "Tyler, the old guy you met in the village. He guessed it, once he got a look at Marshall."

"Boyd," April whispered.

"You've heard of the Boyds?" Luke asked.

April nodded slowly. "I just heard about them. . . . And I know Marshall was related way back."

"The Boyds are distant cousins of mine. We're all related way back. How did you find out?"

She told him then about the computer readout, how her student had found the name in the old courthouse records, and how it had appeared again in Anita Rotherham's ledger.

In a moment of silence, April heard Dylan singing. Then, quietly, as if speaking to herself, April murmured, "Of course. Everyone is kin. Kin of kin. But my husband hates you. And your cousins."

"He's afraid of us, sure. He hated this place from the beginning, but he didn't know why. I didn't either until I started checking. The last Boyd to live in the mountains was Marshall's great-great-grandmother. She left Mad River in 1897 and went down to work in Kingston. She married a French Canadian river captain by the name of Benard in 1902. It's all in the Kingston Court House records. I checked it myself two weeks ago."

"It's my fault. He didn't want to buy this property," April said softly. "Something was telling him it was wrong, but I wanted the house. I wanted to be close for my goddamn research." She started to cry, realizing what she'd done. The same theory that she offered her students was being proven in her very own family. And there was nothing she could do to change things. "They're all out of control, Luke. They've all gone mad. The hills are full of killers. But why?" She stared at Luke without seeing him, trying to figure out what had set her husband off.

"We did it, April. Marshall knows about us. We set him off by having an affair."

"We couldn't have!"

"We did." He stared back at April, and then went on, "Marshall doesn't lose in life, does he? Everything he's ever done has been a success. You don't get where he is in a New York law firm unless you're pretty ruthless. People are afraid of him in New York, aren't they? I've seen his kind up here in the mountains. They walk around like they own the place, and all of us."

"He might be that way in the City," April answered defensively. "But this is the country..."

"That's right. But in the country we feud. Well, Marshall Benard has done us one better."

"But the others followed him! Why? You haven't explained why they're helping him."

"They've been waiting for him, April. They knew who Marshall was as soon as you moved up here. We may have driven Marshall over the edge, but that gang, they were waiting for him." Luke stepped around April and flipped off the wall switch. One small light remained lit in the room, near the chair where Luke had been sitting.

"Stay here," he told her, gently resting his hand on her shoulder, "I heard something." He returned to the armchair and slid down into the soft cushions, spotlighted by the reading lamp.

"Luke!" April whispered, stunned by what he was doing. Another wave of choking fear caught her throat.

"Shhhhh."

"You can't! Luke, please," she begged. "Come with me. Up to the house."

"It's better that I'm here," he said, turning a page.

"You're sitting in the light. You want to get killed?"

"He's a lousy shot with that A-Bolt." Luke looked up. "I'm not going to get myself killed, April. If he's after me, then let him come get me."

April realized then that Marshall hadn't shot any of his victims. He had used a knife, as if he were a mugger in the City, attacking women on dark stairways. She thought of Debbie Kinlin and her mutilated breasts, and of Lynn Grossman and how she had looked, floating in her own blood. "Oh, dear God," she whispered, turning toward the door.

"Where are you going?"

"To my children." April opened the door and stepped into the night. The shotgun blast blew out the porch light beside her head.

Luke hit her from behind, buckled her knees with his tackle, and knocked her off the porch. They fell together into the front yard and rolled over, into the high grass and berrybushes at the edge of the yard. April felt the prick of needles on her cheeks. She was face down against the bare ground and her back hurt from where Luke had slammed her.

"Luke!" she cried and he clamped her mouth with his palm. Then, slipping one arm around her waist, he hauled her deeper into the trees. He was running, struggling with her awkward weight. She could hear his panting, but he didn't slow. She turned in his grasp and hit him. He let go of her mouth to cup her swinging fist.

She screamed then.

Another shotgun blast burst over their heads. She could hear men shouting to each other, and see the thin beams of flashlights sweeping through the branches.

"Shut up, goddammit!" Luke whispered savagely. "You'll get us both killed." The branches whipped her face and cut her skin. She cried and turned her face into his chest and let him carry her away.

They crossed a creek. April heard Luke's bare feet splash through the water. In the trees beyond the creek he stopped, sank to the ground, and dropped her. They lay together on the damp ground. April could feel moss at the base of a tree and she pulled herself up against it and turned around. Her chest hurt from Luke's grip and it took her a few minutes before she could even whisper.

"He was going to kill me."

"That wasn't your husband." Luke was crouched down on one knee, watching the trees at the top of the ledge.

"What?"

"Keep your voice down. Do you want to give them another chance at you?"

April grabbed the sleeve of his wool shirt. "What are you talking about?"

Luke slid down next to her at the base of the tree. His face was inches away.

"That wasn't your husband taking potshots at us. Your husband has a rifle; that was a shotgun."

"Who? Why?" She squeezed Luke's arm, afraid to let go.

"It happens up here whenever there's trouble. If a girl gets pregnant, or someone is killed during hunting season, we're the ones who pay. The locals come up to Mad River Mountain looking for us."

"Debbie Kinlin isn't a local girl!" She was still whispering, but the urgency of her voice made it sound loud and sharp.

"Look at that town. What's keeping it alive? You city people. If you weren't up here purchasing property, buying all those goddamn useless antiques they sell at the firehouse auctions, this area would go under. Without city people, the income in town is welfare and unemployment checks."

Luke stopped speaking and cocked his head, listening to the wind. April kept quiet. All she could hear was creek water rushing across the rocks, and in the far distance men's voices, fading.

"They're gone," he said finally, standing.

"But why were they shooting at me? Or you—they know you didn't hurt Debbie."

"They know I'm the one who helps everyone, keeps them together. Come on, let's get out of here." He turned toward the woods again. "We'll make a circle and come around by way of the barn."

"I've got to call the sheriff."

"No. No sheriff!" Luke grabbed her arm.

"Luke, I have to call him. I have to tell him about the Grossmans."

"The sheriff is related to half the people in this town. He's no better than the rest. Keep him away from us!"

"But I have to tell him Marshall is killing these people."

"No," Luke answered back. "Marshall is one of us." April could not see his face in the darkness. His shadowy body hovered above her. "Your husband has gotten control of my cousins. The Tassel and Holt boys have always done what I told them. They were afraid of me, and they needed me, too, to deal with the city people and get them jobs. Now Marshall has somehow turned them against me, turned them loose on the city people, which is what some of those kids have always wanted. Well, your husband is my problem now, not the sheriff's. He's caused the killings and I'm going to kill him."

Thirty-nine

When they came out of the wood, April and Luke spotted the sheriff's car parked in front of the house. The interior light was turned on and there was a man sitting in the driver's seat. Another man was approaching the front porch.

April started toward them, but Luke pulled her back for a moment into the shadows. "Look—he may know about the killings already and he's come to warn you. Go talk to him. Don't say anything, just listen. If he asks about Marshall, tell him he went for a walk or something. You don't know where he is. I'll go around back and wake Timmy and Greta. Get them out of the house and down to my place."

"Why? What for?"

"They'll be safer there, especially if the cousins come looking for Greta."

"They want Greta?"

"They want you both," Luke answered, then gave her a nudge. "Now go talk to the sheriff."

"Mrs. Benard?" the man asked as April came across the lawn. He was wearing a suit, but it was too small for his frame and he looked stuffed, like a badly made sausage. His badge was pinned to the suit's wide lapel.

"Yes?" April said, glancing past him, noticing that the other cop had stepped out of the parked patrol car. He was holding a rifle in one hand.

"Mrs. Benard, my name is Wirth. Sheriff Joe Wirth. Is your husband here?"

"Why?" April asked, stalling. It would take Luke a few minutes to circle the house and wake the children.

"Mrs. Benard, there have been several attacks..."

"Yes, I know," April said nervously.

"You know?" The Sheriff stopped talking.

"Yes... Debbie Kinlin. My husband told me."

"Mrs. Benard, that's why I'd like to speak with your husband. I have a few questions."

"My husband isn't here."

"Do you know where he is, ma'am?"

April shook her head. "He went for a walk earlier...."

"Ma'am, I hate to tell you this, but your husband has been implicated."

"Implicated? What do you mean? By whom?"

"Implicated by Miss Kinlin. She recovered enough a couple of hours ago to give us a statement. According to her it was your husband who knifed her." He spoke softly, trying to lessen the impact of the news.

"My husband helped that woman. He didn't hurt her," April answered back.

"There's been another attack... a few hours ago," the big man kept speaking softly, watching for her reaction. "A family named Grossman."

"Yes?"

"They were all murdered, I'm afraid. Do you know them? They were city people."

April nodded. "Yes...I...We knew them...slightly..." She glanced up at the house and wondered where Luke was. Perhaps it was a mistake not to tell the sheriff what she already knew. If this were the city, she knew, she would have told the police everything and let them handle it.

"We need to speak with your husband, ma'am." The sheriff was quiet but insistent.

April crossed her arms, feeling cold. "I told you my husband isn't here."

The sheriff nodded, then glancing over at the other police officer. "If I were you, ma'am, I'd think about going into the city for a few days; so far it's only summer people that have been attacked."

April nodded.

"If you like, Mrs. Benard, I could send a man out here. Someone from town, you know, who could guard the place.

You might feel better if you had a man around the place.
You never know . . ."

"No. I'll . . . we'll be okay." She backed away from the
sheriff and glanced nervously across the lawn to the trees as
if half expecting to see Marshall hiding there.

"Sheriff, I think you need to know something else."

He nodded and waited for her to continue. When she
didn't, he moved to one side so the car's interior light might
shine on her face. When he did, he saw her fear.

"He's one of them, Sheriff."

"What's that, ma'am?" The big man stepped closer to
hear her soft voice.

"My husband, Sheriff. He's one of them."

"An inbred?"

"Yes."

"Jesus Christ," he swore. "I'll be . . . Mrs. Benard, if
he's one of them, if he's on Mad River Mountain, it might
take us all summer to find him."

"No, he's going to come out of the woods tonight."

"Why?"

"He's going to come to get me."

The sheriff studied her for a moment. "If you think that,
Mrs. Benard, you'd better leave."

"No," was all she said.

"Then I'd better leave this officer here." He waved to the
other man in the police car, beckoning him over.

"No," she said. She still had her arms crossed, wrapped
tightly in front of her, as if she were freezing there on the
warm summer night. "He'll never come near, not if he sees
you. You have to leave."

"Lady, I can't leave you here like fish bait," the sheriff
protested.

"Then he'll go somewhere else, kill more people. Do you
want that, Sheriff?" she asked. "By morning, you'll have a
dozen murdered."

"Lady, but . . ."

"I know what I'm doing."

"I'll leave Slim with his shotgun." He turned toward his
waiting deputy.

April shook her head. She knew what she had to do.

Timmy and Greta were out of the farmhouse by now, and it was up to her to draw Marshall from the woods. It was her fault. It was she who had brought him back to the Catskills.

"Leave me," she told the sheriff. "If he's out there watching, he'll come to the house. Give me ten minutes alone in the farmhouse and then come back. If he hasn't come by then, I'll leave with you."

The sheriff studied April Benard. The look of fear had disappeared from her face. She returned his stare boldly, "I know what I'm doing."

"Ten minutes," he said, eyeing his watch. "Do you want a shotgun?"

"I have a rifle," she said. "My husband's."

The sheriff's car drove slowly away, April watched it disappear down the country road, the red rear lights dimming in the distance. When it was gone, when she could hear again the sounds of woods, the rustle of leaves in the tall maple trees, she turned from the road and went up the front steps and into the house.

Marshall had kept away from the house, stayed crouched inside the barn door and listened to April talk to the police. The kids he had already tied up, with tape across their mouths, then dumped in the cellar. The girl had screamed when he grabbed her in the dark hallway, and bit into his thumb. He'd had to hit her twice to shut her up and when he slapped the tape across her mouth, she stared up at him, her eyes wild. He wondered whose girl she was.

When the sheriff had driven off, he sat down on the stone floor to sort out his mind. Three of the cousins were with him, and they, too, squatted in the dark of the barn, watching and waiting for him to tell them what to do. They glanced at each other, grinning with anticipation.

Marshall looked over at the cousins. He could smell their breath, their unwashed bodies. They smelled like pig shit, he thought, or cattle dung, when you stepped on a dry pie and broke through the crust, and got a strong, rich whiff. He grinned. They were his, he thought with satisfaction, and they would do what he told them, and that made him immensely happy. He had never felt better in his life. This was fun, he thought. He reached over and affectionately squeezed the knotty shoulder of Beer Mouth, then whispered, "The sheriff. That sheriff and his boy. Let's go get the two of them."

"I want her," Beer Mouth said. He motioned to the dwarf crouched beside Marshall, "Me and Nick, we almost had her once."

"You said we could have her," Nick added, standing anxious to get going.

Marshall grinned. "Okay, she's yours," he told them.

Marshall was out there, April knew. She felt him watching her. She remembered that when they had first started seeing each other, he would just sit and watch her as she cooked dinner, or sat reading quietly in a chair on a rainy afternoon. She would glance up and see him staring at her from across the room. She had laughed at him, embarrassed, and he had innocently admitted he couldn't get enough of her, that he was a starved man when he was in sight of her.

She closed the front door and stood perfectly still and listened to the house. Earlier in the day she had opened the downstairs windows, and now the night breeze off the valley swept through the house, cooling the rooms.

Something moved. A piece of furniture, perhaps. A window. She heard the scraping as she stepped away from the front door and walked into the living room. From there, she saw that the deck door had been flung open. There were no downstairs lights on, and the living room was empty. There was another scraping sound.

Damn it, she thought. Luke hadn't gotten out of the house with the children. He must have waited for the sheriff to leave, and then he had to dress Timmy. She knew how difficult her son was to wake late at night. At the top of the stairs, she stopped and whispered, "Luke? Where are you?"

The piece of furniture moved a second time. Tracking the sound, April turned toward Greta's bedroom, trying to hold her fear in check. She reached to flip on the hallway light, and out of the darkness, two small hands seized her waist and jerked her into the room.

April smelled the inbred before she saw him. He held her

with one arm around her waist and grabbed for her breasts with his tiny fingers.

April kicked and caught the dwarf in the crotch. He doubled over in pain, and, breaking loose, she dove for the stairs. In the dimness of the moonlight, she spotted another small shadowy figure running down the hallway.

"Timmy?" she shouted as a second cousin lunged for her.

Screaming and kicking, she broke loose and ran for Timmy's room. They came after her, as she knew they would, and when she reached the bedroom, she grabbed Timmy's small baseball bat with both hands and, in one quick motion, swung at the approaching inbred. It hit caught him fully in the face and broke his nose.

The second creature was on her at once, diving at her leg. She felt his sharp teeth biting into her flank. Dropping the bat, she beat down at him with her fists, laced her fingers into his long, greasy dark hair and twisted back his head.

In the moonlight, she saw the twisted grin on his face. Then she saw the blood, her blood, on his thick lips. She freed her leg from his grasp and kicked him in the groin. When he let go, she swung the small bat again and hit him at the base of his neck. She heard his spine crack. He didn't even whimper as he crumpled to the floor. She didn't wait to see if he was alive, but jumped over his body and ran for the stairs.

Downstairs, April rushed into her bedroom, seized Marshall's rifle off the mantel, and loaded as she ran out of the house. She ran for Luke's house, kept running as she slipped the cold cartridges into the magazine, doing it all from memory, from having watched Marshall and Luke.

She circled the pond, ran into the woods and up the slight rise to where she had spotted the golden deer in late May. Her lungs and throat were burning. She stumbled on the narrow path and fell forward, certain that she would shoot herself with the deer rifle, and fell forward into Luke's arms.

"We gave the woman enough time, Slim," the sheriff said, glancing at his digital watch. "Let's go." He shifted his big frame in the front seat of the patrol car and reached out for the shotgun, checking the safety.

"You want me to drive up without lights?" his deputy asked.

"That might not be a bad idea. Kill the engine at the crest of the knob and coast down the hill, just in case." He reached over and lowered the side window. The deputy started the car and inched it forward on the gravel road. There was enough moonlight for him to see the length of the road and Joe Wirth grinned, saying, "This is going to be as good as possum hunting, ain't it, Slim?"

"Depends on who we can tree, Joe."

"At least one or two of those little fuckers, once we get that woman off the place. I can goddamn assure you of that. Shit, who's that?" The sheriff leaned forward and peered out the car's window. A man had emerged from the woods. "Is that him?"

"Shit, I don't know!"

Slim moved the powerful car searchlight to the approaching figure, and when it caught him full face, the man jerked and shielded his eyes. But he kept walking toward the sheriff's car.

"Is that him?" Slim asked quickly, getting anxious.

"Goddamn if I know," the sheriff mumbled, opening the door and stepping out. He placed the shotgun across the top of the white car and aimed it at the man. "Hold it right there, fella!" he called out, his voice loud in the silent night.

It was Marshall Benard all right. The sheriff had been told that Benard was dark-haired and six feet. And seeing him stagger, the sheriff guessed that he was drunk.

"Mr. Benard, come on over here, sir. We have some questions," Wirth said gently, and slipped the shotgun off the car roof. He was surprised to realize how tense he was. "Shut the fucking light off, Slim," he snapped. He moved around the front of the car, saying as he approached Marshall, "We'd like you to come back with us to the station, answer a few questions."

Marshall moved then, danced in front of the car, and in one swift and fluid motion, lunged at Joe Wirth, shoved the edge of the broken beer bottle he was carrying into the big man's face. He twisted the glass in the soft flesh of Wirth's cheek, as he drove him back and off his feet.

Marshall ripped the shotgun out of Wirth's hands and turning, fired at the deputy. He hit Slim in the face, splattering the inside of the car in a shower of hair, flesh, and brains. The thin deputy bounced off the seat and slammed the steering wheel, hitting the horn.

Slowly, taking his time now even though the horn blared across the valley, echoing into the hills, Marshall walked around to the driver's seat, opened the door, and with the muzzle of the shotgun, nudged the body enough so that the dead deputy tumbled out of the car and fell to the ground. Marshall stepped away quickly as the blood ran in a steady stream off what was left of the deputy's pulped face, and dampened the dust of the country road. Then, standing in the light of the car, he waved his cousins out of the woods.

"Oh, thank God it's you!" April exclaimed, dropping into Luke's arms, and he held her trembling body, comforting her and letting her gain control of herself. Then he said softly, not knowing how to break the news, "They're gone, April."

"Who?" She pulled back to see his face.

"Timmy and Greta. They weren't upstairs. I thought maybe, you know, they had run down to the cabin to find you."

"No, please!" She tried to pull away but he held her fast.

"I'll find them, April."

"How? How?"

"I told you once. No one can hide from me in these woods."

"He took them. . . . Dear God, he can't hurt them." She thought of Lynn Grossman's body in the pool.

"We'll find them," Luke whispered. As he reached down and took the heavy rifle from her hands, a shotgun blast rang into the valley.

"The sheriff!" April said, relieved. She turned toward the house. The sheriff had to help her. Her children were gone, and it did not matter what Luke wanted. Timmy was gone, taken away by her insane husband.

Luke seized her arm.

A car horn rang out, surprising them both, and April thought at once of the streets back in the city and the constant blaring horns outside her loft. She never even paid attention to them there. But here, deep in the woods, the sound terrified her and she stood perfectly still, afraid to breathe. When the blaring stopped abruptly, the silence of the dark night was even more terrifying. She shivered.

"Let me go, Luke!" April demanded. Looking up, she saw the fear in his eyes, and that frightened her more. Luke was never afraid of anything. "Luke," she said softly, "we have to get someone to help us."

He was staring past her, across the lawn toward the road, and he said, "The sheriff has come back."

April looked around and saw the sheriff's car approaching the house, its bright blue-and-white lights flashing. Thank God, she thought, thank God.

Then Luke grabbed her arm. "Come on, move!" he said.

"But I want to talk to the sheriff—"

"No sheriff. I'll handle this." He seized her from behind, clamping his hand over her mouth, and pulled her into the woods.

Forty

He didn't take her far. When Luke released her, April saw that they had simply circled the lawns and come up on the side of the house, at the spot where she had seen Luke's brother watching her. And then she realized she had been right, that Luke had been the man in the woods that night.

"It was you, wasn't it?" she asked. "You don't have a brother Mark, do you?"

They were crouched together, hiding in the long grass that edged the lawn.

"I wasn't spying. I was trying to protect you from the Tassels and Holts. They wanted you." He kept his eyes on the police car. It was parked in front of the house, but no one had yet emerged from the dark interior.

"What for?"

"You know what for."

"So you did me a favor and slept with me instead?"

"They wanted you. They've wanted you all summer."
He turned and stared at her, as if to make sure she understood him, "And your husband, if he gets his way, is going to give you to them."

April shook her head. "No one is going to get me. I'm going to Wirth. I'm not going to risk my life, the lives of Timmy and Greta, just so you can get even with Marshall." She stood at once and moved forward, toward the lawn. Luke grabbed for her, but she pulled free, and broke into a run. He jumped forward then and tackled her in the rough underbrush.

"Damn it!" She swore, trying to claw her way from his tight embrace.

"Look!" He pulled her up so she could see the road. Marshall stepped out of the patrol car. "That shotgun blast. He must have killed Wirth."

Then they saw three of the Hill People crawl out of the backseat of the white patrol car and run up the lawn to the house.

The front door opened, and Beer Mouth and Nick Holt came onto the front porch. They had hold of Timmy and Greta.

"Oh, no!" April started to stand.

"Stop!" Luke ordered. "They're alive. They're all right."

"They're not, goddamn it!" She tried again to stand and Luke seized her, held her in his tight grip and whispered, "They've already killed a half dozen people. The sheriff, too, goddammit, and they'll do the same to you, given the chance."

He was staring at Marshall and the cluster of his cousins, six of them now, all gathered on the front porch and surrounding the children. April watched Luke's face, waiting for him to tell her what they would do, and she saw the dark worry in his eyes, and thought how he was carrying the responsibility of the whole clan. He was weighted down by it, she realized, by the guilt of all those years of isolation and inbreeding that had produced this mad moment in the mountains.

Luke turned the rifle to one side and removed the safety on the gun. He glanced at April and spoke softly, continuing to talk as he checked the magazine of the deer rifle. "I did have a brother Mark. I told you the truth about him. About six years ago, when Mary Sue Watson Hickey wouldn't marry him, his mind just snapped. He woke up one Sunday morning and went out and killed Burke Hickey, then like I said, killed Mary Sue and dropped her down the spring well. But he never did time in Joliet State Prison. He never got off the mountain."

"What happened to him?" April asked, dreading the answer.

"I killed him. I shot him up on the ridge near Slide Mountain. He was crossing over to Pearl Peak, going after the people who lived up there. And if I hadn't killed him he would have gone off like Marshall did tonight and killed a dozen more. Killed them until someone stopped him." He stared at her a moment, then added, "And that's why I have to kill your husband." He raised the rifle, braced the barrel against the stump of a black oak tree, and took aim at Marshall. His silhouette was clear, towering over the dwarfs and children. A clear shot on the dark night.

"No! Luke, please, you can't." She grabbed his shoulder. "I'm afraid you might miss. . . . Timmy."

"I won't miss," he snapped, shaking her off, but when he looked back to take his shot, Marshall was disappearing into the house, followed by the others.

"Shit!"

"I'm sorry. Can't we get closer?"

"We have to now," Luke replied, lowering the rifle and staring up at the dark house, deciding what to do next.

"Let me go," April offered. "I'll go to the house, get their attention, and you can go around back, slip into the house, find Marshall . . ."

"Marshall's got a shotgun. I saw him carrying it when he got out of the cop's car. He'll shoot you from the front porch."

"He won't. You said yourself that the cousins wanted me. They'll come get me."

Luke kept shaking his head. "You can't fight them off. You can't run from them. They know the woods. They'll have you raped before I can reach you."

"The car! I'll use the patrol car. I'll get inside, shine the lights on the house, and when they come, well, I'll . . . deal with them. I'll run them over."

He stared at her a moment, then asked, "Have you ever hit anything on the highway? A deer? A dog? Do you remember the thump the body makes, bouncing off a fender? That's what it will sound like, hitting the dwarfs."

She answered calmly, without hesitation. "They have Timmy, Luke. They have my son. If I have to kill them to get my child, I will."

Luke watched the dark house. In a few minutes, he thought, it might be too late for April. At that moment Marshall and the cousins might be killing the children.

"All right!" he said, urgent now. "You stay in the trees. I'll go down by the road, and come up on the barn side. If they're watching the road, they won't see me until it's too late. Wait until I have the car going, then make a run for the house. I'll turn on the siren, get their attention. Go into the house through the cellar; there's no lock on that door, and I doubt anyone will think of guarding it. You'll be inside before they realize it's you." He handed her the rifle.

April nodded, but Luke was still watching the house. "How many did you see crossing the road at Pearl Peak."

"Maybe fifteen. At least that many, counting the boys."

"There were five of them with Marshall on the porch."

"Where are the others? Two attacked me upstairs, and I know I killed one."

Luke shook his head. "Maybe they're in the house. Or the woods." He looked over at April. His eyes had adjusted to the night and he looked into her eyes. "We have to kill them all, April. Boys, too."

"Oh, no. Luke, please . . ."

"Everyone. I'll do it, but you've got to know. They're all mad. I can't let them live. These murders are like a virus. They'll spread unless I stop them all."

"Luke!" April pointed. Beyond the pond and above the dark shadow of the woods rose an orange and yellow burst of flame. It brightened the sky like fireworks.

"The cabin," Luke whispered. "Well, we know where the others are." He stood, pulling April with him. "All right, let's go!'' Without waiting, he ran out of the trees, straight through the wood to the road and the police car.

The leaping flames brightened the lawn, made the night sky briefly brilliant with colored light. They would see him, April feared, and she stayed crouched in the long grass, waiting for the flame to die down.

Luke ran, ducking his head and shielding his face with both arms as the thin branches snapped and tore at his clothes and cut into his face. He reached the road, ran down through the thin gully and out onto the gravel, running for the patrol car, parked a hundred yards ahead of him in front of the farmhouse. April couldn't see Luke. The road was below the lawn, but she could see the porch of the farmhouse and she watched the front door, praying that Luke would reach the car before he was seen.

Luke reached the patrol car and slipped inside, locking the door behind him, then he reached over, turned on the engine, and shifted the car into first.

The deputy sheriff stared up at him, wedged between the seat and the dashboard. Both of his eyes had been shot out of his head, and the shotgun blast had blown away his lower lip and jaw. Luke glanced at the backseat. The sheriff was stretched out face down on the seat. His body, too, dripped blood. Luke turned away, looked up at the farmhouse as the front door opened and three of his cousins ran out onto the porch. Luke touched the accelerator.

The big car jerked forward, spraying gravel, skidding as it gained speed. Luke spun the wheel toward the house and drove the car up the grassy slope and straight at the three dwarfs.

One dwarf tumbled over the front of the car. His body smashed the windshield and rolled off the roof. Luke spun the steering wheel, heading the car again toward the road. Another cousin grabbed hold of the side mirror and was trying to reach in and open the door. Luke pumped the gas pedal, picked up speed and ran the car between two closely-set trees, scraping the dwarf off the side of the car.

The patrol car bounced onto the county road and skidded on the loose gravel. Luke hit the brake hard; as the heavy car spun to a stop, he was thrown against the dashboard and, reaching out to brace himself, he put his hand in the deputy's mangled face. When he pulled back, his fingers were wet with blood. He wiped his hand on his shirt, then reached out and searched the dashboard for the siren switch and flipped it on. The sound wailed into the silent night.

Sitting up again, staring through the front window, Luke spotted two more of his cousins coming out of the woods, running for the house. He grabbed the steering wheel with both hands and went up onto the lawn after them. In the bright headlights, he could see the fear on their faces as they saw the car charging them. They were grabbing each other in fright, trying to pump their short legs faster, to get away from the car. One stumbled and fell forward on the grass. He was struggling to his feet as Luke hit him with the right fender. There was a crunch of metal and a thump as the small body smashed the right headlight, then Luke saw his cousin's body flung off into the darkness.

The other cousin had verged left and away from the car. Spinning the wheel, Luke found him again in the single beam of the car's remaining headlight. He was less than twenty yards from the underbrush. Luke thumped on the gas and bore down on him, coming from an angle, and clipped him as if he were a bowling pin. He smashed the left headlight, then bounced off the white patrol car and sailed into the underbrush. Luke heard him scream as he was hit, his small voice lost in the roar of the engine and the wailing siren.

The car was sliding away from Luke, careening on the wet grass. He turned the wheel against the slide, as he would have done on an icy road, but the heavy vehicle was out of control. The pond loomed just ahead of him. He jammed his foot against the brake, but he knew he had lost it. The car flew off the edge of the bank, sailed out over the pond, and he closed his eyes, hung onto the steering wheel and waited for the car to hit the water.

April was running for the cellar door as Luke crashed. "Luke!" she managed to say, seeing the car sink.

"Dear God, no," she whispered. She waited for him to surface, to escape from the sinking car, but there was no sign of him. He must have struck his head; now he was unconscious. She stood paralyzed, wanting to go to help—but this was her only moment to save the children.

She forced herself to keep going. Pushing open the heavy wood door, she stepped down into the dark cellar. It was cold in the dark, low-ceiled room. She shivered and began to cry, then, fearing they would hear her upstairs, she bit into her knuckles, fought herself to keep calm.

She heard footsteps running across the living room and out onto the deck. She listened to the running, tried to guess how many were still alive, tried to count the dwarfs she knew were dead, but she couldn't think, couldn't remember. Afraid that she would bolt and run herself, just run to get away, run for help somewhere on the mountain, she positioned the deer rifle in her trembling hands, and walked carefully toward the stairway to the first floor. Concentrating on the edge of light that seeped under the upstairs door, she nearly screamed when her toe struck soft flesh on the cellar floor. Jumping back, she swung the rifle to take aim before she recognized the muffled whimpering.

April dropped to her knees and with both hands felt along the stone floor for her son. When she found the soft body, she felt for his shoulders and face, felt the thick tape across his mouth, and realized he was tied up in a tight bundle, like a shipping package.

She started to rip the tape from his mouth and stopped. He would be crying, she realized, sobbing hysterically, out of control, and Marshall would hear him, know that he was loose in the cellar. April hugged him against her in the darkness, whispering that he was all right, begged him to lie still, but she kept herself from letting him loose, even while he struggled.

Oh, dear God, she thought, what was she doing to her child? She pulled away from him and reached around her until her hand touched another bundle. She felt Greta's leg and the girl moved. April sighed. They were alive, she thought. The children hadn't been hurt.

"Greta, it's okay. I'm here," she whispered. "Lie still, please. Everything will be all right."

Greta kept struggling.

"Don't! Lie still! I have to get help."

But who would help her, she thought. Luke was dead; the sheriff was dead. She should take the children, go out through the cellar door and hide in the woods until someone came looking for the sheriff. All she had to do was save the children and herself. She didn't care what happened to Marshall or the inbreds.

She started to move back to the children when footsteps sounded through the house. Then the first floor door was opened and light flooded the small cellar. April raised the rifle and when she saw the small dwarf silhouetted in the light, she pulled the trigger. The bullet knocked him against the hallway wall where he slid down to the floor without a sound, leaving a bloody mark on the wallpaper.

The first floor exploded into shouting, Marshall's voice louder than the rest. Full of adrenalin, April threw the bolt of the deer rifle, and braced herself. Then she glanced back at the two children. She saw them in the light from above, saw their eyes wild with fright. She went to them and ripped the tape off their legs so they could stand, telling Greta, "Hurry! We have to get to the woods." Then she grabbed Timmy with one arm and helped him to the cellar exit. She stopped for a moment and fired again at the open door to the first floor, driving away the dwarfs from the cellar entrance.

Half carrying Timmy, and with Greta clinging to her, April ran straight across the lawn and into the woods, to where Luke and she had watched the house. She kept running, pulling the children after her, shouting at them to keep going, to hurry, to do what she said. They were both crying, sobbing behind their taped mouths, and choking on their tears. She stopped when they were fifty-yards deep in the woods and ripped the wide tape from their mouths. Timmy cried out at once and April buried his face in her shirt to muffle his voice.

"Take this!" she told Greta, giving her the deer rifle, then lifted Timmy into her arms and started running deeper into the woods. When she did stop, it was only because she stumbled in soft mossy soil. Greta dropped down beside her gasping for air, and April grabbed her and pulled her closer, so that the three of them lay sobbing and breathless in each others' arms.

They needed to hide, April realized. Although he was too exhausted to move, she knew that they had to find a safe hollow and hide there until morning. In the first light of day, they could go for the gravel road and get out of the woods.

She took Timmy's face in her hands and kissed him repeatedly, then kissed Greta. The children clung to her.

"Daddy tied me up," Greta said, crying and trying to wipe the tears off her face.

"We're going to be all right," April said reassuringly. "We're going to find a safe place. We're going to be all right."

"Mommy! Mommy! Daddy tied me up!" Timmy said.

"Shhhh!" April placed her palm on her son's cheek, gently trying to hush him. "We have to be quiet." As she held him, she glanced around, looked to see where they were in the valley, tried to remember in what direction she had fled. Above her, high in the sky, she could still see the bright flames of the log cabin. Where was the fire department, she thought. Why hadn't they shown up? Someone must have seen the flames from Pearl Peak. But maybe there was no one left on the other side of the mountain. Maybe all of them had been murdered.

April shuddered. "Come on! Run!" She grabbed Timmy's hand and pulled him up, and reaching over, took the Browning from Greta, saying, "Let me." She felt safer with the heavy rifle in her hands.

It was easier going downhill, running on a deer path that curved and descended toward the valley floor, but Timmy couldn't keep up and he stumbled, crying with fright.

"All right, honey. All right." April lifted him into her arms, but still held onto the rifle. "Go, Greta! Run ahead!"

"No! I'm afraid." Greta had hold of her shirt; she wouldn't take a step away from April.

They would never get away like this, April thought.

"This way." April stepped off the path and walked into the trees. She held up the rifle in front of her to bend back the branches. Greta tucked her face into the small of April's back and linked her arms around April's waist to keep from being hit by the sharp thorns of bushes and low branches. April pushed forward.

The Hill People would follow, she knew. They would take the deer paths into the valley, assuming that was the way she'd gone. If she were off the path, anywhere in the thick woods, she might be safer, she guessed. The underbrush was thicker away from the deer paths, and they could find an old maple or cottonwood tree and hide in among the thick roots. She could regain her strength and breath, and decide how to safely sneak off the mountaintop.

A hundred yards off the path, moving slowly, April lost her footing on the steep slope and her feet slid from under her. She held Timmy tightly and bounced down the hillside, stopping at the thick base of a tree when her foot caught an exposed root.

"Shit!" she swore. With difficulty, she reached forward to pull herself free. In the dark, she felt her left ankle. It had already begun to swell at the joint. She would not walk out of the woods, she knew. The ankle was broken or at least twisted. She sat back against the rough bark of the trees and suffered the pain in silence, knowing now, that they couldn't go any farther.

"Mommy, I'm scared," Timmy whispered, coming into her arms and hiding his face in her lap.

"It's all right, sweetheart. We're going to be all right."

"Luke will help us," Timmy said, raising his face. April saw in the shadowy moonlight a glimpse of hope flash in her son's eyes.

"Yes, Luke can help us." She smiled at her son, even as she remembered how the car had catapulted into the pond.

"April?" Greta whispered, crawling closer. "What are we going to do?"

"We're going to stay here, honey. We're going to wait until morning and when it's light enough, we'll go out onto the road and get someone to help us."

"He's going to kill me," Greta whispered. "Daddy wants to kill me!"

"Greta, your father isn't well. He doesn't know what he is doing." April reached over and gently touched the girl, and Greta moved closer, came sobbing into April's embrace and she held both of the children, let them cry against her. How could she tell Greta the truth about her father? And what would she do if Marshall found them? She hoped that she would have the strength to shoot him before he harmed his daughter. Then she leaned back against the tree and forced herself to relax, to dismiss the pain of her ankle. She closed her eyes and tried to rest as she waited for the break of day in the Catskills.

Forty-one

Just before daylight the temperature dropped, waking April from a light sleep. She woke shivering. Both of the children had curled tightly against her, seeking warmth. When she moved her arm to check her watch, Greta stirred. Timmy curled down even closer to his mother.

Greta sat up and rubbed the sleep from her eyes. "I'm cold," she said.

"It's always cold before dawn. We'll be warm once the sun clears the hillside," April whispered, not wanting to wake Timmy. There was a thin blanket of fog surrounding them. April thought back to that night on the rainy highway when the deer appeared from out of the foggy woods, smashing their car and killing her Tom. She had thought that nothing could ever be as bad as that night, lying pinned beneath the twisted car, her husband's warm blood dripping onto her face, her baby screaming at her breast.

She glanced around to get her bearings and realized with astonishment that they were just below Luke's cabin and the clearing of white birch trees. Through the trees she could even see the few cords of wood Luke had stacked in the woods.

She must have simply traveled in a wide half circle around the property. Marshall would find her easily, she realized. When he and the Hill People went searching at dawn, they would take the path down to Secret Lake and see them in the woods, less than two thousand yards from the farmhouse.

Using her free hand, April searched her pockets and pulled out the few extra shells she had grabbed when she ran from the house.

"What are you going to do?" Greta asked.

"I don't know." She lifted the rifle and took off the safety.

"Are you going to kill Daddy?"

April glanced at Greta. There were no tears. The child seemed to accept what might have to be done to save her life.

"I don't want to kill anyone." April lowered the rifle into the thick leaves beside her, keeping it within reach, then she looked up, toward the hillside, where the deer path came down through the woods.

"He tried to kill me and Timmy."

April glanced again at her stepdaughter.

"He didn't know it was me," Greta said softly. "I could tell he didn't." A flush of tears glistened in her eyes, and then her face broke down as she lost control. April reached out to pull Greta into her arms and gently stroked her hair as she kept watching the woods, alert for any sound.

Gradually, the light of day came down off the mountaintop, seeping through the trees and into the valley. April watched the dawn spread through the forest. She heard birds begin to sing, first far off, then closer, as the woods woke. It would be another beautiful day in the Catskills. Then she spotted the cousin.

April did not move. She did not even stop stroking Greta's hair. But her heart began to race and she closed her eyes briefly to pull herself together. When she looked again the dwarf had moved, slipped from behind one tree to the next, still coming downhill toward her.

She slowly moved her hand away from Greta's head and felt beside her for Marshall's rifle, slipped her fingers around the stock.

"Don't move, Greta," she said softly, calmly. "I'm going to pick up the rifle and shoot."

"They're here?" Greta asked, not moving. Her face was turned sideways and away from the hillside. She did not open her eyes.

"Yes. Just one of them," April answered, thankful that Greta had not become hysterical. The child had grown up, April realized. April kept her head steady but shifted her eyes and took in the whole ridge. She saw then that she had been wrong. There were three dwarfs in the trees, running soundlessly. They were like the rats she'd found in the cupboard, she thought. They kept breeding, kept producing their own kind. Luke was right. Now it was up to her to get rid of the whole nest of monsters. "Listen to me," April whispered to Greta. "When I lift up the rifle, I want you to roll away from me. Don't stand up, just keep rolling through the leaves and get out of the way."

"What about Timmy?" Greta asked.

"He'll be all right," April answered quickly, keeping Greta calm. Two of the dwarfs had reached trees close to where she sat. They thought she hadn't seen them in the wood.

They would probably come as close as they could, then rush her across the open space and attack from different angles.

She gripped the rifle, thinking of what Luke had told Marshall about squeezing the trigger slowly. She took a deep breath.

"Okay, get ready." She felt Greta tense against her. April scanned the trees. All three had reached the last cover of trees. They would have to run across twenty yards of open brush to reach her. She would wait until they all left the safety of the trees, then she'd move. Timmy stirred in her arms and stretched. Please don't wake, April prayed. Don't sit up and get in my way.

The last of the night's shadows faded away. Daylight swept through the valley. April felt a soft breeze of warmth, and then the dwarfs came at her, all running downhill at once.

"Now, Greta!" April sat up, pulled the rifle from the leaves and aimed. She did not panic. She felt as if time had slowed, that she had endless time to aim at the small man,

and pull the trigger. The bullet hit him in the face. April did
not even pause. In one smooth motion, she shifted left,
brought the second man into her sight and fired. The shot
knocked him off stride. He was still moving when he died,
the way a chicken runs wild with its head chopped off.

The last of the dwarfs dove at April. His watery pink eyes
were up close, blazing with rage as she pulled the trigger,
spraying her and Timmy with blood as the bullet hit him
point blank and tore a hole through his chest. He fell on top
of them and, as Timmy screamed, April grabbed the bleeding body and shoved it away.

The rapid gunfire echoed across the valley, then the
woods were quiet. Still gasping for breath, April reached for
her son and used her fingers to wipe the dwarf's warm
blood from his small face.

"Greta, come," she called. "We have to get out of here.
Help me up."

"Where are we going?"

"Back to the house," April said slipping her arm around
Greta and using the rifle as a makeshift cane. "Timmy,
come on. No more crying. You have to be a big boy for
Mommy." She touched him affectionately. The little boy
wrapped both his arms around her legs and hugged her
back.

"You shot Daddy's gun," he said, eyeing the bodies.
"You killed those guys."

"Come, sweetheart," April urged him.

"No!" Greta protested, "Why should we go back to the
house? He's there."

"Honey, I can't walk." April took hold of Greta by the
shoulders. "We have to get help, and the only way to do
that is to use the phone."

"Daddy . . ."

"We'll be all right. I have the rifle." April remembered
then that she hadn't reloaded the Browning, and she pulled
out more shells from her jeans. "Come on, you two!" She
made herself sound confident, and again using Greta's
support, hobbled up the slope and out of the trees.

"What's that?" Timmy asked when they came to the
back lawn and saw the sheriff's car in the pond. Only the

top was visible. April looked away, afraid she might see Luke's body.

The lawn was empty. The house looked deserted. He was down in the valley searching for her, April guessed. If she hurried she could get inside and lock the doors, then call the police.

"Hurry!" she told the children. "Hurry." And pushing herself, biting down on her lip at the pain in her ankle, she forced herself across the mowed lawn, up onto the deck and into the house.

It was silent inside.

"Shhh," she whispered, standing in the dining room and listening. She held up the rifle, ready to shoot. She was no longer afraid of killing anyone, not even her husband. Then she said to Greta, "Go lock the front doors. And all the windows. Upstairs too. Go on. Timmy, help Greta." She turned around and locked the deck door behind her, and then bracing herself against furniture, she hobbled into her office and picked up the phone.

She was dialing 911 when she realized the line was dead. Of course, she realized, and saw where her husband had ripped the cords out of the wall.

Then she heard Greta screaming, and she knew. Stumbling out of the office, she saw what she knew she'd find: Marshall holding the children. He had both of them in one arm; his other hand held a kitchen knife. He had been hiding upstairs all the time, waiting for her to return.

"Hi!" he said to April, grinning.

"Let them go, Marshall," April said calmly, raising her rifle.

He kept grinning, shaking his head. "I want her." He nodded at Greta.

"Marshall, she's your daughter," April spoke softly, approaching.

He brought the kitchen knife up beneath Timmy's throat. April stopped. Her little boy was staring at her, his eyes wild.

"Marshall, please," she whispered.

"The boys want him," Marshall said, stepping toward the deck door.

"You can't, Marshall. Please. They're our children."

"So what? You know what they say up here, April—everyone is kin, and kin of kin." He grinned again.

"I'll kill you," she said.

"And I'll slit Timmy's throat." Without warning he glanced Timmy's soft cheek with the knife blade. The child screamed as the blood squirted out. April grabbed the back of the dining room table to keep from falling.

"See?" Marshall laughed.

He no longer looked sane, April saw. The sickness had distorted his face, tore up his muscles, and in a brief few hours, made him look old and sick. She was thankful for that, she thought. When she killed him, she would not be killing the man she'd married.

He was on the deck, walking backward toward the stairs. April kept following him, still holding the rifle. At some point, she knew, he would look away. He would lower the knife. He would make a mistake, and she would kill him.

Beyond the porch, coming out of the woods, she saw Beer Mouth and Nick Holt with three more dwarfs. These were the last of them, she knew. Well, good. She would finish them off as well, just as Luke had wanted.

And then she saw Luke. He came running across the road and onto the lawn. He had survived the crash, she realized, and had gone into the valley to search for her. When he saw her with Marshall, he sprinted toward the deck. Thank God, he was alive, she thought, sighing with relief.

Marshall, too, spotted Luke, and he shouted at her. "Kill him! Kill Grange and you can have your kid." He let go of Greta and seized Timmy by his thick blond hair, holding him up like a trophy.

"No!" April raised the rifle. Marshall was less than ten yards from her. She had already killed four of the inbreds at that distance; she knew she would not miss her husband.

"I'll kill your kid unless you shoot that bastard!" Marshall shouted. The rage in his eyes, April realized, had turned wild.

"No, please," she whispered, "don't." Her hands were trembling. She glanced at Luke who had reached the deck. She pleaded with her eyes for him to help her.

"Let the boy go, Marshall," Luke said softly, approaching him.

"Stay away or I'll cut the kid!" Marshall shouted, and then he did it anyway, jabbing Timmy with the point of the kitchen knife, drawing more blood.

"Stop!" April screamed. Her legs buckled.

"Let Timmy go!" Luke said. "You can have me."

"I don't want you, Grange. They do," he nodded to the dwarfs who also had reached the deck.

"I'll kill you!" April shouted.

"Kill me," Marshall answered back, "and Beer Mouth will kill you." He had Timmy hung up by his hair, and was using the little boy as a shield, as he backed himself toward the deck stairs.

April kept moving, trying to get a clear shot at Marshall.

"Don't shoot," Luke warned, raising his hand. "You might hit Timmy." He was coming at Marshall from the other side, and then without warning, he dove, hitting him below the knees and knocking Marshall into the house.

Marshall let go of Timmy and swung the long blade knife at Luke, digging it into his right shoulder. Luke cried out but didn't let go. He raised up and in desperation, slammed Marshall against the house a second time, knocking the knife loose.

"Get away, Luke!" April shouted, raising the rifle and trying to take aim.

Marshall swung at Luke, hitting him low in the stomach but Luke grabbed Marshall's hair and pulled him down, too, as he doubled over in pain, and pinned him to the boards with his body.

Thank God, April thought, seeing Luke had hold of her husband. Then in that split second, Beer Mouth jumped onto the deck, grabbed the kitchen knife and pushed the long blade into Luke's side.

Luke reached out and grabbed his cousin with both his hands and squeezed his throat. He glanced at April and shouted, "Go! Get out of here! I'll stop them!"

April fired at her husband and missed. The bullet broke a window above Marshall's head. She fumbled with the bolt, backing away, trying to keep her distance on them, and when she was loaded, Marshall had grabbed his daughter, had his arm around the child's neck as he pulled her after him.

"Mommy!" Greta managed to say as her father squeezed her neck.

April ran forward, ran at Marshall, and took dead aim at her husband's face. But when she pulled the trigger, the heavy rifle jumped in her arms and the shot went wild. Marshall fell back and let loose of his daughter. April dropped the rifle and grabbed Greta.

"Inside!" She shouted as Marshall hit the deck rail. She grabbed Timmy and Greta and pulled them after her into the house. Slamming the door, April locked it just as rocks from the garden were picked up by the dwarfs and thrown at the windows, breaking glass. She pulled the children away from the window and herded them toward the cellar door.

"Downstairs!" April ordered. At the cellar door, she flipped on the light, then said to Greta, "Wait for me." The dwarfs hadn't thought of coming around the house, of getting at her through the cellar.

"No, I'm scared," Greta clung to April.

April glanced around. Marshall and three more cousins were at the windows, breaking glass and ripping the screens. She had only one way to kill them now.

"Go ahead," she said calmly. "I'm coming after you." She ran to the fireplace, took down the two antique oil lamps from the mantelpiece, and smashed the glass jars against the walls, spraying lamp oil across the hardwood floors of the living room and dining room. Then she grabbed the fireplace matches and reached the cellar door just as Marshall tumbled in through the downstairs windows.

She was calm and in control. Her fear had passed. She waited until all of them had scrambled into the house and tumbled onto the hardwood floors, and then she scraped a thick match across the box. It lit in a quick burst of blue flame, illuminating her face for a moment as she knelt and touched it to the pool of fuel. The flame flared up and spread, racing its hungry way across the waxed wood floors.

Marshall screamed as he tried to dance away from the licking fire, but the flame caught his pants legs, bit into his flesh. The fire spread wildly through the house, raced to all the rooms, cornering the Tassels and Holts and setting them all on fire.

April jumped through the cellar door and slammed it behind her, wedging a garden rake through the handle. She ran down the wooden steps and, lifting Timmy into her arms, shouted to Greta.

"Hurry. The house is on fire!"

Forty-two

April led the way through the cellar toward the slanting sunlight that filtered through the hinged door. She felt her way up the steps, slipped open the latch and, using her shoulder, lifted up the door, flooding the room with light.

Standing at the top step of the cellar, she looked first at the farmhouse. Heavy smoke and licks of yellow flame were visible in the windows, and out across the back lawn, she saw two inbreds racing to the pond, their clothes and hair on fire. Their bodies hissed when they hit the water. She could see another one already dead. His body floated in the water like a charred log. With Timmy still in her arms, April turned and ran for the car.

Opening the door, she pushed Timmy ahead of her, then reached under the floor mat for the extra ignition key and started the engine as Greta scrambled into the backseat. Without waiting for her to slam the door, April backed the station wagon from the parking spot and onto the gravel road. From the corner of her eye, she saw that the whole house was aflame, saw flames eating through the tar-paper roof shingles.

April hit the gas pedal and the heavy car spun and sprayed gravel as it raced off the mountaintop and down to the highway. She didn't slow down until she came out of the woods. Ahead, she saw the expressway to the city.

She would stop at the State Highway Patrol office and tell them what happened. Tell the police how the Tassel and Holt cousins had killed Marshall, killed each other. They won't ask too many questions. This was the mountains, April reasoned. And in the mountains there was always bloodletting. In another season or two, she knew, all of these killings would fade into memory. New city people would come up and buy houses. And no one would remember this summer's tragedy.

"Mommy?" Timmy asked.

"Yes, darling?" She reached to stroke his cheek with her fingers, and seeing the blood on his face, pressed her handkerchief against the cuts.

"Mommy, are we going to be okay?"

She smiled at him reassuringly. "Yes, darling, we're going to be okay. We're going home, back to the City, and nothing terrible will ever happen to us again." She glanced then in the mirror and said, "Greta? Honey? Are you okay?"

Greta looked to April and said quietly, "Am I going to be all right, too?"

"Yes, darling, I'll take care of you. You have nothing to fear."

April glanced again in the rearview mirror to encourage Greta with a smile, and saw that Greta was looking away, looking out across the field. April turned to see what Greta was watching and spotted the deer. It was grazing in the meadowland beside the expressway and it raised its golden head as the speeding car raced past. April gripped the wheel, then relaxed as she saw that the deer was too far away to harm them. All of it, she realized, all the Catskills and Mad River Mountain was too far away to hurt any of them, ever again.